# FORGOTTEN LIBERTY

## ALESSIO CALA

# Acknowledgements

To the friends and family who generously gave up their time, reading various drafts, providing editorial improvements, and critiquing elements of both narrative and design. Your input, support and encouragement helped me to see this story through to its completion.

Thanks to Sofia Cala, Charlotte Mason-Mottram, Winifred Greenfield, Adrian Greenfield, Sam Foot and Caitlin Titmus.

Thanks to my parents, Maria and Salvatore, for supporting me in every goal I've set myself throughout my lifetime - and for being patient when those aspirations occasionally changed from time to time.

Particular thanks to my auntie Charlotte, for stopping me from naming a horse 'Jane.'

# MAP OF AUTARK

"A crowded society is a restrictive society; an overcrowded society becomes an authoritarian, repressive and murderous society."

- **Edward Abbey, Dispatches and Salvos from an American Iconoclast**

They were surrounded. The raiders closed in on all sides of the log cabin. The ten of them, including the dog, kept low as a chilled silence overthrew the inside of the cabin. For the first time along his journey, the bearded man had reached a dead end. He sat pressed up against the wall below the window, eyes locked on the nurturing woman hiding beneath the wooden table in the centre of the room. His eyes tilted down to the boy held closely in her arms, their faces mirroring that of his own, riddled with anticipation and terror. His heart rattled his rib cage, thumping raw and hard between his lungs.

He knew that she had developed a tender relationship with the boy over the short period of time they had been together and the boy was comfortable around her. The bearded man understood that, he had known it the moment she laid eyes on him. When she received the child, she received something that she had always wanted in her life but never had. For she was infertile, and although the boy had fulfilled an overbearing void in her life, the bearded man pondered whether the discovery of the child had been a blessing or a curse.

"What the hell are we waiting for?" barked the larger man in the black beanie sitting beside him. The bearded man caught a whiff of the oaf's perspiring body and did well to ignore its ripeness. The oaf pulled the .38 revolver up to his chest in both hands and craned his neck to peer outside.

"He's still out cold," a voice muttered from the back of the room. The plump man with the round spectacles had been unconscious behind the table the entire time. The bearded man glanced at the two men kneeling over him but his view was somewhat obstructed by the table legs.

He also saw the other woman, huddled with the border collie, eyes fixated on nothing in particular as she sat frozen in the far corner.

The bearded man tilted his head up to the window but all he saw was the dreary sky. It drifted over the moulting maples and pines that shed their leaves and needles to the bitter cold.

The oaf shifted onto his side and used his knees to elevate his body.

"Don't you dare," hissed the red-haired woman kneeling beside the table. "There's too many of them out there."

The oaf's head snapped back over to her with piercing eyes. "I'm not gonna sit here and wait to die over some goddamn kid."

"We are not handing him over to them!"

They argued in low, hushed tones, their throats dry and exhausted. The nurturing woman held the boy tighter. The bearded man saw dread envelop the boy's face, but his blissful innocence distanced him from their discussion. Outside in the woodland's clearing he could hear the raiders barking their demands.

*Diez.. Nueve... Ocho...*

The oaf continued to stare at the red-haired woman in defiance, his gaze drifted from her, to the boy, and back again. Her eyes bugged wide. She could be just as stubborn as him. Her hand gripped firmly to the sling of the sawn-off shotgun over her shoulder. A final warning. The bearded man felt an overwhelming sense of detachment from the scene unfolding before him. He sat still beneath the window sill and watched.

The oaf's face churned with anger. His nostrils flared like a boar, teeth clenching with true grit.

*Siete... Sies...*

The oaf lunged forward. The red-haired woman jolted back in surprise. She felt the weight of his shoulder plunge into her, throwing her aside like a worthless ragdoll. He dug in under the table and snatched the boy with his fat greasy fingers. The nurturing woman cried out and held on as tight as she could. She tried to fight back but could not match the oaf's brutish strength. He wrestled against her and ripped the boy out from under the table. The bearded man's eyes lit up, his body began to rise without full consent. He felt disconnected, as though a spectator to an out of body experience. He acted upon instinct and impulse and the cries of his loved one only fuelled his will to protect. He pounced on the oaf from behind. The oaf stood firmly on his feet, his stance widened to stabilise himself. The bearded man's forearms wrapped around his neck. He felt the brute shake violently in his arms but the oaf could not contain both himself and the struggling boy.

*Cinco... Cuarto...*

Time slowed altogether. The bearded man saw the red-haired woman snatch the boy's hand in an attempt to pull him away from the oaf's grasp. They pulled each arm in opposite directions, almost tearing him in two. Tears streamed down the boy's face, his cheeks red raw as he called out to the nurturing woman reaching out to him from beneath the table.

The bearded man yanked back hard, causing them both to fly back into the window.

*Tres... Dos... Uno...*

Together they dropped to the wooden floorboards. Glass and woodchips shattered all around them. All at once, the deafening crack of automatic gunfire shook the cabin. The oaf grunted as the bearded man's arms wrapped even tighter around his throat.

Frank began to choke him.

# ONE

*Autarky:*

*A country, state, or society which is self-sufficient or economically independent.*

A lot of the time, we as a species strive to better ourselves, to improve our capabilities and advance the world as we know it. We keep building on our existing creations, tweaking and improving every aesthetic aspect of our lives to its utter perfection to the point where it raises the question, 'are we going *too* far?' It is very rare for us to have ever felt the need to revert our evolutionary advancements. That is until the discovery of Autark.

Autark wasn't just an island. It was the basic structure for a soon to be practiced ideology. It was an old way of life that many felt was lost through our modern age of technological advancements. Roger Bullon was a historical and geographical professor at the University of Cambridge, England. He set out to explore the North Atlantic waters with a marine biologist in search for alternate behavioural patterns in certain species of fish. The well-known marine biologist who had already been studying this particular area of the ocean was Javier Paraíso of Costa Rica, a man well-respected in his field.

Their collaborative project continued for several months, discovering successful findings that would improve our knowledge of the ocean and its inhabitants. One evening they sent their crew diving to research the activity of Hexanchidae, or 'cow sharks', to compare their activity at night to that of the day. During their study, an unexpected storm threw them off course. Their boat was separated from the divers and their equipment and research was either destroyed or lost to the ruthless storm and sea. Although several divers were never found and later pronounced dead, the storm did manage to bring Bullon and Paraíso *some* level of fortune.

The boat had managed to wash up onto a sandy shore. Paraíso woke first to the morning sun shining through the needles of nearby pines. He found Bullon injured and unconscious in the wreckage but managed to carry him out onto this unknown territory. As he carried his groggy partner through the pinewood forest, he contemplated where exactly in the world they could be. He questioned how long they had been unconscious. Could the waves really have taken them half the width of the North Atlantic? He pondered as to whether it could be the islands of Faial, Pico, or one of the other islands in the central Atlantic Azores group, but it could not have been. This land was far colder. It was untouched. There were no roads, no settlements, and no structure. The two researchers had stumbled upon an uncharted island.

European coastguards managed to locate their position through the intact emergency tracking device in the wrecked boat's GPS system. Bullon and Paraíso were rescued and returned to the United Kingdom where they would share their findings with the university. The original project had been a disaster, but this new discovery would change their lives forever.

Bullon used this misadventure to begin something he had wanted to do for a very long time. He pitched a meeting with the university board of directors for a project that would need government funding and unbiased public volunteers. The idea was simple: revert to the analogue age. Roger Bullon had spent decades of his life studying the ancestors, liberating groups and movements of numerous cultures and felt that we were now missing something that held so many people together all those years ago; Community. Bullon expressed that in the modern world, we as a society do not engage with each other as we used to. We do not speak to our fellow man as we once did. We do not even exchange more than a simple *'hello'* to our neighbour. This wasn't a generalisation but more of an observation of the wider general public.

Bullon did not state that this had occurred globally, but rather pointed out that the majority of people in densely populated towns and cities had lost touch with the essence of the word community, society, togetherness. He had also spent several years of his studies with members of self-sustaining communities based in the outback of Alaska, U.S.A. Bullon wanted volunteers from around the globe to devote their lives and volunteer to live on this island and its primitive nature. In return the people would receive the necessary materials and basic requirements needed to sustain an independent lifestyle. He couldn't expect people to drop everything for nothing, so giving them the basic essentials to start with was a must if he ever expected people to commit to such an experiment. He prepared a pitch with help of some of the country's most respected psychologists. The aim of the study was to see if people would interact more and help each other in this new environment; to see if they could build something from the bare minimum and form structure, form a community.

Initially the project was declined, but after Bullon's persistence and careful consideration the British Government decided to fund it under two conditions. The first condition was that the study may only appeal to British citizens; the reason being that the government didn't want to be held responsible for funding a study that essentially paid the cost of living for people who were from countries outside of the UK. They didn't want the public backlash, the retaliation and questioning as to why taxpayer's money and university budgets were being used to transport and fund basic materials and means of living to non-British citizens. Then there was the second condition. As this land was not under any jurisdiction over international waters, they needed to ensure the U.N. was prepared to sign ownership of the land over to the UK. The U.S. appealed at first, but the island was situated outside the two hundred mile territorial limit, thereby committing the claim for ownership up to annexation. The U.N. took interest in the community project, and was prepared to sign ownership under the condition that the project was a non-profit based organisation. They could export to the island, but nothing, and they meant nothing, could return. The other members of the U.N. fought long and hard over the ownership of the island. The major opposition being that of South American representatives demanding a fifty percent share in the land for the purpose of oil excavations. They didn't want to miss out on the opportunity. Paraíso had every right, just as much as Bullon, but in the end, the U.N. favoured the community project. It was less of an economic threat to their individual countries.

The UK was granted access and ownership to the island under certain restrictions and conditions. No economic profit was to be made from the island. Mining for oil and other valuable materials was strictly off limits. Nothing was to be returned to the UK under any circumstances and ownership of the land would fall under the U.N. after a certain limit of time.

Few people knew the deadline for the call of handover. Some speculated years, others decades. Whatever it was, it must have been a long time for them to allow people to relocate and devote their lives to this community project.

Another crucial aim of the project was the idea that currency did not exist. Bullon wanted to reintroduce the means of trade, meaning that your trade was your means of surviving. Life was fair in Autark. You could come to the island, but you had to offer something. It was the perfect way to deter the lazy. Everyone had some form of contribution. Whatever you did was eligible for exchange with other settlers. Half a dozen apples could buy you two legs of a rabbit and so on. This archaic way of life was about to become the way of life for selected UK citizens looking for a change. The project appealed to elderly citizens, primarily because they either agreed with the purpose behind the study or they were just looking for somewhere overseas to spend the rest of their days.

The British Government sent UK military forces to Autark to begin construction of an airfield for air landings. The soldiers sent to Autark would be stationed there over the project's ten year study period to ensure safety and reinforce stability. They were encouraged not to intervene unless the circumstances were life threatening for the sake of validity in the study. Due to eventual budget cuts, they too would live by the lifestyle of Autark settlers.

Bullon was a member of university board which meant he would not be able to leave the country for extended periods of time. He was a man with many responsibilities. That's where his partner, Javier Paraíso, came into play. Paraíso became his front man for recording all findings within the study. He would live alongside the test subjects without their knowledge of his objective and observe first-hand how the people would interact with one another. The plan was for Bullon to visit once a month and they would meet within the military base stationed inside the airfield to relay his findings.

The media were hooked during the first few months. Thousands of volunteers had signed on. British citizens of all ages and backgrounds packed their bags in search for a new and simpler life. Paraíso worked closely with the settlers of Autark. Together they built houses, designed ways to access clean running water and implemented solar energy with the materials available to them. It was a huge success right from the start. He pinned it all down to the fact that everybody was in the same boat. They'd given up their life in the UK and this was all they had now. Things in Autark grew quickly, settlements expanded and although there was no television, a radio specialist joined the project and built radios that could connect to the airfield's radio tower for settlers to tune in on second-hand news back home. A few volunteers thought they could dedicate their time to hosting a radio show to increase morale around the island. There were three frequencies, a private station dedicated to the military which was strictly off limits to settlers, one for news updates and topical debates and a final one for music. The analogue radio was really the only technology available to the settlers. Vehicles were hard to come by because of fuel, so horses were the norm, unless you were with the military.

People from all over the world caught on to the success and praise Autark was receiving. They too wanted a piece of the pie. Refugees from eastern countries experiencing ongoing conflicts and civil wars migrated west through Europe. Riots ensued when EU border forces refused entry to the overwhelming masses, thus sending them further down the river and exposing them to something that would only be seen as a utopia. Migrants soon made their way over to isolated Autark by any means necessary. The UK military forces were not prepared for additional numbers and soon lost count and touch with what was really going on. Little did Bullon know, Paraíso had a different view towards his position in the project. As much as Paraíso loved the concept, he felt neglected and envious of the praise Bullon received back in the UK. Paraíso's reputation among the people led him to become their leader, a charismatic vessel of wisdom and hope. The migrants approached his people and not only did he go against the U.N.'s wishes and welcome them with open arms, but he also contacted the western world and advertised Autark to the people of his home nation of Costa Rica.

# TWO

8 YEARS LATER.

The middle-aged couple sat hunched and huddled together under the harsh release of late autumn's downpour. Their horse-drawn carriage trudged through the damp dirt track. Wooden wheels clung jadedly to their structure with every trembling rotation. Raindrops tapped and glided off of hooded waterproof ponchos that sheltered their bodies in the cold. Tall grasslands on rolling hills stretched for miles either side of them with pocketed tree lines scattered throughout. Amidst the darkness of the man's bearded face sat a burning cigarillo between dry lips. The scorching orange light illuminated the greyness of day's gloomy afternoon. Between the couple, further back beneath the carriage's tarpaulin canopy sat a friendly canine companion, a border collie who answered to the calling of Max. The canine's head jolted up as he heard the sounds of teeth crunching through apple.

"Frank?" the woman mumbled through chunks of fruit.

"Yes Annie?" he replied.

"You think we should have waited for the rain to stop?"

"Can't."

"Why not?"

"You know why. Market closes at midday. If we miss this then we'll have to wait another week till the next trade."

"I know."

"Then why'd you ask?"

"I don't know. This weather worries me, that's all."

"I know," he said, allowing the tobacco infused smoke to seep from his mouth. "Me too."

Holding the apple between her teeth, Annie tied her long brunette hair back up into a bun and tucked it back beneath her hood. She sensed Max's interest in the apple and could not defy those eyes of adoration and utter intrigue. Piercing the apple's skin with her incisors, she took the piece of fruit from her mouth and offered it to the dog. He sniffed curiously to investigate before taking it and chewed through the soft, juicy texture. In the cart behind the trio sat rows of crated fruits and vegetables; onions, parsnips, carrots and apples were among several other various choices on offer.

Dying embers and dusty ash fluttered down onto Frank's lap as he moved the cigarillo away from his mouth. The reins of the horses rested loosely in one hand, the cigarillo in the other. Annie fiddled with an old antique radio beside her. Its wooden carvings and overall appearance were a sight to be appreciated. Sadly the same could not be said for its performance.

"Still no good?" Frank asked abruptly.

"No," she sighed in defeat. "Can't seem to get the thing to work."

Frank pushed the end of the cigar into the side of the cart and twisted the light out before tossing it to the mud. "I'm telling you, Annie. Old bastard sold us a lemon – thing's a piece of crap. Kinetically powered radio my arse..."

Annie studied the wire running from the radio to a conductor attached to the wheel's spindle but could make neither head nor tail of the problem.

"Maybe it's the rain."

Up ahead, a man on a horse emerged through the misty wall of rainfall. His hair was drenched in straggled curls that hung in front of his face and his damp shirt clung tightly to his body. It was obvious he had not prepared for such a downpour. As the man's proximity drew nearer, Frank recognised his familiar face through the grey. Frank tugged back on the reins and the carriage stopped parallel to the man. The man sounded his command, a release of air through taut cheeks that sounded like the quack of a duck. The horse stopped immediately. It was obedient and well-trained. There was only one man Frank knew in the whole of Autark who could train horses so well.

"Hello Annabel. Frank," said the man.

"Oh, Henry. Look at you. You'll catch a cold out here," Annie replied. Although they never had any children of their own, Annie always seemed to possess the caring qualities of a nurturing mother.

"That's quite all right, Annabel. Not far to go now." Henry replied in his thick Irish accent. Frank studied Henry's horse, a healthy silver mustang that glistened in the rain.

"How many did you bring in this morning?"

"Just the one today. A snake oil merchant lost one of his two horses to some angry customers last week."

Annie's eyebrows rose unexpectedly, "sounds terrible."

"You should pop in for a drink on your way back. I'll tell you all about it. Don't want to be keeping you out in this rain."

"We should really say the same for you," said Frank.

Henry looked down at his shirt, almost surprised he hadn't noticed just how drenched he really was. Together they laughed, exchanged goodbyes and departed on their separate ways.

The brute force of the weather began to pick up along the damp trail. Puddles consumed the earth. The cart's canopy began to thrash and sway with the wind's quick change of pace and direction. The couple said very little to one another as they drew closer and closer to Merribank village with every rolling stride of the squeaky carriage. Annie tossed the bruising core of the apple into the track below and the smell of tobacco still lingered as the carriage proceeded onwards.

The core of the apple was left lodged into the soaking mud. Several minutes passed. The dirty rainwater splashed up against it, revitalising what was left of its tender juices. The soaking mud slowly began to solidify, attracting panicked insects who sought both nourishment and refuge from drowning. Though the harshness of rainfall surrounded the core, the repetition of each tapping drop evoked a stillness and tranquillity like no other. The insects abruptly scurried away from the track and into the brush. Tumbling vibrations shook the ground, drawing closer and closer to the core as every second passed. The vibrations soon transmitted to the frequencies of galloping hoofs and the squeaking of loose mechanisms.

The apple core was obliterated and disappeared beneath the hurtling force of yet another horse-drawn carriage. Its rickety wheels ripped through the rising puddles along the dirt-ridden track. Unlike the one before it, this carriage bellowed out an aura of ferocity and anguish. The horses were whipped and hollered at by their riders. Four men wielding automatic firearms fired wickedly into autumn's sky. With every shot flashed light from their muzzles and piercing echoes from their chambers. The men chanted and hollered in rebellion and the rumbling engines soon followed behind them.

A convoy of three military trucks made passage behind the cart, but these men were no military. Windshield wipers fought desperately against the thrashing rainfall, now heavier and more frightening than moments ago. Driving the trucks were men of the same nature. Their brutish physique and rough skin; their battered, scarred bodies reflected the hatred within their tormented souls. One in particular stood out from the others. He sat in the passenger seat at the front of the pack. The entire right side of his face was scarred with wrinkled flesh of a past disaster. The burnt man stared out into the bare fields, consumed with burdening thoughts.

Within the darkened canopies of the truck's cargo sat rows of children. Most appeared age ten or eleven, while some were as young as four. Each child was equipped with a firearm far larger than they could carry. The children's fragile minds were poisoned, corrupted by those same men who had been damaged long before them. Sitting quietly, they too were scarred and dented by the world around them. There was nothing but the rain and engines to drown out the silence. Among the children, one stood out as a vessel of childlike innocence. Rather than wielding arms, this young boy held a small black book, and in that book he scribbled and sketched with a blunt pencil. This boy could not have been older than four or five but the other children only appeared to repel his magnitude of potential.

# THREE

Between high wooden beams the hanging lights of Merribank illuminated the market place. Crowds of settlers and merchants exchanged their trade. Rays of light shone multi-coloured apparitions through crystal glass decor more poignant in the gloom of an afternoon most grey. Merribank market was the village's main attraction, a calling point to all those looking to trade in the south-west of Autark. Its grand stone archway tunnel was a spectacle in itself that took the settlers of Merribank two years to complete. Those travelling into the village set up their stalls while merchants opened their doors to anyone seeking only the best value. The scent of freshly caught fish, aromatic spices and exotic perfumes generated a musky aroma that entwined the crowded marketplace. A row of elderly widows bartered and haggled with the local butcher for the finest cutlets of venison the island had to offer.

Situated atop several pillars scattered throughout the market were megaphone polls. They regurgitated distorted renditions of music through Radio Autark. It was the same orchestral piece that had been on the air for the past four years. It droned endlessly but the villagers of Merribank had listened to it for so long that they somehow tuned it out completely. Although it had been turned off from time to time, a group of children who resided the village found amusement in switching it back on when the adults weren't looking.

Established on the corner of the market's street was a boutique tailor with fine leathers and practical accessories displayed proudly behind the window's chipped wooden frame.

Annie closed the door as she and Frank stepped out onto the street and she wriggled her hands into her new leather gloves. She took a sip of water before placing the canteen back into Frank's knapsack. Frank carried a crate with leftover fruits from the morning's trade. Upon their return to the cart, they discovered Max standing watch, deterring all those who dared to help themselves to the contents of their cart. Frank smiled at the dog and the dog looked back with that same adoration he always did.

Frank hauled the heavy crate back into the cart and pulled the canopy back over the top to cover the goods. They had bartered their trade of fruit and vegetables in exchange for ten bags of compost; half a dozen freshly cut steak fillets, a case of shotgun shells to deter the crows and a new machete that Frank planned to use to maintain next year's cornfield.

"What's for dinner tonight, darling?" Frank asked.

"Roast with veg and lots of salad."

"Again? Jesus Annie, I'm not a rabbit. A man can only eat so much lettuce."

"Then stop bloody growing so much and we won't have to eat it," she snapped back playfully. Frank turned to her and put his arm over her shoulder. He thought about when they were younger and first getting married; how they struggled to make ends meet just to put food on the table. Once they both had a taste for this new life, every other way just seemed overcomplicated and unnecessary. They struggled back then, but they managed to get through it all because they were together. To Frank, that was all that mattered. She was all that mattered. He pulled her closer and laughed, kissing her forehead softly. "Was there anything else you wanted to do before we head back?"

"No. My hands are warm now." She smiled and rested her head upon his chest.

Distant screams of women drowned out the tunnel, reverberating against the walls and flooding the inner market. Both settlers and merchants turned to face the distant cries, peering over one another to observe the commotion. Frank stepped out into the road to get a better look but a crowd had already formed to block his field of view.

The blast of automatic rifles flooded the marketplace. Frank flinched at the sharpness of their resonance and when he looked again, the sea of people had parted, scattering in all directions. He turned to see his wife but was blocked by the sheer chaos of scarpering settlers. Bodies dropped all around him. He felt a great force push against him suddenly, a cowering merchant shoved through with neither thought nor care. Frank fell back into the road. His back thumped hard against the stone floor. The wind shot out from his lungs and he could do nothing to retrieve it.

He stared up into the glowing colourful lights above. Panicked legs flew past and their feet trampled over his body. Turning over onto his stomach, he pushed himself to crawl through the sea of chaos. Gunfire blared in the distance. It was getting closer. His fingers were stamped on beneath the filthy boots of panicked settlers. The pain was sharp and the blood pumped harder through to his fingertips. Frank used the fallen bodies to drag himself over to the roadside. As he caught his breath, the sound of smashing glass combusted the nearby market stalls into a blazing inferno. A merchant bolted into the road, doused in the flames of a Molotov cocktail that danced all around him. His screaming cries would scar the minds of all those who heard for an eternity.

He wondered if this was a nightmare, if he would wake up any moment at home, sitting next to Annie in their matching armchairs. The pain was too real, his body ached and bruised. Through the obstructed view he caught glimpses of children bearing arms. They fired their weapons into the market's stone shelter. No remorse, blind to the nature of their actions. He heard her calling. It came from across the road but he could not see through the desperate stampede. He brought himself up to his feet and pushed through the masses, barging shoulder to shoulder with every step.

Annie saw his face and reached out over the others to take his hand but she couldn't reach. Instead, Frank shoved through and swept her to the front of the carriage. Together they quickly climbed aboard. The horses reared up wildly and whinnied amidst the madness. Frank held the reins tight and the cart swerved out into the road. He felt the bumping of pedestrians hitting the back of the cart as they were shoved from its path. Another banquet of fire erupted behind them, bullets ricocheted and snapped up from the dirt and stone below. Dozens of settlers dropped, folding to the ground. A bloody mist sprayed up into Frank's face. He whipped the reins but could not see ahead of him. The carriage jolted over the jagged stone floor and fallen bodies and soared out into the clearing of the open trail.

They had made it out into the desolate trail between the village and their home. They would have gone the full stretch but the cart dragged to a sudden halt. One of the horses collapsed. It was the older of the two, twenty-three years of age. She dropped to the ground, her legs folding beneath her exhausted body. They sat isolated in the middle of the dirt track. There was nothing but the light patter of rain and swaying trees shedding their leaves. An array of vegetation gently floated over the cart. Warm yellows, ambers and dark decaying browns fluttered to the ground around them; and in those colours he saw the burning flames of Merribank marketplace.

"Are you okay?" he asked her. She nodded but her face said otherwise, eyes wide, darting from one side of the tree line to the other. He hopped down into the road and detached the injured horse from the cart. It struggled to walk, limping towards the tall grass on the other side. Frank marched to the back of the cart. He reached inside and pulled the shotgun out from inside the canopy. He cracked it open and checked the breech. Two shells. He flipped the barrel back up and it locked into place. Frank stood there beside the cart for a while, watching the horse traipse and whinny softly. He started to approach it but stopped halfway. He couldn't do it, couldn't bring himself to put the suffering creature out of its misery, not after what they had just been through. He stood there in the rain and the injured horse shambled away into the open field. Frank turned back to Annie and said, "you think we can make it back with just the one?"

She didn't reply. She didn't even hear him, her mind was elsewhere.

"Annie," he repeated, much louder this time.

Finally, her eyes engaged his own. He moved to her side and looked up at her closed body sitting up on the carriage beside Max.

"I know you're scared. I'm scared," he admitted. "But I need you here with me now. I can't get us back on my own."

She nodded again; this time in short, rapid bursts. She closed her eyes but no matter how hard she tried she couldn't shake the horrific images from her mind. Frank glanced back over to the field and noticed the wounded horse lying on its side, its weary lungs expanding and contracting with every numbered breath. The croak of the raven distracted him from behind. It called to him from a low branch, staring at him, cautioning him.

Frank and Annie walked round to the back of the cart to check on the stock. Frank pulled back the tarpaulin blinds. Annie nabbed the box of shotgun shells with shaking hands and stuffed them into Frank's knapsack.

"When we get back, I'll warn Henry while you go inside and get your sister," Frank ordered. "I don't think it'll be safe in the house for the time being. Not until we know what's going on."

She didn't reply. He felt her tug on his arm like an infant calling for attention.

"Frank?" she called out wearily.

"What is it?" he asked, still focused on the stock.

"Frank."

"What?"

This time he looked up at her but she wasn't looking at him, she was looking dead ahead. He followed her gaze to the back of the cart. Crouched in the corner of the cart was a small boy. His knees were tucked up into his frail chest, hands firmly clasped on a book of some sort. At first glance he did not appear armed or dangerous. He had tanned skin, straggled black hair and eyes of emerald green. Tattered rags held by a rope at the waist were all that clothed his naked body. They stared at the boy and he stared back. The dull droning of engines loomed in the distance behind them. Terror struck their hearts. They looked at each other, then back at the muddy trail they had just taken.

"Just grab him," Frank ordered. "We won't make it back fast enough on this thing."

"But what about the other stuff?"

"Leave it."

He snatched the machete, looped it to his belt and placed the shotgun sling securely over his shoulder.

"Come with me," Annie called out to the boy. "I won't hurt you." She gestured to the child with open arms. He was apprehensive at first, but when he heard the engines closing in; his mind was quickly made up. Though Frank could not see the trucks, there was no doubt in his mind that they were heading their way. He detached the only remaining horse from the cart and helped Annie and the boy up onto the saddle.

"You ready to run, boy?" he asked Max as he mounted the horse. The dog tilted his head to one side, gazing at the new companion that sat between his masters. Frank and Annie looked back one last time. The rusty military trucks rose swiftly over the horizon through the damp drizzle. Frank kicked his heels into the horse's sides. Annie sat behind him with the frightened boy between them, holding her arms tightly around Frank's waist as they set off down the track. He looked back and saw Max sprinting fast, doing his very best to keep up.

The horse was through the gate and up the trail before they even had a chance to gauge their surroundings.

"Tracy!" Annie called out to the house. It was a little rough around the edges and could have done with a lick of paint but it was home. She hopped off the horse, up the front porch and disappeared up the stairs. Across the landscape, Frank spotted clouds of black smoke rising. *The stables.* Scorching flames parried the drizzle of rainfall. Henry's home, once a beautifully handcrafted wooden stable was now a blazing inferno.

"Oh God..."

The stench of reeking gasoline lingered out from the burning stables. The fire spread rapidly across the tall pastures between them, creeping closer and closer toward the rich fields of Frank and Annie's livelihood.

"Frank!" he heard her call to him from inside.

He went for the door but remembered the boy, still sitting atop the mount. He looked petrified, the distant flames dazzling the whites of his eyes. Frank took the boy into his arms and headed into the house with Max on his heels.

He found Annie sitting on the bed beside her older sister Tracy. She was pale, shaking and withdrawn from the others. Annie felt obliged to look after her older sister and she cared for her very much. She remembered when their mother died and how hard Tracy took it. It was the first time they discovered her symptoms. While most grieved for the loss of a loved one; Tracy shot through phases of grief, anger and uncomfortable bursts of laughter that worried them all so dearly. She was never the same after that, but Annie was always there to care for her.

Frank stood in the doorway with the child in his arms. His soaked jacket and waterproof poncho dripped onto the warped wooden floorboards below. He hesitated momentarily, not knowing whether the child could be trusted alone. He wanted to pack additional supplies and time was running out. Tracy needed Annie by her side and he feared he might learn to regret leaving the boy unsupervised. He sat the child on the bed next to Tracy and began stuffing his knapsack with extra clothes and two blankets that lay at the foot of the bed.

"Who is this?" Tracy asked.

Frank didn't look back. "We're not sure."

"What do you mean you're not sure?"

"There's no time. We need to get out of here right now."

The child's eyes bounced around the room, dazed and confused. He was unsure of his surroundings but continued to remain still.

"Annie, I need you downstairs in one minute. Can you do that for me?" Frank asked.

She didn't acknowledge him but he knew she heard. She took hold of Tracy's hand and carefully helped her up onto her feet. Frank bolted down the staircase, through the kitchen and out the back of the house. He packed some rope from over where he tied the ladders together and ran back indoors. Once inside, he took to his knees and scrambled around the lower cabinets. Various cast-iron pots and pans spilled out onto the kitchen floor behind him. He took a small boiling pot and tied it to his knapsack with the rope. He wrapped the pot in scarce rags to muffle the clattering sound of metal. He checked the cabinet above the sink – a single tin of homemade tomato soup, a box of matches and a container of leftover strips of grilled rabbit jerky – it would have to do. He took his canteen from the knapsack and filled it at the sink before stuffing it back inside. He would have to boil it some other time. The bellowing rumble of engines shook the house. He froze for a split second, as if to double-check that his ears were not deceiving him, but the engines grew louder with every passing second.

"Annie!" he called out from the kitchen. He held onto the shotgun and tossed the knapsack over his shoulder.

"Annie, we have to go right now."

"We're coming," she hollered back.

Annie and Tracy rushed downstairs and through to the kitchen. Annie held the boy in one arm and he held on tight whilst fiddling with his ear. Frank tossed Tracy her coat and bag. She caught them in a flustered mess and put them on amidst the madness. Frank swung open the back door. It clashed against the stopper and reverberated back on its hinges.

"You get them down the field and into the tree line. You don't stop, understand?"

"What about you?"

"I'll be right behind you. Just go."

The trucks stopped outside the front of the house and the engines cut to dead silence. Frank heard Annie and Tracy's footsteps cutting through the tall grass of the allotment out back. He peered into the hallway and saw shadows emerging through the frosted glass panels in the front door. A sharp set of knocks startled him and he instinctively raised the shotgun. Max barked at the silhouettes.

"Stay!" Frank muttered, slowly backing further into the kitchen.

"Frank?" a familiar voice called out to him from the other side. He lowered the shotgun in bewilderment. "Henry?"

"Frank, you need to open the door."

"Henry. The stables..."

"Don't worry about that."

Frank sensed a disturbing inflection in Henry's voice. He stopped, eyes fixated on the silhouette of his neighbour through the glass.

"Henry?"

"Yes Frank?"

"You're not alone, are you?"

"No Frank."

He felt a lump in his throat, a single bead of sweat dripped down his temple.

"I'm so sorry," he choked. It was all he could muster. He struggled to leave from that spot; to turn his back and leave his neighbour, his friend, knowing that he would never see him again.

"You should get out of here, Frank."

Frank took several retreated steps before turning his back on Henry. He darted out the back door as fast as he could and hurtled down the hill. Max sprinted ahead of him. Frank felt his equipment weighing him down with every step, his lungs peddling overtime. The crack of gunfire tore shreds of wood and glass from behind him. He felt his legs speed up to the downward momentum but his body failed to keep up. He stumbled forward and his hands slammed hard into the earth below. His legs flew back over the top of his body. He tumbled down the grassy hillside and crashed through the cane pillars of the tomato patch.

All the pain shot to his ankle. He laid there on his back, the rain water splashing against his dirt-ridden face. Gunfire snapped by overhead. He turned onto his belly and crawled towards the tree line. Henry's tortured screams carried out for miles across the raided valleys. Frank heard men hollering to one another in a foreign language but he struggled to distinguish it over the echoing gunshots. Annie emerged from the shrubbery. She stalked over to Frank, pulled him up onto his feet and guided him into the forest.

"Where's the horse?" he asked. Annie's only response was her faltered loss for words. "I thought you were going to get her? That's why I thought you told us to go on."

"Forget it. We can't go back."

"What about your ankle?"

"I'll be okay. Just grab the boy."

They trekked a few miles downhill through the forest. Frank didn't stop in fear of their pursuit. The constant rain caused the forest floor to become a stodgy marshland. His ankle throbbed and began to swell but he carried on nevertheless. Exhausted. Through the gentle patter of rain and squelching of their boots, they each lifted their weary heads to the unmistakable sound of running water. Tracy reached the peak of the valley and took a moment to breath. "There's a river," she called out to the others falling in behind. Frank caught up beside them. He noticed the approach of nightfall and recognised the river.

"Kiors Creek. Carries down from a stream far west. The other end flows north to Elkford,"

"I've never seen it," said Annie. "When did you come up here, when we first came over?"

"Not quite that soon. Maybe four years ago or so."

"What for?"

"Was stocking up on medicinal plants, and it was a good excuse to give Max and the horses a walk. All we have to do is follow it."

She knelt by the river where the rain beat against its surface. She scooped the water up and brushed it across her face. She then did the same for the boy standing beside her. He remained silent, yet to speak, but allowed her to wash his face for him. They filled their canteens by the river but Frank could see Tracy was hesitant. "It's safe to drink once we've boiled it. Waters never met the ocean, rain won't do much harm."

All at once they heard Max's call not far up at the face of a nearby cliff. They followed the sound of his bark up through the trees and rocky crevices. When they reached him, his front paws stood raised against a dying pine, barking up at a panicked squirrel that spiralled up the diseased tree trunk. Max had discovered a small convex dip in the side of the moss-engrossed stone cliff, a shelter in the form of a cave. It was a poor excuse for a cave, maybe more of a small cavern, only five metres deep but Frank wasn't in any position to complain. It appeared unoccupied. No signs of leftover carcass lay within its depths, nor any faeces or disturbance of nesting. Frank contemplated the risk of staying the night. The light was fading fast and the cavern sheltered them from the rain that appeared to have no end in sight. He knew there was no way they could continue through the dark, especially with his ankle that had been overworked since they had left the house. His throbbing fingers and aching chest made the prospect of rest all too tempting. The cavern was tucked away from the open stretch that followed Kiors Creek. Although it was cramped, it would have to make do as their camp for the night. There were no alternatives. The wilderness of Autark could be a dangerous place for drifters and travellers alike; but if there was one thing Frank was certain of, he would not sleep well that night.

# FOUR

Frank lay in utter darkness, completely still within the cramped conditions of the cave. He felt the cold in his bones and the temperature dropping in the night. In the corner of his eye he could see the last haze of the campfire's smoulder drift outside, lost to the forest.

He couldn't sleep. The weight of the world was on his shoulders, the mass of the earth flooding his mind. He thought about the boy; how he had not spoken a single word since their discovery. He wondered what had led him into their lives. That night they had pitched a fire inside the cave, surrounding it with tall rocks to aid in the concealment of its light and flame.

They had no bedrolls, only the clothes on their backs and two blankets between them to keep them warm. Annie and Tracy shared one, pushed up against one side of the cave. Frank could just about make out the boy, wrapped tightly in the other. He was curled into a ball and Max lay beside him in a similar fashion, his nose tucked round into his scruffy tail.

Frank couldn't help but wonder if they were being followed. His mind flooded with questions. *What do they want? Is it the boy?* He gazed out into the bitter darkness. Moonlight shimmered off naked branches that whistled and cracked in the cold.

The cackle of the pestering crow stirred Frank from his indefinite slumber. He had barely slept at all, maybe two hours at best. Rays of sunlight beamed into the cavern. He felt his heavy eyelids hang as though they were being held shut. For a split second, he imagined he had woken in the comfort of his own bed. The sudden realisation was like a fist in his gut. A flushed sweat triggered across his brow. He shot up and looked back over his shoulder but there was nobody there.

He scrambled up to his feet but dropped back to one knee. He'd forgotten about his ankle. His body fought desperately to catch up with his eager mind. The monotonous croak taunted him from a treetop outside the cavern. He listened to it again and knew he was mistaken. It was not a crow but rather a raven. He had recognised its call from before on the road back from Merribank. At first it irritated him, mocked him from afar, but the more it croaked the more he believed its call was that of unsettling woe. His head lifted, eyes squinting against the rays of light and once he gauged a clear view into the clearing, he was filled with an overwhelming sense of relief.

The boy sat peacefully atop the stone's flat surface. His feet did not touch the ground and instead kicked freely, back and forth as he scribbled into a black leather-bound book. Max sat beside him, stripping away layers of bark from a fallen tree branch with his teeth. His fur was still damp from the previous day. He sensed his master approaching and stared up at Frank with those glistening brown eyes, his tongue bouncing with every pant. Frank hobbled out from the cavern's shelter.

"Where's Annie?" He asked the boy.

The boy pulled his attention from the illustrations but remained silent. He caught sight of the bearded man and glanced sheepishly over towards the river.

"I'm going down to speak with her," said Frank. "You stay right here with Max, you understand?"

The boy nodded. Frank patted Max on the head and set off downhill, clinging on to each tree that he passed for support.

With the sun shining through the pines, it was as if Frank was seeing the river again for the first time. The light reflected off the water's surface, flowing down the river's course with such natural grace. He spotted Annie and Tracy filling up their canteens where they had done so the previous day. They noticed him hobbling down and he could tell Annie was none too pleased to see him up and about on his feet.

"You should be resting," she called out as he covered the last twenty yards.

"You should have woken me. It isn't safe out here."

"Why aren't you with Sam?" Tracy asked.

Frank looked back uphill and caught vague glimpses of Max and the boy through the branches above.

"He's okay. Max is watching him."

"He's certainly taken a liking to him awfully fast."

"I know. Strange. He's usually more careful with strangers."

Tracy knelt down to fill her canteen. She held the top against the water's current so it flowed in with minimal effort.

Frank rested both hands on his hips and turned back to the ladies.

"So what we gonna do?"

"What do you mean?" Annie asked.

"Well we have a stray child on our hands and it isn't safe to head back home."

"I thought you said we were heading to Elkford?"

"We are. I'm talking after that. After we hand him over."

"Hand him over?" said Annie.

Frank sensed the sudden disappointment underlying her tone. "Well what did you think we were doing? He belongs to somebody, Annie."

"He's right, Annie," Tracy piped up, her back still turned as she capped the canteen shut. "His parents are probably worried sick."

"I know, but what if his parents aren't around anymore? Who will take care of him?"

Frank glanced to Tracy and knew that she too shared his concern. He rested his hand upon his wife's shoulder and moved in closer.

"We'll figure this out once we get to Elkford, okay?"

Her opinions had not been reciprocated among the others. He saw her saddened eyes shy away. He was drawn to them, so deep and full of disappointment and his heart sank low in his chest.

Frank made his way back up to the cave ahead of the others. He aimed to pack up their supplies to start heading north as soon as possible.

*"Are you an incomer?"* a soft voice whispered.

Frank stopped. He turned to face the boy who sat with the blanket wrapped around him. His cheeks a rosy complexion and eyes so wide you would think he had seen a ghost.

"Am I what?"

The boy struggled to look him in the eye, intimidated by Frank's rugged exterior.

"An incomer; a person from outside." he repeated once more. His accent was remote. Frank had never heard anything like it.

"So you do talk?"

The boy nodded. Frank moved closer to him, ignoring the aching pain in his ankle. "Yeah, I guess you could call me that. What's your name?"

The boy glanced up, unsure. "My *name*?"

"Yes, your name. You must have a name?"

The boy shook his head.

"Do you know where your mother and father are?"

The boy ignored the question and returned to his book. Frank quickly lost his attention and could tell he was no longer comfortable with the subject. If they were going to find his parents he would need more information. They had the entire journey to Elkford to find that out. The boy just needed time to warm up to them. Although he had seen the start of something between Annie and the boy, he couldn't help but feel the urge to pass the child on as quickly as possible. Their home had been destroyed and the only thing on his mind was keeping his family safe and seeking amends for the damages.

Frank began to learn more about the raiders every day. He had heard stories and rumours of their existence from the merchants of Merribank but never believed them to be true. Although they had no official name, they were said to have been pirates of the sea, claiming that the island of Autark had previously belonged to another. Even though Autark was situated in the north Atlantic, their numbers consisted of men and women from all over the eastern coastlines of South America. He remembered a fisherman in Merribank who once claimed they had overthrown the military base four years ago. He claimed that all communications with the outside world had been destroyed, that the raiders were using the base as a fort. People in the west rarely ventured east. There was little need and if they ever did, it would only ever be to visit Wolvendale to purchase building material in bulk.

Few people believed the fisherman, including Frank, but now he began to see things differently. The raiders were closing in from the east, slaughtering the innocent and kidnapping their young to force them into slavery. They took advantage of their fragile, impressionable minds and moulded them into soldiers, into killing machines.

"You ran away from those men, didn't you?"

"Yes."

"You were scared?"

The boy nodded.

"You didn't want to do the things they wanted you to do."

"No."

"Are you scared of me?"

The boy shook his head. The throbbing in Frank's ankle returned suddenly. His leg gave way but he managed to catch the large rock to break his fall. He leaned against the rock where the boy sat and lifted his trouser leg to take a closer look. His ankle was swollen. It had discoloured, bruised to a deep purple but he was certain that nothing was broken. He noticed the boy staring at the ankle for some time, but he couldn't quite make out what he was thinking. Annie and Tracy returned from the river. Like a sixth sense, Annie spotted Frank immediately. He was leaning to one side, wincing in pain.

"Are you okay?"

"I'm fine," he replied, stubborn as a mule. She helped him across and sat him down on the rock beside the boy.

"He just spoke," Frank said, and just like that Annie's face lit up in excitement.

"Is that true? Did you speak to Frank?"

She knelt down beside him and was filled with a new lease of energy. The boy smiled back at her, enticed by her showering praise and light-hearted tone. She took his small hand into her own. "What is your name?"

"He doesn't have one," Frank interrupted through grunting and moaning.

"You don't?" she said. She spoke in that same voice she used with Max. In fact, Max was caught up in all the excitement, his front paws resting on the rock as he sniffed out the boy beside Annie, tail wagging like a helicopter preparing to take flight.

"Well we'll have to do something about that now, won't we?" Annie continued. The boy smiled and tilted his head forward bashfully. Frank saw the connection between them and he knew the boy's innocence warmed her kind heart. She had taken to him so naturally, using extravagant gestures and a pureness in her speech that he rarely ever saw anymore.

"What about Phil?" Tracy suggested.

"No, he's not a Phil, are you?" said Annie. She laughed and the boy's smile grew wider.

"*Phil*", he giggled back to her.

"What about Sam?" she conferred with her sister.

"Sam's nice," Tracy agreed.

She went ahead and pitched the name to the boy. "What do you think?" He nodded in approval but a name meant nothing to him. The concept was alien to him. He had always been used to being nothing more than a number. As he stood over them, Frank felt conflicted, joy and concern. She was getting too attached. Now she had *named* him, and he feared that the more time they spent with the child, the harder it would be to part.

# FIVE

They followed the river north that day, taking the path along the embankment in the hope that it would lead them directly to Elkford. The terrain was rough and uneven – gravel littered over smooth stones that stuck out of the muddy earth – a steep drop on either side of the river. Frank heard the rumbling of his empty stomach before he felt it.

All they had eaten over the past day was the single tin of tomato soup. They shared it between them the night before. Frank served Annie and Tracy a fair portion, leaving the meagre leftovers for himself. He fed Max some of the jerky and saved the rest for later. He gave the majority of his own share to the boy. His thin arms and prominent cheek bones suggested malnourishment. He took it as an example of the kind of treatment dealt to all those under the enslavement of the raiders.

Max followed close by. Frank treaded carefully across the rocky terrain. Annie and Tracy followed close behind. Sam walked between them, arms raised as he held onto their hands. Annie had cut the blanket in half and cut a hole big enough for the boy's head. He wore it like a poncho over his tattered rags. It wasn't much but at least it was an extra layer. The boy's feet were caked in mud and cracked leather sandals were all that covered them. They had spoken on and off with the boy. It was nothing more than small talk about minor things. Things they had seen by the riverbed along the way, the weather, but it soon trailed off for several minutes of silence.

"Frank, do you think they made it out okay?" Annie asked.

"Who?"

"Henry's family; Callum and the girls."

Frank hadn't even thought about it. His mind was elsewhere. He thought about Elkford and wondered if the raiders had already travelled north to make their mark on the wooden fortress. They hadn't seen a single soul their entire time in the forest and that only agitated him further.

"I don't know," he replied. "I'd like to think so, but I couldn't say."

They reached a natural obstacle ahead and Frank soon realised the dangers of their position. Over the years, the rise in the river's water level had gradually worn away the riverbank, turning their path ahead into a steep downward slope towards the river. He looked up at the bold rock formation covered in moss and hanging ivy that separated them from the rest of the forest. It followed parallel to the river and had finally caught up with them, curving its way in front of them and stopping at the water's edge. A lone, warped pine leant over the river, its roots somehow growing in the sheer face of the sloped rock. Below the tree he noticed the increasing speed of the water's current. A simple creek had cultivated into a wider, more aggressive river.

"Maybe we can go back and find the road?" Tracy suggested.

He glanced back along the bank where they came from. There was no way they were going back after covering all that ground.

"The roads aren't safe anymore," said Frank. "I mean we've come this far and we don't know how close or far they are." He studied the rock formation blocking their way once more. It was steep to begin with but the top was a flatter surface that reconnected to the rest of the forest.

"We'll have to climb over," said Frank.

"How on earth are we going to scale that?" asked Annie. Frank carefully climbed up to the obstacle, scaling a boulder that stuck out from the damp earth between the rocks. He turned his back and leant against the rock's jagged surface, spreading his legs and bending them at the knees.

"I'll boost you one at a time."

"Frank, your ankle," said Annie.

"It's okay, come on."

She rolled her eyes and shook her head. Frank had always been a stubborn man. He intertwined his fingers, locking his hands together and presenting his curved palms to the others.

"Tracy, let's go," he persisted.

Tracy looked to Annie, both ladies frustrated with his hustle, but together they knew he was right. There was no way of knowing if they were being followed. Going back now could resort in finding themselves face to face with their pursuers.

Tracy lifted herself up to the boulder and placed her foot in the pocket of Frank's palms. Annie watched nervously with the boy who buried his head into the material of her waterproof poncho.

Frank boosted Tracy up over his shoulders and felt her weight lessen as she pulled herself up to the rock's flat surface above.

"Come on, boy," Frank said, clapping his hands and gesturing inwards towards his chest. Max hopped up to the flat boulder and jumped up into Frank's arms. He turned, passing Max up to Tracy.

"Annie."

She let go of the boy's hand and raised her own, *stay put*. He nodded and watched her follow suit of the others. As Frank hauled Annie up, he felt a slight movement below him but his feet were sturdy on the rock. Once she was up, the feeling had departed. He stepped forward and helped the small boy up to join him on the boulder. When he took hold of the boy, the weight of the boulder dipped to one side beneath his feet.

The boulder was moving.

The boulder popped straight out from the face of the incline. It detached from the wet mud. The slanted edge dipped suddenly toward the river and knocked Frank and the boy along with it. He slammed down into the pebbly slope below ahead of the rock and began to roll uncontrollably towards the rapid waters below. He barely heard Annie call out to him over the sounds of his body scratching and thumping down the incline. He crashed hard, breaking the water's bubbly white surface and plummeted deep into its depths, the boy tight in his arms. Frank opened his eyes and could see the dirt from his clothes wash away into the murky water. Tiny bubbles shot up to the surface. His eyes followed them down to the boy in his arms. He thrashed back and forth violently, his screams muffled through the water. Frank fought hard against the current, flipping in all directions as he tried to direct them up.

He pushed for the surface, holding the boy up to catch the first breaths. Frank gasped for breath the moment his lips broke the surface, a mixture of oxygen and water drowned his lungs. He coughed on impulse, eyes popping wide in shock as he regurgitated the water back up his windpipe. He could do nothing to repel the strength of the water's current dragging them downstream. Frank caught sight of the treacherous rapids ahead. He glanced back, glimpses of his wife and sister in-law rippled through the frothy water but there was nothing to stop him from taking this inevitable detour.

They plummeted through the rapids, the water swallowed them whole. Frank tried to hold the boy above the surface but was tossed around like a rag doll in the sheer force of the current. A losing battle of endurance against mother nature.

The further they travelled downstream, the narrower the distance between the rocks. Frank felt his jacket tear. His body scratched and thumped against the rocks' edges. They bobbed up and down through the water, gasping for pockets of breath at any given chance, Frank's lungs tightening in his chest. Plunging further down, he caught sight of a giant boulder that rose out of the water and split its path. He could move neither left nor right to stray its path. All he could think to do was protect the boy. Thrashing against the current, he turned his back to the boulder and closed his eyes. His body tensed. He held the boy out in front of him and the waves crashed furiously around them. The boy remained silent, too shocked to resonate the faintest of utterances. Frank waited. The anticipation killed him. He thought it to be worse than the outcome, but he was wrong. The bluntness of the boulder rattled his spine – knocking the wind out of his restless lungs –

delivering the final blow as his vision faded away into complete darkness.

Frank opened his eyes. His vision was blurred, obscure and liquefied. The sky overhead came to his foreground and intertwined the branches of the pines above. All he could hear was the vibrations of the water running its course past the pebbles and stones around him. A small figure came forward into view. He studied it just as intensely as it stared back. It was the boy. It was Sam.

Frank shot up. He felt the water in his lungs rush up his throat and coughed impulsively. Sam jumped to one side, nearly tripping over into the shallow water of the riverbank. Frank gagged on the water and a hollow regurgitating sound emitted his throat. Tears formed in the ducts of his eyes, his throat straining from the sheer reflexes of his gullet. Long deep breaths followed the water's passing. He stared at Sam who stared back in fear. Frank found it near impossible to figure out what was going on in that head of his. Looking around, he could see that the creek flowed far smoother now than it did before. Far up the valley was a final rapid where water plummeted into a shallow spring and cruised downhill in a zigzagging motion.

Annie, Tracy and Max were nowhere to be seen. Frank felt the bruises running up his body. Although his back felt frail, there was enough movement to reassure him it wasn't broken. He shuffled back to the edge of the riverbank below a collection of hanging willow trees. The boy followed. His hands were close to his chest, insecure of what he should do.

"How long I been out?" Frank asked.

The boy shrugged his shoulders nervously. Frank used the nearby rocks to help him up to his feet. The water in his clothes weighed him down. He noticed the boy in his soaking rags and damp stringy hair that now swept across his forehead.

"We need to get you some new clothes."

Sam nodded. "I'm cold."

"Me too."

Frank removed his poncho, jacket and shirt and rested them on the nearby rocks that were lit by the sun. The temperature was still low but he couldn't tell if it was just the cold water on their bodies. He untied one of his boots, tipped it upside down and watched the water pour out into the damp earth. After untying the other, he removed his socks and ringed them out before placing them with the other clothes to dry. Frank sat down on one of the boulders. They sat together, filthy and drenched like drowned rats.

"Take off those rags, you'll get hypothermia."

"What's that?"

"You'll catch a bad cold," Frank said.

The boy shook his head, arms stiff by his sides in protest.

"Suit yourself." Frank rummaged around the pocket of his jacket atop the rock, studying the boy's rags as he did so. It was only after close examination that he realised it was merely a potato sack. It had holes for arms and a head and was tied at the waist with a piece of frayed rope. The sack was ripped across the torso and made the boy look square and rigid. Frank pulled a small wooden box wrapped in a leather slip case from his jacket pocket. He untied the damp drawstring and opened it carefully, checking no water had gotten inside the box before pulling out a cigarillo and placing it between his cracked lips. The boy watched in amusement. Frank caught on to the boy's gaze. He took the box and pushed a small release near the bottom of the box. A secret compartment slid out from beneath. It contained matches and a piece of flint. Frank peered up at the boy as he took a match and struck it across the flint.

The match snapped in two and the boy made no effort to contain his amusement.

"That's not funny," said Frank.

The boy smiled and watched some more. Frank took another match - one that appeared to be the most superior - and struck again. *Success*. The phosphorous ignited. Frank quickly shielded it from the wind with his free hand and pulled it in to the tip of the cigarillo.

"They should be following the river. We'll just have to wait for them to catch up."

"Okay."

Frank noticed the boy's face drop. "What's the matter?"

The boy reached inside his potato sack rags and pulled out a black leather-bound book and pencil. He opened the book of wet pages and handed it to Frank. The book was filled with primitive child-like drawings of stick figures in all kinds of situations. Frank turned each damp page with care, examining the sketches the boy had created while mouthing the cigarillo into the corner of his lips. There were dozens of sketches. Stick-figures, trucks of them all armed with rifles, a burning village and several other violent sketches. There was one with a figure lying face down with a smaller figure in its arms.

Behind the figure was another person aiming what could only be depicted as a gun to the back on the figure's head. He wondered whether the boy had seen all of these images, and if so, he felt pity for the child. No child - or human being for that matter - should ever have to witness such incidents.

Frank felt the dampness of his jeans chafing. He adjusted them at the ankle and as he did so, he noticed a black sluggish creature gripping to his calf. It was a leech. He couldn't even feel it and knew the local anaesthetic must have already begun making its way through his body. Sam's face dropped, shocked eyes darted back and forth between Frank and the leech. Frank took the cigarillo from his mouth and aimed the burning tip down at the leech. He lowered it and placed the tip onto the leech. Sam watched it drop and squirm back down the riverbank. Frank noticed something on the boy, his eyes squinting to gauge a clearer view.

"Lift up your arm," he said, waving the cigar in his hand.

Sam did as he was told and spotted the large leech clinging to his elbow. He began to panic, hopping up and down, not knowing what to do.

"Calm down," Frank said. He clutched the boy's wrist tight and held him steady. Holding out the cigar, he could feel the boy pull away. "Stop squirming. The longer you leave it there, the worse it'll get."

Sam nodded, reluctant at first, and then he shut his eyes tight. The cigar sizzled as it made contact with the bloodsucking parasite. The leech dropped instantly. Frank took a handful of his vest and stretched it up to wipe away the blood. It continued to gradually ooze out of the sucker marks. Frank rose to his feet, scanning the surroundings as he spoke. He was looking for something. Something in particular.

"Okay I need you to stay here. I'll be right back, understand?" he mumbled sternly past the cigarillo between his teeth. Sam nodded again and stood awkwardly beside the sprawl of damp clothes on the rock.

Sam watched the bearded man just a little farther down by the creek's edge. He knelt in the shrubbery and picked some plants. He analysed them, stared at them, sniffed, and even tasted them before hobbling back over to the boy.

"Okay. Listen up, this is good to know."

"Why?" Sam asked, sitting cross-legged on the boulder's surface.

"What do you mean, 'why?' It's good for you to know this. It's important."

"Okay."

Frank held up the plant for Sam to observe. "See this plant? It's called a Melastoma. It'll help stop the bleeding on that little bite you have there. You can tell it from other plants because of its long thin leaves and red stalk, you see there?" Frank ran the tip of his finger along the stalk and then handed the plant to Sam. Taking another, he continued the lecture. "You'll find these along most sunlit riverbanks. What you do is, you chew the leaves there and you stick them on your wound. That'll coagulate the blood for you."

"What does *cogolots* mean?" asked Sam, his voice both confident and enthusiastic.

"Coagulate... it means to harden or solidify."

"What does solidify mean?"

Frank sighed, "It means to– look, you put the plant on the wound and it will stop the bleeding, okay?"

"Okay."

An entire hour had passed. Frank began to worry about Annie's whereabouts. He buttoned his shirt and draped his jacket over his forearm.

"Are we going now?" Sam asked, holding out his hand. Frank took the boy's hand and helped him up, taking one last look around.

"We have to go back," he said. *Calm down, Frank.* He couldn't help it. He needed to reassure himself. He took one last glance to the north before turning back.

"Come on," he said, guiding the boy back upstream. Moving uphill took its toll on his ankle. He slipped his jacket between his back and knapsack, freeing both hands to steady himself on the rocks. The misconceptions and panicked thoughts lingered in his mind. He was agitated by his surroundings. Every noise echoed in his ears; the birds, the river and the rustling of wind in the bushes caused him to startle easy. He blew away the sweat dripping over his upper lip and pressed onward.

They had been walking for some time, maybe no more than a few miles from where they initially fell. Frank stopped, his vision blurred as he witnessed the swarm of a hundred men waiting for him at the top of the hill. The terror struck his heart. Something tugged his leg and he looked down at Sam who wondered why they had both stopped. Frank's head snapped back up to the hilltop, but there was nobody there. He had to blink a few times to assure himself, deceived by his own imagination. Frank picked up the boy in his arms and pushed on. He took three more steps before another set of noises stopped him in his tracks. It was real this time. He was certain. He knew it existed because the boy heard it too. They dropped to the ground and lay still, concealed by rocks that surrounded the riverbank. Minuscule streams of water flowed soothingly between them, brushing little stones and fallen leaves against their bodies. Frank peered over the rock, he could hear voices ahead. Sam burrowed his head into Frank's torso and shut his eyes tight. A figure emerged from the valley's horizon about seventy metres upstream. A second figure followed, then finally a third. The three raiders were difficult to make out from such distance. He saw the rifles in their arms.

A single sharp clicking noise startled him stiff from behind. His body tensed up and he recognised the distinct cocking of the weapon's hammer.

"Easy, old man," a female voice spoke softly. "Turn around, nice and slow."

Frank gradually turned his head as instructed. He knew no window of escape was in order. There was nowhere to go. A young red-haired woman stood before him. One hand rested against the bark of a tree, the other wrapped tightly around the grip of a sawn off shotgun. Frank's eyes lined perfectly between the twin barrels only inches away from his face. The young woman noticed the boy in his arms. Her expression remained firm, well aware of the approaching party ahead and seemed eager to lead them away.

"Let's go, come on," she ushered Frank over with the shotgun. He had no alternative. He took the boy and followed her orders without question.

"Crawl over here until I say it's okay to stand," she continued.

Frank did exactly that, inching closer toward the tree line. He kept his eyes on her the entire time, examining her every feature. Although she had strapped an olive drab bandana around her head, it did little to stop her long red hair flowing in the breeze. Behind her field jacket was a black vest that draped loosely around her slim figure. Her olive cargos were tucked into a pair of scuffed up black leather boots. An intimidating bandolier of shotgun shells draped across the front of her torso and she wore a lightweight knapsack on her back. Frank held Sam close in his arm while using the other to shift them closer to the woman by the tree line. She waved the shotgun upward promptly, signalling for him to rise to his feet. He complied with her demand and noticed her step back to create some distance between them. She motioned with the shotgun once more; deeper into the forest. Frank took the lead, sensing the end of the shotgun on his back at all times. He heard her whisper directions to him as they moved further away from the river. Sam sobbed quietly. He looked down and saw the boy staring up with those petrified glassy eyes.

"You best keep that boy quiet," she hissed. "I don't want to hurt you, and I won't if you don't make me." Frank nodded without looking back, it wasn't worth the risk. He held the boy closely and shushed him softly as they delved deeper into the woodlands.

As they departed from the forest, she made them wait by the roadside. Knowing she stood behind him with a loaded gun made him nervous.

"Have you seen my wife?" he asked. His voice was desperate and frightened.

"You're not allowed to talk till we get to where we're going, understand?"

He didn't respond.

"You're a fast learner," she said. He didn't fear her but rather feared for the safety of those he sought. She noticed his hunched stature. His dread flushed her with guilt, she could have continued with the facade but it wasn't necessary.

"Listen, I know where your wife is."

Frank turned to face her. "Is she okay? Where is she?"

"Calm down. I'm going to take you to her but for this to work I need you to trust me. It isn't safe out here anymore. All you need to know is that you're safer in my hands than the hands of those bastards back there."

Frank nodded again.

"You're Frank, right?"

"She tell you that?"

"No, I guessed." She grinned smugly and he realised just how ridiculous his question was. She overtook him.

"I'm Kara," she said without looking back. "Your wife said you were out here so I came looking."

"You came all the way out here just for me?"

"Hey don't be fooled, I'm no good Samaritan. I'm getting something out of this wild goose chase."

"From my wife?"

"No. Now enough with all the questions already. You're starting to give me a headache."

Frank didn't know how to react. He wasn't sure about the whole ordeal, but what he did know was that this woman could lead him back to his wife.

Kara looked both ways before stepping out into the deserted road. Frank waited patiently at the roadside, holding the young boy up in one arm. He watched Kara kneel down in the middle of the road. She ran her fingertips through faint markings in the dirt.

"What are you doing?" he asked.

"Tyre tracks. Fresh."

"Is that bad?"

"Not really, it means they've just done a round. They'll do another in an hour so we'd best get a move on."

"Where are we going?"

"Elkford."

# SIX

Not a word was spoken between Frank and Kara on their journey up to Elkford, nor was another soul to be seen. He had only seen Elkford once before during the early years of the island's development. It had changed immensely since and was now surrounded by a vast wooden fortress. Tall tree trunks towered in unison around the perimeter. As they approached the gates, Frank saw the guards armed with wooden bows and rifles posted high on the walls. They recognised Kara and yelled something out to the other side of the wall. Two guards opened the gated archway. Kara led Frank and Sam inside and the guards stared intently as they passed. Frank speculated their unusual gaze, he couldn't tell if it was himself or the boy that they observed so studiously. Kara slung the shotgun over her shoulder and strolled on into the village of Elkford.

"If this is your first time here, welcome to Elkford. If it's not, then sorry I brought you here."

Frank's initial thought when laying eyes on the village was how eroded it had become. Wilting fruit trees lined in rows either side of the main strip. Where children once played in the streets now adults stacked boxes of supplies to be rationed. The rain stopped but the grey sky left a gloomy residue over Elkford in this time of oppression.

"What happened here?" Frank asked.

Kara ignored his question and led them into the village tavern. Evening was approaching and the tavern was full of diverse groups sitting together in mild chatter. Frank felt the stare of a dozen men and the room quickly fell to near silence. An old dusty piano sat in the corner of the room with nobody to play it. Kara ignored the stairs and sat them down on a vacant picnic table in the corner of the room.

"Sit here and wait for me."

Frank did as he was told. He sat down and propped the boy up beside him, watching Kara as she spoke to the bar tender.

They exchanged words for a while and every now and then they would look back over to Frank and the boy. A few moments later she returned with a burlap sack and a glass of rum.

"Where's my wife?" Frank asked abruptly. He was exhausted, famished and most of all, impatient. Kara took a sip of her rum before replying.

"She's talking to my boss at the barracks. We'll go there when I finish this."

"No I think you'll take me there right now. You can finish your drink later." Frank's posture tightened up. He leaned, his index finger perched demandingly on the table. Kara set her drink down and examined Frank for some time, unravelling him with her eyes.

"How long have you known this boy?"

"What's it to you?"

"Just curious. How long you been out there, Frank?"

"I don't know, two days?"

"You haven't seen your wife in two days?"

"Well, no. I lost contact with her earlier this morning."

"So you get this worked up when you haven't seen your wife for less than a day? Sounds a little obsessive to me,

Frank." She raised an eyebrow and took another sip of her drink. Frank paused for a second. His patience was wearing thin and he didn't take kindly to her straight forward spin on things.

"I want you to cut through all the bullshit and tell me what the hell is going on here; but first of all, for the last time, take me to my wife!"

His voice rose uncontrollably. More heads turned inside the tavern. Kara downed the rest of her rum. She stood up, wiped her mouth with her forearm and threw the burlap sack over her shoulder.

"All right. I've finished my drink. Let's go see your wife."

Frank snatched Sam up by his wrist and followed her towards the door. As they got halfway across the tavern, he felt something quickly clamp his arm. He looked back at the podgy hand holding a wad of his jacket and followed the tattooed arm up to see that of a larger man, a gristly oaf in a black beanie.

The oaf's gaze never left Frank as he spoke. "There a problem here, Kara?" Frank could see it in those deadpan mackerel eyes, the type of man just itching to cause trouble.

"Let go of him, Derek, this has nothing to do with you," said Kara.

Frank held Sam away from the oaf. "You want to listen to the lady and ease up there, friend?"

Derek stared at Kara, then back at Frank and finally down at the boy. He grumbled like a wild bear and released his grip before lowering back down into his seat. Kara led Frank back outside and shut the tavern door behind them.

She escorted him through the strip and down some steps that lead to a stone lodge. The sky was already far greyer than it was when they entered the tavern and it would soon be night. Frank wondered if he could really trust the woman. She seemed to know almost too much, but her blunt honesty and reasoning was enough for him to believe her. They passed a stone archway and entered a courtyard where a few guards sat, smoking and playing cards around a small wooden table. They exchanged brief greetings with Kara as she passed before noticing the boy. One man was left stunned; his cigarette dropped from his mouth and rolled straight off the table. It was only then that Frank truly understood why they reacted this way. It only just occurred to him in that moment. He had not seen a single child in the village of Elkford.

They walked through the courtyard, flourished in weeds and limestone sculptures that were in dire need of amends, decayed and discoloured from being exposed to acid rain. A sculptured Elk stood gracefully; one of its antlers had chipped away and lay in a messy clump of rubble on the ground beside it.

A booming set of barks echoed through the courtyard. Frank turned and saw the beloved dog jump up at him. He struggled to juggle the boy and contain Max's excitement all at the same time. He settled Sam down and ruffled the dog's cheeks and patted him on the head.

"Sorry, he can't come inside," Kara said, holding another door open for them.

"Sorry boy," said Frank.

The dog yawned and wheezed as his master and the boy followed Kara inside. Kara shut the door behind them. She strutted ahead through the hallway and pushed past a set of fabric drapes that led them into yet another room.

The room was filled with various items of a logistical nature. In the centre was a flat stone platform with a large situation map of Autark sprawled across its surface. The map was littered in markings and small wooden units dotted around each major settlement. There was a chalk board mounted to another wall, plastered in various statements, drawings and arrow points crossing each other in all directions. It was a planning and management room. Several men and women stood around discussing amongst each other. Another wall displayed a weapons rack, ranging from knives to bows to rifles and handguns and finally; sitting to one side on a bench, was Annie.

"Frank," she stammered. She shot up from her seat and ran into his arms. He felt her tender embrace and the scent of her hair flourished the inside of his nostrils. He hugged her tightly and then placed both hands on her shoulders.

"Are you okay? What happened?" Frank asked, flustered with questions.

"Am I okay? What about you, I've been worried sick," she replied. "Kara heard us hollering for you, she brought us here to safety."

Frank turned back to Kara, no longer anxious of her motivations.

"Thank you," he whispered.

"Don't mention it."

Frank paused, scanning the room around them. "Where's Tracy?"

"She had a brief tumble in the woods," said one man over by the map. "Our medical assistant has tended to her and she is resting in one of the guest quarters across the yard." The man strolled over to them. The spurs of his boots jangled with every step. His dark brown hair was combed back and a thin moustache sat across his upper lip. He sported a welcoming grin and held out his hand.

"It's a pleasure to finally meet you. My name is Javier Paraíso." His voice was both clear and articulate with a South American flare. Frank shook the man's hand hesitantly, exhausted and overwhelmed with everything that had happened over the past two days.

"Frank."

"Frank, your wife has spoken of nothing but you since she arrived here in Elkford."

"All good I hope."

Javier chuckled in amusement. There was a charming manner about him but it almost seemed too apparent, too forced. Javier's attention drew lower to the boy by his side. He took a moment to ingest what he was seeing, surprised by the sight of the child.

"My goodness. Is this your grandson?" said Javier.

"No, he's not ours," Annie piped up.

Javier's charm soon faded. After hearing Annie's words, four guards stepped forward in unison and snatched the boy from Frank's grasp.

"What the hell are you doing?" Frank hollered.

He wanted to pull Sam back but it all happened so fast. He was caught off guard, the boy was already in possession of the guards. Frank and Annie did their best to push past the towering guardsmen but their age and strength was no match. Frank heard the boy crying out over the broad shoulders in his way. Javier yanked him away from them and led him into the circle of guards on the other side of the room.

"Check his back," he ordered

Frank's arms were held together, locked behind his back, Annie's too. They watched as Kara lifted the boy's rags to expose his bare back. Frank's jaw dropped. He stared, mesmerised at the sight that would remain with all who laid eyes on it. Tormented scars ran parallel across the child's back. They were fragile, a rubbery texture of sagging tissue grazing in diagonal motions. Even lower at the base of his back was a burning imprint, the surrounding skin red raw as it read, '027.'

"He's a raider boy," yelled one of the guards. Kara noticed the black book tucked into his rags and ripped it free. She tossed it up to Javier for closer examination.

"He's harmless. Please, leave him be," cried Annie. Frank struggled against the guard but a swift rifle stock to the gut knocked him back down to his battered knees.

"Stop this violence!" Javier demanded. "If this boy really is a spy for the raiders, he would not have allowed these two to live for so long."

"Could've led the raiders to us, left a trail for them to follow?" suggested Kara.

"For Christ sakes, he's just a child," Frank croaked under the throbbing pain in his stomach. He struggled to breathe, his head low as he gasped for breaths. Javier opened the book. He skimmed through each drawing, his eyes scanning them as though deciphering an ancient relic. He flipped the page again, and again, until he reached the most recent of sketches. His eyes widened, he stared at the image and the room waited in anticipated silence.

"Impossible..."

"What? What is it?" Kara asked. She stared up at Javier, holding the boy steady beside her. Javier held the book out to

Kara, she took it carefully to inspect and after some time her face soon mirrored that of Javier's. Frank and Annie shared an unsettling glance.

"Release them," Javier ordered.

The guards hesitated, looking at one another for reassurance.

"I said let go of them," he repeated sternly. They released their grasp and so did Kara. Sam ran back into Annie's arms, tears streaming down his face. Javier snatched the book back from Kara and approached Frank. He squatted down and held the book up for the couple to see. There on the page was a sketch that Frank struggled to fathom.

The scribbled illustration revealed a room filled with people. To one side there was a figure that knelt beside a smaller figure. Next to it was a standing figure with a book in its hands. Finally, on the other side of the page, were two figures being held back on their knees by what could only be perceived as guards.

It was them. It was all of them at this precise moment in time. He didn't know what to say. Sam hadn't taken the book out since they left it out to dry by the river. Then it hit him. He remembered the drawings before, the one with the gun. It was a near identical depiction of their first encounter with Kara. These were two occasions he had sketched something before it had actually happened. The boy had illustrated events prior to the time they had truly taken place.

The room lay still, stunned in utter silence. Although they saw it, felt it, no one was prepared to accept the wave of supernaturalism that lingered in the atmosphere around them.

# SEVEN

Later that evening, Annie, Sam and Max had returned to their assigned quarters for the night. Javier had asked Frank if they could speak privately. They sat down at the table where the guards played poker earlier that day, cards still strewn across the table.

A luminous silver sheen was cast over the two men under moonlight. They sat across the small round table from one another. Javier offered him a drink which he kindly accepted, but Frank wasn't really there for the drink. He watched Javier swig the warm whiskey around his glass in a circular motion, crossing one leg over the other.

"Frank, I apologise for the way you were mistreated today. I shall be blunt with you as I sense you prefer a direct to-the-point approach."

Frank took a gentle sip of the whiskey and leaned back in his seat. "All right."

"The truth is I have no leadership experience, but these people have always looked to me for answers. I have managed to band together the remaining settlers of this island and bring them hope, hope that they can conquer these demons that torment our land."

"Hope is a dangerous thing, Javier. You've got these innocent hard working people under your spell. You've made them believe that you can save them from what's coming their way. You and I both know that as soon as the first shot is fired, that spell will be broken."

"You know what? You are absolutely right. But what can I do?"

"That's not my problem."

"I never asked to be their leader. I was appointed this position. I was okay with running a village, not an army, Frank. After two months these raiders have nearly engulfed our land and claimed it as their own."

"What do they want?"

"The same as everybody else, freedom, but their idea of freedom is riddled with a selfish and twisted ideology that only those with poisoned minds can comprehend. They know these lands are not governed. The British want to wash their hands of the situation. There is too much political backlash for them to reveal what is really going on. If the U.N. truly found out, the only thing they would have to say is, 'we told you so.' Politics are fickle, Frank."

"You mean to tell me that the reason there hasn't been any basic supply shipments over the past few months is because the Brits have turned their back on Autark? The rest of the world doesn't know about all this?"

"They know nothing. No governing body is sending help, Frank, which is why I had to send for help myself."

"What do you mean?"

"I sent my last party of fishermen out west to deliver a message to my contacts in Costa Rica. When they received word of our attacks, a group of individuals formed an assembly of freedom fighters known as 'Libertad Para Autark,' or, 'Freedom for Autark,' as you would say in English. These fighters have managed to recruit people from all over the globe, not just soldiers, but citizens looking to make a difference. I received word this evening that the LPA forces have landed on Autark's shores. They entered in the south west through Merribank village and are heading north to aid in the defence of Elkford as we speak."

"I was in Merribank when it happened."

"Then you know what these people are capable of. They've been here for years, but in the space of just a few months they've overrun the military base, run down the eastern industrial town of Wolvendale, across the south through Merribank and are finally circulating towards the last village in Autark: Elkford."

"Why are you telling me all of this?"

"Because I need your help. I have spoken with Annabel and she is eager to partake but she wanted to discuss it with you first."

Frank sat up and brushed the dirt from his jeans. "I'm listening."

Javier pushed the bottle of whiskey and glasses aside and removed a tatty piece of stained paper from his pocket. He unfolded it over the table to reveal a hand-drawn map of

Autark with a red circle in the north east corner. It circled the military base.

"I have lost contact with my scouts at the military base. It is said that the raiders have up to one thousand people under suppression working as slaves, women and children included."

"They're moulding children into soldiers, Javier. The kids I saw couldn't even carry the damn rifles in their arms."

"Which is why I need you to escort some of my people there to find out what is going on."

Frank sat quietly for a moment, ingesting the revolutionary figure's proposal. "Forgive me for saying so, but have you completely lost your mind? I'm an old man for Christ sake, I mean do I need to remind you what is out there? What could I possibly offer your people?"

"The boy, Frank. The boy. He needs to be kept safe. He has been there himself. He will know the layout."

"That doesn't mean he-"

"Frank, listen to me, please. In just a few days, Elkford will be lost. I am being realistic with you now because I see that you yourself are a realist. In the past four years the raiders have completely overrun the east of Autark. Nobody believed the rumours and now we a paying for it with our lives.

Nowhere is safe anymore. The LPA can only do so much. We both know what the child is capable of. We both saw it."

"I'm not sure what I saw back there."

"We saw the future, a living and breathing prophecy."

Frank knew what he saw. He just struggled to believe it. While the other children wielded arms, Sam wielded parchment. The boy was a diamond in the rough, and Frank wasn't sure he truly understood just how remarkable he was.

"You want me to trek across two hundred and sixty miles of raider infested territory to save a thousand slaves? What then? Free them into the wild to be re-captured? This is absurd."

"I'm not asking you to free them. I'm asking you to buy us time, time to regroup with the LPA. The raiders will think you are being held up here and by the time they've raided our village you will be miles ahead of them. If we win the fight it will scatter their forces and when the time comes, we shall meet you there and together we can put an end to all of this."

"Even if you were to survive a fight, how are you going to free all those people?"

"As a unit. We may not have many weapons and we may be outnumbered but I will do whatever I can for this land as I have done for the past eight years. Listen to me. The raiders have stolen our fishing boats; they've burnt our crops and fields and have kidnapped our farmers. There are many ways in, provided you have a boat, but there is only one way out of the island. Autark Harbour is on the other side of the base. Take the boy and your wife far from here to Newfoundland and send for help. It is only a few hundred miles north-west of the island. Autark isn't safe anymore. I will wait here and prepare for siege with my people. The LPA should be here soon. If we do not reach the military base by the time you are gone then we will wait for your return but your priority is the safety of that child."

"This is not my fight, Javier. I want no part in this. I've lost my home, my livelihood, even watched my neighbour die by their hand. All I have left is my family. I'm not putting the only thing left in my life on the line. Get someone else to do it."

"That boy has developed something of a bond with you and your wife. You may not want to believe it but you know it to be true. You are the only ones he trusts, when you are not present, he does not speak. If the raiders are aware of his powers, they will no doubt be looking for him; and the first place they will search? Right here. He won't go with anyone else. It has to be you."

Frank leant both elbows on the table, his head in his hands.

"I never asked for this."

"Look around you. You think any of us asked for any of this? These were the cards you were dealt." Javier held up the pack of playing cards and tossed them across the table in front of Frank.

"This is our island, Frank. We, the people, we built it; and although you wish to cast yourself aside, whether you like it or not, you too are a part of the people. When will you take responsibility and stand up, fight for what is yours?"

"All I care about is my family."

"Then will you go the distance to protect them?"

Frank didn't reply. He sat quietly, defeated. He knew Javier spoke the truth. The island was being overrun and the settlers who built Autark were now forced to slave away for the raiders who took it from them. He could run, maybe go into hiding, but eventually the raiders would catch up with him and when they did, he knew that surrendering to them was a far worse fate than death itself. He sat up, confronting Javier's judgement head on.

"You're saying Annie wanted to do this? *My* Annie?"

"Yes. She wanted to discuss it with you first but she seemed willing."

"If I do this, and we can restore Autark to what it was; I want you to make amends for what I've lost." Javier held out his hand, "consider it done."

Frank took his hand and shook it firmly.

He spoke with Annie upon his return. She was eating at the time, sharing her food with both Max and the boy. He watched her wipe the stains from the boy's mouth as though she had been doing it her whole life. Frank had second thoughts about their task. Annie would never place the boy's life in the hands of another, nor would Sam allow anyone else to take care of him. She knew that there was no home for them to return to, that Elkford would soon follow the harrowing fate of Merribank. All they could do was comply and hope that they would survive their journey to Autark Harbour.

Frank sat at the end of the bed. He was grateful for the hospitality they had received from Javier's people. The room was basic but a warm bed was better than the cold hard floor of a cave.

"How's your ankle?" Annie asked.

"Better, thanks. Kara took a look at it."

He caught a few hours sleep that night and had the whiskey to thank for it. For the rest of the night his mind was burdened with the images of Henry's death. The distant screams, gunshots, everything echoed in his mind like a recurring nightmare. It was maybe four or five o'clock in the morning, he had already packed their things the night before and was ready for the journey east.

Since the roads were heavily patrolled by raiders, they would have to stray their course and use the forests as their means of navigation. It would surely double their time out in the wild with limited resources. Frank thought about Tracy. She was an emotional person. The reason she had managed to subdue her overwhelming emotions over the years was down to the care of her sister. She was okay for now but the extended pressure of travelling across Autark scared the hell out of him, not just for Tracy, but for himself.

Later that morning an abrupt series of knocks struck the door. Annie opened the door to reveal Kara, the sling of her shotgun over one shoulder, her knapsack over the other.

"You guys ready to go?"

"You're coming with us?" Annie asked.

"That's right."

Tracy strapped on her backpack and Annie took a quick check to make sure they hadn't left anything behind. The people of Elkford had donated some equipment for their journey. Attached to the strap of Frank's knapsack was a kinetic torch which allowed for hands free access. They were also supplied with bedrolls, handcrafted by the settlers and crafted from the hide of the renowned elk that roamed the surrounding woodlands of the north. Additional supplies included rations and ammunition. The quantity was scarce but the people of Elkford were lacking in their usual numbers and the group was grateful for whatever they could spare.

Kara guided Frank and the others back out through the courtyard towards Elkford's main gateway. Frank spotted Javier and some others by the arched gateway. They were performing last checks on their equipment and weapons before their departure. Frank took hold of Annie's arm and stopped her. He looked over to Kara. "Can you give us a second?"

"Sure, come on over when you're ready," she replied. Tracy and Annie stared back, he couldn't beat around the bush any longer.

"What are we doing here, Annie?"

"What?"

"Listen, I get it."

"I don't think you do."

"You're worried about him," he said, gesturing to the child who was none the wiser, gazing out to the masses of people waiting by the gates of Elkford. Annie put the boy down and took his hand.

"Tracy, you understand, don't you?" she said, turning to her sister.

"Actually..." Tracy stammered. "Look, I was all for getting him to safety, but going along with this suicide mission? I have to side with Frank on this one."

"This isn't us, Annie," said Frank. "We're not equipped to deal with this kind of thing."

"That's exactly what I'm talking about," Annie continued.

"If everyone thought like you then nothing would get done. Don't you see? We either get out there and do something to contribute or we sit on the fence and lose."

As much as Frank didn't want to accept it, he knew that what she said was true. He didn't want to do this. He wanted to be at home, tending to his garden and shutting himself away from the world but that wasn't reality. His reality had been flipped upside down. This was reality, a threat to their land, their freedom. There was no way he could go back until this whole ordeal was over and done with.

"Something doesn't sit right with me. I don't know if we can trust these people."

"What makes you say that?"

"Can't put my finger on it. I get the feeling they know more about what's going on than we do. He knew to look for that marking on the boy, and he's got settlers wrapped around his little finger. Let's just keep a close eye on these people. Autark isn't safe anymore, not whilst raiders are around. We get to the harbour, find a boat and get out of here until we know things have been sorted. Just promise me you'll both be careful."

"Good morning," Javier interrupted from afar.

Tracy waved back as the leader of Elkford walked over to them with open arms. He escorted them to the gate and introduced them to the volunteers who would escort them on their journey. Altogether there were four people who would lead them across the raider infested Autark.

The first was Kara.

Although they had gotten off to a rough start, Kara had a pureness to her that Frank couldn't describe. Maybe it was that she said everything as it was, a straight shooter with a fighter's spirit. In addition to Kara was another familiar face. The second person was Derek, the oaf that had manhandled him in the tavern the night before. Frank wasn't pleased to see Derek, and Derek made it all too clear that he was none too pleased to see him either. Derek's shoulders slouched and his head hung low. Sweat patches seeped through his jumper around his armpits. Frank spotted a snub-nosed .38 revolver tucked diagonally into the oaf's belt. Frank was promised a refurbished home at the end of their voyage. He wondered what was in it for the others, especially Derek. Whatever it was, it must have been well worth their while.

The third companion was a Hispanic man, somewhere in his late thirties who went by the name of Carlos. Javier sung Carlos' praises that day at the gate. He went on and on about how he personally selected Carlos to lead them on their journey and how he was a crack shot with a rifle. Carlos' predominant feature was his long straggly hair that he tied back into a bun. He wore a doeskin tunic and breeches and his boots were layered with a soft rabbit pelt. Rumour had it that Carlos was a blood relative to Paraíso. Kara had briefly mentioned it the night before but it was something that the two men were never open about themselves.

The fourth and final member of the group was quite the character at first glance. He was an older man, maybe even older than Frank, oozing remnants of a time period that the U.S. had fixated on for many years. He wore a long brown leather duster with a matching wide-brimmed hat. He sported some vintage leather boots and attached to his hip was a bandolier and holster. Inside the holster was a classic black single-action army revolver, a peacemaker that appeared to sustain a valuable history. His name was John. He tipped his hat, his smile barely visible beneath his valiant grey moustache that grew outwards and upwards.

Curious settlers gathered around Elkford's front gate. Strangers shook Frank's hand, even embraced him. He could hear the widows sobbing, begging the group of voyagers to bring back their lost sons and daughters. Frank felt the nerves tightening in the pit of his stomach, a mix of fear and anger. Javier had provided the settlers with false hope, made them believe that Frank and the others were off to free the slaves of the military base. That was the LPA's job, not theirs, but Paraíso needed to keep morale up for the time being. Frank watched the people beg and grovel at their feet and the guilt of uncertainty riled up inside of him. He was anything but the right man for the job but now the people looked to him to grant them their redemption.

"I wish you all the best," said Javier. "When you find the contact, he should guide you the rest of the way." Javier embraced Tracy and Annie. He turned to the gathered settlers and raised his fist in the name of revolution, chanting words of encouragement and justice. The guards opened the gates and Javier embraced Frank and whispered something into his ear. He didn't quite catch it all over the masses of people congregating and rejoicing around them.

Frank was at a loss for words and he wondered whether Javier's whisper even deemed a response. Not knowing what else to do, and not wanting to endure the embarrassment of asking the man to repeat himself, Frank simply nodded along, staring down at his own feet. Javier Paraíso held both hands on

Frank's shoulders and took one last look at him before his departure. Javier smiled and nodded. Frank wasn't sure whether it was sincere or an alluring charismatic smokescreen. The group sauntered out of the gates of Elkford and set off on their journey east. The crowd of people waved their goodbyes, Javier among them. As he listened to the settlers chants of gratitude, Frank couldn't help but feel played. This was a task for soldiers, for fighters, not a farmer. He knew the risks after experiencing what the raiders were capable of. He feared for Annie, for Tracy and Max. He also feared for the life of the boy, an innocent being whose talent or gift, or whatever it was, had led them on a path that would put their lives in grave danger.

# EIGHT

The first day was spent pushing deep into the depths of the forest. They had abandoned the roads, veering from any sign of civilisation to better their chances of concealment. The rural environment was harsh, the ground uneven. November's rain showered the forest floor. A collection of puddles flooded downhill to form ponds in the lower regions of the valleys.

Their goal was to locate a solitary huntsman, a man who supposedly knew the eastern side of the island like the back of his hand.

"The guy is bat-shit crazy. Nice enough fella, but a fucking loony," Derek had described him.

The group debated how long it would take to reach their contact. Derek thought a week, Carlos only a few days. Frank and Derek exchanged a few intolerable glances along their journey. Something about the larger man rubbed Frank the wrong way. They had managed to steer clear of the major raider convoy heading north to Elkford but the thought of running into reinforcements travelling from the east was his greatest fear.

The wind droned endlessly through the cold nights. They had managed to secure shelter in the valley from a natural overhang. Derek, John and Frank took watch in the night. Shifts were split into roughly three hours each but there was no way in keeping such a precise check on time. Having Max close by through those slow hours of the night eased Frank's mind ever so slightly. He hadn't made much time to speak with the others that day. Getting too close for comfort was always something he chose to avoid but Annie convinced him otherwise. She spoke to him that night after his watch. He had swapped over with Derek and she waited for the oaf to reach his post outside the camp. With the others fast asleep, together they lay, their bedrolls huddled close together in the cold dark night. Annie leaned in closer and pushed her cool lips against Frank's frozen earlobes.

"Not sure about that one," she whispered. "I spoke a bit with her today though."

"And?" he whispered back softly. From then on they conversed in hushed utterances.

"She seems alright."

"I wasn't sure at first, but I think she's okay."

"You should speak to the others, find out more about them."

"Yeah…"

The surrounding area was far more open the second night. Carlos and John built noise traps around the perimeter of the camp. They tied rope between trees and hung discarded cans from previous meals. Kara gathered twigs and branches and laid them at the feet of the traps in the hope that they would increase their chances of hearing an intruder. They were going to be together for some time and Frank was slowly beginning to see a routine form over the course of their travels.

Carlos was not just a scout for Paraíso. He was a frontiersman and fur trapper for the people of Elkford. He knew the surrounding woodland of the north-western part of the island better than anyone. He was very economically driven, the man hunted for trade, not necessity, and pelts were very costly and proved a rather profitable business. On their first night in the forest, Carlos had shown Frank a handcrafted map he had built over his years in the wild. It was inscribed with ink and contained greater detail than the generic map that Javier had provided him with back in Elkford. In the mornings, Carlos would set out ahead about an hour earlier than the others. This gave him a chance to check the route ahead as well as hunt if the opportunity were to occur. The others would follow his tracks and regroup around midday.

Around noon on the third day of their journey, they had yet to see a raider or any other living soul. Derek took point, stomping his boots rhythmically ahead of the others like an elephant. Frank walked alongside Tracy and watched Annie feed Sam a pear, wiping the juices that dribbled down his chin with a handkerchief.

"Would you stop that kid from slurping so loudly?" Derek grumbled back over his shoulder.

"Kids gotta eat," said John. "We're running low on food as it is and Carlos says he's gonna rustle up a buck or something."

Derek tilted his head back. Frank only saw the back of his head but the motion was enough to assume he was rolling his eyes. "You really believe that? Guy wakes up early, tells us he wants a head-start so he can go hunt. Anyone even seen him aim that rifle of his since we've been out in this shit?"

"Enough, Derek," Kara said. "We haven't been in a situation where we've had to use our weapons yet. Let's hope it stays that way."

They reached an area of the forest that was seemingly untouched. Moss covered the earth and scaled the trees. It blended with the ivy that spiraled up the rotting pines, sucking the life from its natural host. Brambles and thorns scattered their path, forcing them to weave in and around the prickly obstacles. Frank and Derek went to work with the machetes, hacking and slashing at nature's burden. They listened as the swishing of the blade whipped against the foliage and watched it rustle limply to the ground. Broad stems and holly crunched beneath their boots as they pressed on. The distance between the trees narrowed up ahead. Branches intertwined and blocked out the sun, casting sinister shadows that played tricks on the mind. The dampness of the roots and lack of sunshine caused them to give off a clammy aroma. Derek leaned back against an enormous fallen oak, both hands on his hips. The oak had been there for decades, its inside completely hollow and rotten from the inside out. Derek's cheeks puffed with every gasping breath. "Fuck me."

"Is that really necessary?" asked Tracy. She made a meagre attempt to cover Sam's ears but the damage was already done.

"What? You think he hasn't heard anything like that where he's been? Boys come from the shit pit."

"What is your problem?" Annie added. Derek grumbled dismissively. He was too out of breath to give them the time of day. Kara exchanged a brief apologetic smile with the ladies.

The rustling of leaves amplified. Frank stopped hacking away at the brambles and listened. It wasn't him. It was just ahead of them and approaching fast.

"They're coming!" a voice hissed from within the brush. Carlos burst through the shrubbery. His tunic snagged on the thorns; he ripped it away with one hand and the others flushed with panic.

"How close?" Frank asked firmly.

Carlos frantically staggered over to the fallen oak. "No time, come on."

Kara snatched Annie's hand. She steered her and the boy towards an opening in the ancient tree. The damp trunk's thick dusty roots raised outwards into the air. Frank heard the muffled voices heading their way. He called Max over and joined the others. Together they hunkered down in the darkness of the fallen oak. The inside of the trunk was swarming with insects that claimed it as their own. They lay still amongst the dirt and the rot. Carlos gathered the freshly cut brambles and was the last one in, shoving the plants between the roots to conceal the large opening in the base of the tree.

They remained still, listening to the voices that grew louder with every passing second. Frank could hear the altercations between Spanish and English. He lay upright against the inside of the tree and held Max tightly in his arms. He begged for the dog to stay quiet. His face was only inches away from Annie and the boy. Their expression's mirrored that of Franks; fear dominated every muscle in their complexion. He could feel the tickling legs of the millipede crawling over his arm. Twigs snapped just a few feet away. He tried to control his breathing but his nerves got the better of him. He exhaled in staccato spurts. Soil smeared the side of his face, the pressure of the soft bark pushed against his aching body. He felt Carlos' back huddled up against his own in the cramped darkness. Deep grizzly voices spoke where they had previously been standing. The ongoing conversation was muffled through the bark of the oak.

Frank noticed dirt brushing away only inches away from his head. A scuffling sound that spread outward. The foot-long millipede tunneled through the gap in the bark and crawled into the aging oak. Frank's eyes were drawn to it but slowly drifted back over to the hole it had left in the bark. A beam of light shone through the surrounding darkness. He shuffled up and craned his neck to peek through the microscopic hole. Obscure shadows passed by, far too narrow to decode any details. He listened to what sounded like the trickling of water. A dark shadow obstructed his view. Heavy grunts and breaths ensued only inches away. Frank gently slid back down and curled up, clamping one hand tightly around Max's mouth. He shut his eyes tight and wished them all away. All they could do was wait.

It took twenty minutes for the raiders to move on. They had listened to the raiders chatting, smoking, eating, pissing and shitting until they finally moved on. The group clambered out of the decrepit oak. Frank felt the cramp in his lower back and arched backwards, both hands compressing the aching pain. The floor was littered with discarded bones and half-eaten fruit. Max picked at the scraps of meat left on a dirty chicken leg before realising that the group were moving on.

They continued east, their pace slower than before. It had been a close call, a stern warning to keep their guard up from there on out. Tracy and Annie took turns holding Sam. Although he could walk, he tired easily and struggled to keep up with the others. Frank studied the surrounding woodland carefully. "We've been walking for days now. You sure we haven't passed it?"

"We didn't pass it," said Derek.

"Are you sure?"

Derek spun around. He dug both hands firmly into Frank's shirt and pushed him back into a tree. Frank's shotgun fell to the ground, his hands clamped onto Derek's forearms.

"Derek!" Kara shouted.

"You listen to me, old man," Derek barked. "You don't know shit. You're only here because that shy little prick won't move without you."

Kara yanked the oaf back by his shoulder. Frank's grip eased off and John wedged himself between them. "Listen fellas. I don't know what your problem is, but we're here for one job: to protect that kid."

"Spare me the bloody lecture, cowboy," said Derek, waving it off. He stomped ahead, cursing beneath his breath.

Before his relocation to Autark, Derek was a fisherman who worked mostly along the English Channel. His mother passed when he was just a boy and he decided to make the move shortly after the passing of his father. Derek had spent most of his life out at sea; he never married or started a family of his own. He was married to the ocean. With the haul of a recessive economy threatening his livelihood, there was soon nothing left for Derek. He sought change and set sail for Autark, however, it was not the simplest of tasks. The deadline for the Autark project had long gone, four years beforehand to be exact. Autark was no longer accepting candidates, but that didn't stop people finding their way to its prosperous shores.

By owning his own boat; Derek saw a rather profitable opportunity and decided to snatch it with both hands. The coast of England and France was littered with gold just waiting for someone to take it, and that's just what Derek did. He landed a deal that he knew would reward him handsomely. Hundreds of eastern migrants desperately sought transport to the utopia that was Autark. Derek agreed to transport those most desperate and they would forever be in his debt. One Malaysian family took him in as an undying token of gratitude. They fed him, clothed him and even gave him a place to sleep.

Working non-stop for thirty years eventually took its toll on the fisherman. He arrived on the island with the intention of using his skills as a fisherman to trade, but first there were desires that had been bottled up for a very long time. Deep in the backstreets of Wolvendale - the eastern industrial center of Autark - lurked a discreet and distasteful establishment. Prostitution was inescapable, even in Autark; it would always be seen as a form of service, a service that required payment. The Wolvendale Brothel was where Derek spent his early months. The oaf's new lifestyle had made him lazy, demanding and violent. He ate, drank and fucked to his heart's content. He was completely taken care of, but soon the magic began to wear off. Derek's newfound lust for harlots led him to abuse the kindness of his Malaysian hosts. He stole grain from their harvest, rare sentimental valuables and priceless family heirlooms in order to pay for his affairs. When he ran out of things to steal, the tables soon turned and he quickly owed the brothel a large outstanding debt.

When the Malaysians found out, they tried to throw him out and he responded with clenched fists. He saw red that night and strangled the father with his own fishing line. He then beat the wife and children and forced them into slavery. Fortunately for the family, things didn't stay that way for too long. One night, the five heads of the Wolvendale Brothel came knocking. When Derek answered the door, they dragged him out into the street and beat him with thick, heavy metal chains. The settlers of Wolvendale rallied up but Derek had fled before they could drive him out themselves. The brothel returned the stolen heirlooms to the family as a gesture of peace and goodwill for the lost father.

Derek fled west to Elkford, a village where he was known as nothing more than a stranger, and offered his services as a fisherman to none other than Javier Paraíso. After proving himself as a sustainable source of income, Paraíso helped Derek set up his own fishmongers by the docks on the outskirts of Elkford. He and his new crew spent their days either out fishing at sea or bartering at the mongers. From then on, Derek soon found himself in the eternal gratitude and debt of Javier Paraíso.

The rain had stopped but the clouds remained. The sun was at its highest point - concealed by clouds - the sky as pale as a blank canvas. Annie felt Sam slipping and hoisted him up. He sat in her arms, facing back over her shoulder and ogled John's bold facial hair. He nearly dozed off at the rocking rhythm of Annie's pace. His head slowly sank down into her shoulder before jolting back up in the fight to stay awake.

Something behind John caught the boy's attention. He trained his eyes on the approaching silhouette and a flash of light reflected a glass lens. John's ears were burning. He recognised the metallic slide of a rifle's bolt clicking into place. He span around, his duster flapping in the wind as he pulled the single-action army from his holster and slammed back on the hammer. Legs apart, he held the revolver by the hip and aimed straight ahead of him. Annie stopped and turned around to face the commotion. Sam's neck whirled rapidly in her arms; he didn't want to miss a single second. The others caught on fast and watched in silence. The figure stood in the shade of a shallow pine. The light of the sky reflected a white beard and shimmered off the surface of round spectacle lenses. The brim of a hat concealed the figure's facial features but his plump build was one that could not be veiled. The plump figure aimed the hunting rifle directly at John, locked in a Mexican stand-off. Frank reached out slowly and edged Annie and Sam behind him, shielding their bodies with his own. Kara raised her hands in surrender, but before she could even take one step forward the rifle's barrel landed square onto her.

"D-d-d-don't even try it," the figure shouted.

Frank recognised the voice. *That stutter...* He was so confident that he knew the plump figure that he stepped forward without even realising. The rifle panned to him faster than it did to Kara.

"I'll shoot your b-b-b-bloody head off!" cried the man. Frank peered into the shade to gauge a better look. "Barry?" The plump figure hesitated for a moment before lowering the rifle. "*Frank?*" he mumbled back. Two dark green wellington boots stepped out from the shade to reveal the plump man, somewhere in his mid-fifties. His mouth gaped open.

"You know this fella?" John asked Frank back over his shoulder, eyes locked on the plump man. His voice was tough and authentic, a beaten up voice box that sounded as though it'd been through thick and thin. Frank let out a sigh of relief. He stared at the man who he had not seen for over four years. Max lunged forward and jumped up at Barry. Frank's first instinct was to stop him but he quickly realised there was no aggression in Max's actions. Max hopped up and licked Barry's podgy cheeks and his tail wagged wildly.

John holstered his piece and the others stood idly by, still cautious of the stranger. Frank and Barry shared a welcoming and long overdue embrace. He smelt of mothballs and raw flesh, a God-awful blend that was enough to put anyone off their next meal. Frank felt Max's light paws claw across his jeans. He hadn't seen Max so full of energy since he was a pup. Carlos overtook the others and approached with haste.

"We've been sent by Javier Paraíso of Elkford. Are you the huntsman?"

"Th-that what they call me up there? I suppose that would be me. Although I have to say, I-I-I wasn't expecting so many of you," Barry replied. He shook Carlos' hand and addressed Annie and Tracy. Frank sensed Carlos' agitation. The scout scanned the wet woodland grounds around them, eyes twitching in all directions. "Pardon my interrupting, but it is not safe out here and we are losing daylight fast."

"He's right," John agreed. "You got someplace safer we can talk?"

"M-m-my cabin is just over this here hill." Barry walked past the others and led them through the last few hundred metres of the forest's overgrowth.

Kara had offered to carry Sam. It was the first time Frank, Annie or Tracy passed the responsibility over to someone else. He seemed okay with it, somewhat unsettled at first but at least he was opening up and giving the others a chance. Frank held Annie's hand firmly and could see her smile in the corner of his eye. They stepped out of the tree line and felt the wind of the open field sweep across their bodies. The grass stood tall, surrounded by a collection of yellow and white daisies and dandelions that shook violently in the wind. The tree line curved around the perimeter of the field and the forest continued along the other side of the lonely log cabin.

"This is it," Barry announced contently. The grass was notably eroded around the cabin where the space had been used to make room for various workstations. A blue tarpaulin sheet covered a pile of chopped logs beside the cabin. The blade of an axe embedded deep into a lone tree stump. About twenty metres from the house was a single makeshift wind turbine rotating in the breeze. Frank put one arm around Annie's shoulder and held her close as they moved through the field towards the cabin. The wind picked up rapidly and continued to thrash the cold air into their faces from all directions. Dark clouds crept over the bright sky and the distant thunder rumbled overhead.

"E-e-everyone get inside," Barry hollered over the whistling gusts of wind. The others picked up the pace, pushing themselves against the thrashing gales. Carlos was first up the steps of the wooden porch. He clamped the doorknob and pushed against it with his shoulder but it wouldn't budge. Derek trudged close behind and nudged Carlos aside, using his entire body weight to barge through the flimsy door. The door flung wide open. Shards of wood chipped and cracked around its hinges. Derek hurtled through and landed on the cabin floor. The others kicked each other's heels as they hurried inside. Barry slammed the door shut but it didn't latch. The sheer force of wind flung it back into his face. He fought back, holding it shut as Frank came to his aid.

"Who broke my door?!" Barry shouted over the intruding gusts of wind.

"It wouldn't bloody open," replied Derek. He got up to his feet and dusted himself off, readjusting his beanie upright upon his bald head.

"G-g-get the nails in that tin," Barry demanded, gesturing over to the window sill. John snatched the tin and offered them out to Frank in a hurry. Frank took them and watched Barry rummage around the pile of wooden planks piled in the corner beside the door. He turned back around with two small planks of wood and a hammer. Frank held the door shut, it was already dark out and the squall of air pushed against the door like the force of another human being. Barry slammed the nails straight into the planks and locked everybody inside. They took a few steps back and sighed heavily. Frank had only just noticed the smell. More raw flesh, this time more pungent than the last. He turned to see the inside of the cabin and was greeted by several chains hanging from the ceiling. Their hooks pierced the dangling carcasses of freshly skinned game, a collection of rabbit and deer. A stained mattress was shoved up into one corner where linen sheets tangled in a clumped mess. Several tools, nuts and bolts sprawled across a wooden table, a single handcrafted wooden chair sat beside it. The static of a dead radio frequency hissed sharply in the background. On the floor to one side of a vacant fireplace rested the pelt of a black mountain wolf. The head was squashed, diluted with no expression. Chopped logs of wood lay in a messy pile beside it.

"You'll have to excuse the mess," Barry said. "I w-w-wasn't expecting so much company."

Everyone set their things down to one side. Barry lit the fire and cooked the venison he had saved up from his hunt. He passed the meat around for everybody and sat himself on the only wooden chair in the room. Frank sat on the floor with Annie and Tracy by the fire. Annie's head drifted onto Frank's shoulder. He felt her soft hair bundle up to his cheek. Tracy stared gormlessly into space. The thrashing bright reflections of the fire fanned over her face. Annie worried about Tracy. She hadn't spoken much since they left their home down south and she was only getting quieter.

Max laid beside Sam on the wolf skin rug, sleeping blissfully, eyes squinting from the warmth of the fire. Frank knew the dog had been pushed to his limits and he was content to know the dog had the opportunity to rest. The boy lay on his stomach and scribbled into the black book, his feet swaying up in the air. Frank held the chunk of cooked meat in his bare hands. He chomped into it and tore it apart with his teeth. He had eaten little over the past few days. Food was limited to preserved soups and bruised fruit and they were already running low on both. He glanced over to John who sat peacefully on the edge of Barry's bed. He held a greasy rag and worked away on polishing his sidearm. There was a stillness to the room. Although everyone was doing something or other, all Frank really heard was the monotonous crackling of the firewood and the gusts of wind moaning across the window. He took another bite out of the venison, his hands greasy from the fat. The rain drummed down on the corrugated iron roofing. Derek stood by the window at the front of the cabin. He tapped his fingers against the window sill and stared out into the darkness. He seemed restless, agitated, as though waiting for something but Frank chose to ignore it. Kara and Carlos stood over Barry by the table. They filled him in on the massacre of Merribank and told him about the raiders heading north to Elkford.

"...Paraíso sent us to you, Barry. He says you're the only one who knows the current state of the east," said Carlos.

"W-w-would anybody like some more venison?" Barry asked. He stood up and approached the large skewer suspended over the fire.

"We can't use the roads, Barry," said Kara. "We need you to tell us another way to get to the harbour." Barry bent over by Tracy and picked up the chopped logs. "The roads are no good," he said, half listening to their words.

"I know, I just said that."

Barry tossed the logs into the fireplace.

"Barry," Kara persisted.

Barry shuffled over to the front of the cabin. "Hopefully this storm clears by the morning." He drew the curtains, snapping Derek from his hypnotic trance as the oaf stood awkwardly by the front of the cabin. Kara glanced over to Frank. He shared her concern. Barry seemed distant, evasive towards Carlos' questions. Frank hadn't seen the man for over three years but much had changed and his behaviour only drew more attention toward him.

"Why don't we leave this until the morning?" Frank suggested. More silence. Frank continued. "Barry, you remember the last time we saw each other?"

Barry mumbled to himself, picking up the nuts and bolts on the table into his palm, *"four... five... six."*

"Barry," Frank repeated, much louder this time. Barry's head snapped up. His beady eyes peered over his round specs.

Annie's head jolted up with a stir. Frank felt guilty for disturbing her but made the most of Barry's short attention span while he had it.

"You remember Paul, the butcher?"

"Yeah I rem-m-member," Barry said, smiling at the not-so-distant memory. His smile led Frank to persevere further . Annie turned to Frank, now intrigued to know more. "The butcher at Merribank?"

"Yeah," Frank replied. "Was back when Barry lived down south; he had just bagged himself this deer, huge thing. I give him a hand taking it in to Paul who had a ton of fuel that Barry wanted for his old pickup." Frank chuckled to himself as the images flashed to the forefront of his mind. Barry released a bellow of laughter that shot him back into his seat. His cheeks glowed red, glazed with sweat.

"What? What's so funny?" said Kara.

"He hoists the deer over his shoulders, front hoofs in one hand, back in the other. I said, *'Let me help you.'* He struts off trying to be all macho about it. I insisted to help him carry the damn thing, but no. He says, *'I shot the bloody thing, I'll be the one to carry it!'*" The others listened in, all eyes and ears on Frank and his story. Frank stood up, imitating Barry's poise and holding up the imaginary deer. "He marches up the steps into the butchers, next thing I hear: Bang. I run up the steps and when I go in, I see Barry toppled over, his face sliding down the front of the counter." Frank struggled to finish, trailing off with laughter. Barry cried out in hysterics, wiping away the tears. Annie slapped Frank playfully, eager to hear the end of the story.

"I go the other side of the counter and see Paul. He's lying there unconscious with this deer on him. Barry only went and slipped on some blood leftover from an earlier delivery. The thing lunged out of his hands and nearly took Paul's head clean off." The cabin shook with laughter, all eyes on Barry as he squirmed with the estranged sensations of both embarrassment and nostalgia. The laughter soon faded and Frank let out a long final wheeze as he sat back down by the fire.

"I think we should call it a night," said Derek. Carlos leaned on the table. "I think so too." He looked exhausted. They all did. Barry crossed the cabin again and sat on his bed beside John who expressed an uncomfortable glance.

"Excuse me, mate," said Barry. He took hold of the grubby quilt and wrapped it around his plump body. John stared at the man getting into bed only a few feet away. He stood up, raised his eyebrows and wandered over to the chair to finish off his handy work.

The group took to the floor and laid out their bedrolls. Frank laid still, the hard wooden floorboards did his back no favours but at least he was warm. He cuddled up to Annie and held her close to him.

"Did we do the right thing?" she whispered into his ear.

"I don't think we had a choice."

"Do you think we can help them?"

"Who, the slaves?"

"Yes."

"I don't know," he said. "You were right though before. If we don't do something, nothing will change. As long as we're together, everything will be okay."

Silence.

"I love you so much."

"I love you too."

# NINE

Frank's eyes opened. The sound of rainfall was replaced by the harmonic notes of redwings and thrushes. It was the early hours of the morning and a monotonous knocking woke him from his light slumber. He reached out and felt Annie beside him. She was fast asleep, the warmth of the Elk skin wrapped tightly around her body. Frank turned his head to the repetitive knocking and as he did so it stopped. He could see an outline of Barry's plumpness through the darkness of the cabin. He had closed the door and placed the wooden board back to keep it shut. Frank wondered why he had been out so early. He was carrying his rifle but there was no animal or other signs of game. *A bad hunt perhaps?* He laid still and the cold air lingered. The others were still resting; some asleep, others groggy from the sound of Barry's commotion, but all chose to return to those valuable few hours of sleep before the wake of dawn.

Frank woke to the harsh hissing of a dead radio frequency. He sat up hastily in a stir. For a moment he forgot where he was. The cabin's wooden interior appeared strange and foreign to him until the sudden realisation shot to him in the form of a dull headache.

"No wonder you got nothing, it's on the wrong frequency," said Kara behind him. He turned to face the others and realised she was talking to Barry.

"I thought it was w-w-one-four-one point two-five?"

"No they changed it a few years back because of interference."

Derek remained on guard by the window. The others gathered around the table. Frank slowly rose to his feet.

"What's going on?"

"The main station has been dead for about a month or so," Kara explained. "We're checking if it's back on the air." She fiddled with the radio dial. A harsh tenor squealed high and low until the faint strings of a harp faded through the cabin. It was a soothing orchestral piece with violins and the voices of angels.

"Well, at least we know the music station's been left on," said John.

"It's on a loop," said Frank. "That same piece was playing when I was in Merribank."

"What the fuck?" Derek muttered. He span from the window and marched over to the table. "You son of a bitch." He shoved Tracy aside and snatched Barry by the collar. Kara caught Tracy before she fell. "What the hell are you doing, Derek?"

"This bastard sold us out."

"What are you talking about?" John asked. Frank moved to the window and peered outside to where Derek was looking. His thumping heart drummed against his body. He spotted them immediately.

Five men stood broadly in the middle of the marshy clearing. They had already seen him, staring back into his eyes, their wicked gaze a piercing symbol of dread. He wondered how long they had been waiting there. They held automatic rifles and the man in front held a megaphone. On either side, more men and child soldiers made their way around the outside of the cabin.

They were surrounded.

"I-I-I didn't do anything. I swear." Barry cried.

"Then why are they out there?!" Derek screamed into his face. Annie spotted the veins bulging through the skin of the oaf's neck. Derek raised his fist and swung a right hook across Barry's jaw. Max pounced onto Derek's leg. The dog's teeth sunk into the oaf's calf and he shook his head violently. Derek hollered through gritted teeth. Frank jumped in and snagged Max back by the collar. "Heel!"

Derek raised yet another fist, this time aiming for the dog. Another hand snatched hold of his wrist. It was Kara. "Stop. It doesn't understand."

"L-l-listen, please," Barry piped up. "I have a weekly d-d-deal with them. I supply them with meat and they spare me. They're a day early, I don't know why. I just wanted to get you on your way before they got here."

"You should have told us," Carlos added. Barry's eyes darted in all directions. He began to breathe erratically, gasping for air until his eyes finally rolled back into his head. The chair swung back and Barry crashed into the wood flooring below.

John knelt beside him quickly, checking him once over. "He's out cold."

Frank's heart pumped faster and faster. He grabbed Annie's arm and pulled her to the floor with him. Everyone hit the deck. Frank ushered Annie beneath the table with Sam, a blubbering mess amidst the confusion. Frank saw the open book dangling in Sam's hand. He took Sam's hand and held it up so he could see. A new sketch: A scribbled house covered in hundreds of dots from where he had stabbed the pencil into the paper. Outside of the house he had drawn people bearing arms.

Derek marched back over to the window. Frank yanked him down to his level. Derek's eyes shot like piercing daggers but he didn't care. They sat still, only the repetition of the heavenly choir was there to fill the silence. A distorted, thunderous voice called out to them. Carlos listened intently, eyes fixated in concentration of the foreign language. "They want the boy."

"What?" Annie stammered.

Derek held the .38 close to his chest with both hands. John and Carlos hauled Barry's body over to the bed and flipped the bed over on its side before cramming him into the corner. John loaded his revolver. He spun the cylinder into place and cocked back the hammer. Max's instinctive yapping argued with the intruders. He paced impatiently by the door. Tracy took hold of his collar and guided him back into the corner of the room by the fireplace. She sat down and held him close in her lap. The distortive click of the megaphone rang in their ears. *"Sabemos que estás ahí. Danos el niño y nadie sale herir,"* the threat repeated. It was calm but something about its sinister tone sent shivers down Frank's spine.

"The fuck did he say?" Derek muttered from beneath the window sill. Kara edged herself back to the table and got up to one knee. "We give them the boy and nobody gets hurt." Derek shifted onto his side and used his knees to slowly elevate his body.

"Don't you dare," Kara hissed.

"I'm not gonna sit here and wait to die over some goddamn kid!"

*Diez... Nueve... Ocho...*

"It's bullshit. We hand the kid over, they'll kill us anyway," John barked from the back of the cabin. Derek wasn't having any of it. He dived under the table and wrestled Sam away from Annie's arms. Sam's high pitched squeal pierced Frank's ears.

*Siete... Sies...*

Tears streamed down the boy's face and Annie begged for Derek to stop. All Frank saw was red. He couldn't even remember leaping forward, but he did and he was on Derek in seconds. He hung tightly onto Derek's back and wrapped his arms around him, struggling to tame the wild oaf.

*Cinco... Cuarto...*

Frank yanked back hard. He released a booming roar of pure adrenaline. His force and weight pulled Derek and sent them both plummeting into the window. The glass shattered into a thousand pieces. He felt tiny fragments fall around his face, delving into every wrinkle and crevice. His back dug into the sharp base of the window, pivoting haphazardly both inside and out of the cabin. He opened his eyes and glared up at the porch from the outside of the cabin. All he could see was the dreary sky through slits of warped wooden beams above.

*Tres... Dos... Uno...*

Only then did he realise his arms were still securely locked around Derek's neck. He was pulled back inside and together they tumbled to the floor below. The booming rhythm of machine gun fire pumped the cabin full of lead. Chips of wood stripped away from the walls and splinters flew wildly. Frank felt his forearm tighten in a release of bottled up tension.

He began to choke Derek.

He held his eyes shut and felt the shards of glass graze the surface of his face. The deafening gunfire reverberated off the walls. Kara dived down to the side of the cabin. One of the table legs where she had been kneeling cracked off and took flight somewhere across the room. The satanic gunfire strayed from left to right in the form of the devil's windshield wipers. Bullets tore through the mattress and feathers flung up into the air. Frank could hear Derek's throat guzzling for air. The gunfire stopped all at once and he felt a tremendous force separate him from the oaf.

Frank was dragged back and tossed to one side. He used his fingertips to brush away the glass in his eyelids and opened them for the first time since the attack. Carlos had pulled him away. He stood over by Derek who was lying down motionlessly. Frank took in short, rapid breaths. Complete disbelief. He stared at Derek. More gunshots echoed outside. The group flinched at the shots, covering their ears, but not a single bullet entered the cabin.

The front door swung open on its rusted hinges. A single raider rushed in, screaming with a rifle in hand. Before they could even gauge a clear view of him, a gunshot flashed through the cabin. The raider's head snapped back at the force of the bullet embedding his skull. Brain matter splattered across the walls. The raider's body slumped down into a lifeless clutter. Tracy screamed to the top of her lungs. She released the dog and tucked her head down into her knees. Open palms shook violently in front of closed eyes. She screamed to forget what she had just witnessed but that brief moment would stay with her forever. Frank looked to the back of the room and noticed the smoking barrel of John's single action army.

The cabin was completely destroyed. Sunlight beamed in from all directions through hundreds of tiny bullet holes. Carlos stared back at Frank, also riddled with disbelief. Frank's eyes drifted back over to Derek, his face dripping in sweat. *Did I kill him?* The oaf did not move. He laid face-down in the shards of glass and timber. A voice called out from the clearing but nobody could make out what was said. Carlos peered up through the smashed window. His eyes widened, spotting something out in the clearing. He snatched his rifle by the door and charged outside.

Derek soared up as if shocked by a defibrillator. He gasped for breath, long and deep. Frank hesitated to breath. The man had risen, as if from the dead. He dropped his head back and exhaled deeply. Frank's legs grew stiff, overwhelmed with the dull drumming of pins and needles. He lay still, staring back into the eyes of the oaf. Derek rose to his feet, his taut fists wringing the flesh of his own palms. His arms tightened, shoulder's locked. He breathed through his nose with flared nostrils. He was going to go for him, or so Frank thought. Derek reached for the .38 lying amongst the glass. Frank laid still, nowhere to run. Derek grabbed the pistol firmly and marched out of the log cabin. Frank's heart dropped suddenly and the others stared in an uncomfortable silence. He crawled to Annie through the debris.

"You okay?" He held her face in his hands and stared into her vacant eyes. She nodded. He could feel her face trembling in his hands. The boy sat quietly in her arms and looked back and forth between the couple.

"Sam, what about you, you okay?"

Sam nodded. Frank couldn't gauge the boy's expression. He seemed more confused, not scared or shocked by what just happened. His mind drifted into the endless realm of possibilities as to what the boy had been exposed to in his life. *Had he really seen worse?* At first he was saddened, but shortly after, anger took over. He realised that the people who did this to him deprived him of his innocence, his purity. The boy believed that what they had just witnessed was normal, and that was what angered him the most.

Carlos sprinted across the open plain. A single man stood, dead raiders littered his feet in cold blood. The man dropped his weapon, hands raised above his head in surrender. He got down on his knees in the tall grass. The rest of the group poured out of the derelict cabin. Carlos stood over the man, his rifle raised toward the man's heart. "Who are you?" He leaned in and pushed the barrel of the rifle closer to his chest. Frank staggered down the steps and joined the others. The man wore a combat BDU and an armour plated chest harness.

"Answer me," said Carlos. Derek struck the man's nose with a right hook. He jerked back, his nose busting wide open. Blood spewed out across Derek's knuckles. He grabbed the injured man and pulled him back up to his knees.

"What the hell are you doing?" yelled Frank. "He just saved our lives."

Derek pushed the man away and turned straight for Frank. His teeth clenched with rage, eyes near bulging from their sockets. John and Kara held Derek back. He desperately tried to reach out over them, snatching the air with open claws.

"You think I'm fucking finished with you?" Strands of saliva discharged from his mouth, his nose a snotty mess.

"Get out of here Derek," Carlos ordered.

Derek turned back to Carlos, stunned by what he had heard. He backed away from Kara and John and channelled his suppressed anger into a wicked stare. Frank could tell from his glance alone that he was saving all that aggression for later. Carlos was right however, there were more important matters to be dealt with right now and Derek's behaviour was only making matters worse. He backed away from the group, cursing under his breath and sat himself down on a fallen tree by the edge of the clearing.

"I'm with the LPA," said the man on his knees. He lowered his head and rubbed his bloody nose into his jumper. He was physically fit, somewhere in his late thirties, American accent.

"What's your name?" Carlos asked.

"Mike."

"You alone out here?"

"Yes."

"You're full of shit is what you are," said John.

"I assure you, I'm not."

Carlos leaned over and tugged something out from Mike's belt. He held it up for the others to see. A bright orange flare gun.

"You want to assure us about this? How do we know there aren't more of your people waiting out in the bushes ready to ambush us?"

"Carlos..." Kara interrupted. "He saved us."

Carlos' head hung low, he was growing more tired and impatient by the minute. "What do you want from us?" he asked Mike.

"Our company were heading north to Elkford when we got run off the road by a group of raiders. I lost my entire squad and got separated from the others. I decided to head east, toward the mountains. I heard there's an abandoned radio tower out there, thought maybe it's worth trying to reach an outside signal. I spent the night out here scoping out the place to make sure you guys weren't more of those assholes. Then I saw the kid." Mike leaned to one side. He looked past the rows of legs until his eyes met with the boy, huddling sheepishly behind Annie.

"Raiders force rifles into the hands of their young."

"If you're LPA, you're here because the world shut us out.

There ain't no outside signal giving two shits about us," said John.

"It's worth a shot at least, don't you think?"

"Sounds like a waste of time if you ask me," Carlos added. The kneeling man turned back to Carlos. "Well maybe we could help each other?"

"No can do, sorry." Carlos turned his back and began walking toward to the cabin. "Pack your things, we're moving on."

"Wait a minute," said Kara. She turned with haste, doing her best to keep up with his determined stride. "This guy is a trained fighter, he could be useful."

"We can't trust him, Kara."

"You don't trust anybody but sooner or later you're going to have to."

"We've already got enough people to babysit, you want more? Be my guest."

"But he can help us."

"Fine." Carlos replied bluntly. He handed the flare gun over for her to take care of. "Anything goes wrong though, it's on you. You know that, right?" That passing of responsibility hung over Kara like a vulture. Carlos made his feelings clear and he wanted the group to know that if anything happened, he was in no way accountable.

Barry sat forward, nearly coughing up his lungs. He was covered in feathers and sawdust and was left alone in the ruins of his once peaceful log cabin. He observed the state of the cabin and felt tears well in the ducts of his eyes. He tried desperately to hold them back; knowing the others were outside. He didn't want them to see, but the change around him was far too overwhelming for him to comprehend.

Tracy entered the cabin. She spotted Barry sat up in the corner by the overturned mattress and rushed over to him.

"Did you get hit?"

"My home..."

She didn't know what to say. There was nothing *to* say. His cabin was ruined. The walls were shot up, the mattress ripped to shreds and the meat he had collected over the past week was now rendered useless. The hunted game had been torn apart by bullets, sprawled out into pieces across the room in a fleshy massacre. Everything demolished. The only thing that had managed to survive were the items stored in his steel chest at the foot of his bed. It would take him at least a month to get the walls fixed, and even then, he now had no means of trade in order to purchase such materials needed.

Tracy could hear the others walking in and out of the cabin collecting their equipment. They would have to move on quickly. If the raiders had come from a nearby camp, there was a strong chance that more were on their way, especially after hearing the shooting. It was a risk Carlos didn't want to take and neither did Tracy.

"You have to come with us."

"I can't leave." Barry wiped his nose on his sleeve, sitting hopelessly amid the rubble.

"I understand, Barry, but you have to listen to me. When those men come back here they'll leave you for dead. I can't leave here knowing that will happen to you, I won't. You don't have a choice in this."

Barry's head tilted up to Tracy's eyes for the first time. He paused, as though silently grieving for a lost relative, but the cabin was all he ever had and now it was gone. He had no real alternative. He could join them on their journey east, or wait for more raiders to arrive and deliver his cruel, impending demise.

Frank told Annie, Tracy and Sam to wait with Kara by the tree line while the others packed their things as quickly as possible. He didn't want either of them to have to look at the dead any longer. He had caught sight of Sam glancing at the deceased children by the cabin. He stared at one of the teenagers lying in the mud. For a moment Annie thought he might have known the child, but there was no expression, no emotion. Barry knelt by the steel chest and crammed all the accessible provisions into a rucksack.

"What about their rifles?" Derek asked.

Carlos picked up the rifle by his feet, stained with the blood of a fallen raider. It belonged to the raider John had shot after the raid. He studied it thoroughly. "No ammo."

"The others outside are low too," Mike added.

"We can't afford to carry the extra weight."

It took them just five minutes to collect everything. They packed more blankets, some medical supplies, a hunting knife, compass, matches and Barry also hooked some snare traps he made to the outside of his rucksack.

Consumables were scarce but water wasn't a problem. There was always the fresh water streams scattered around the island and frequent spells of rain continuously added to the island's already rising water level. Food was what they really lacked. They had managed to eat a decent enough meal the night before, but not knowing where their next meal would come from was a frightening prospect. Frank felt somewhat reassured to know they now had a huntsman with them but he also worried. Barry's mind strayed far from their existing situation. Frank wondered if he knew just how much of a threat the raiders were and what they were capable of. He remembered the assault on Merribank; the burning bodies, deafening gunfire that mowed down hundreds of settlers at a time. He thought about Henry, and whether his family ever made it out alive. He shook the nightmarish memories away. He was here now. There was no point in dwelling on the past. He knew he needed to stay strong, to reassure Annie and tell her that they were doing the right thing, even though he too had his own doubts. He now had Derek to worry about. He never meant for things to go the way they did. The oaf seemed calmer for now, but Frank knew this was not the end of it. The oaf would come back, but for now he would keep his distance and sleep with one eye open.

The group was deflated, traumatised by the death and destruction around them. Frank couldn't blame them, especially Carlos. The man was under a lot of pressure. He was specially selected by Javier Paraíso himself, to guide them and now their numbers had increased. Carlos' experience as a fur trapper was invaluable. He was guiding ten others - including a boy and a dog - through treacherous territory infested with savage beings and ever-changing weather conditions. Winter drew closer and was fast approaching. The distant snow-capped mountains were vaguely visible, flat against the misty white sky. The brisk winds shrilled through the swaying pines, their branches rocked back and forth in a paranormal fashion and the sounds of the wind against the dreary backdrop only emphasised the notion of a dark and eerie presence. They regrouped by the tree line. Frank caught sight of Barry who took one last glance back at the cabin. He heard the others setting off behind him and placed a friendly hand on Barry's shoulder.

"I'm sorry we both got dragged into this."

He didn't reply. He just turned around, empty. They turned their backs on the log cabin and proceeded with their endeavour. The more time they wasted, the more the raiders engulfed Autark.

# TEN

They had made their way east from the cabin. Carlos kept Barry's directions in mind and led them along a narrow path through the forest. Frank glanced back over his shoulder and noticed Annie, carrying the child in her arms.

"Annie, put the boy down, he's got two working legs."

"But he's-"

"The grounds fine here, not as wet. Put him down."

Annie reluctantly abided. She gently put Sam down and continued walking alongside Tracy. Frank offered to stay with Sam. He caught the boy's attention and craned his neck to one side to indicate for him to follow. Sam followed him closely but his attention was elsewhere. Frank's eyes darted constantly from left to right and back again; searching for any sign of raiders.

"What's a penguin?" Sam asked sheepishly.

"What?"

"A penguin. I heard the angry man say it to Barry. He said he waddled like a penguin because he was fat. What does he mean?"

"He said that?"

Sam nodded.

"A penguin is a kind of bird. You don't get them around here though, they're out in the arctic."

"Where's that?"

"South of here, some way away."

"Can they fly here?"

"No they don't fly."

"Don't all birds fly?"

"No. Penguins waddle around. They uh- they slide on the ice, swim and catch fish.. I don't know much else."

"Birds that swim?"

"birds that swim, that's right."

Frank watched the boy process the thought, staring down at nothing in particular. ".. I think the angry man waddles too."

Frank smiled. He also agreed with the boy and his honesty which made it all the more amusing to him. *What am I doing?* Frank's face dropped immediately. He was letting him in. He said it to himself right from the start, that he wouldn't allow himself to get too close. It was distracting him from the very reason he was there in the first place; to find him safety, find his parents.

"We need to keep up with the others," said Frank abruptly, cutting the rest of the conversation short. He began to march forward but quickly felt the child's grasp around his open palm. Frank's head whipped back. He stared at the boy, confused by his anxious little eyes. The crack of wood echoed throughout the forest. Something whooshed down past the corner of Frank's eye. He flinched as the rush of the passing object prickled his senses. He whirled around to find a thick heavyset branch at his feet. He stared at the branch for some time, then looked up to see where it had come from. He remained still and without words. He glanced back over to the boy who gently released his grip from Frank's hand.

"How did you-?"

Frank was lost for words, his head shaking in disbelief. Sam said nothing. He looked down at his feet but his eyes drifted up to peer at the bearded man through timid eyes. Frank spotted the others making some distance ahead. He grabbed the boy's hand and guided him over the fallen branch to catch up.

The sound of rushing water was now audible over the crunching pinecones and brushwood beneath their feet. Barry pushed himself between two thick pine trees, clearing a pathway to an opening. He and Carlos held the foliage back in the form of an open gateway for the others to pass through. They were greeted by the breath-taking sight of Autark's Grand River. The water flushed dead ahead into the face of a sandstone cliff, forcing it to alter its course. It curved round and disappeared behind the concealment of the overgrown forest.

The Grand River flowed from the eastern mountains of Autark. Its waters travelled down and split off into two different directions at the base of the mountain. One diverge travelled east while the other ran down past Wolvendale and circulated back south, towards the coast. It was the first major water source discovered within the island's perimeter. This was said to have been checked during the first planned national expedition conducted by Roger Bullon and Javier Paraíso nine years ago – a year before the community project began. Frank had never ventured to the east of the island. Despite relocating to Autark, he never felt the need to explore or travel outside of his comfort zone. Wolvendale was known for its industrial construction trades. It was the largest town in Autark and to Frank; it defeated the purpose of the community project. He knew he was a hypocrite for establishing his home away from communal settlements though he did feel his trade as a farmer and grocer served a contribution to Autark's western settlers. He had heard tall tales of Wolvendale's fifty foot concrete walls and luxurious housing accommodations but none of it was for him. He didn't see the point.

As they looked out across the breadth of the river, Frank was reminded of the reason that he and Annie initially decided to move to Autark. Although the river itself gushed at a precarious rate; everything surrounding the water; the calmness of the swaying pines, the distant songs and calls of the local wildlife, even the group themselves as they stood gazing into the outlook, everything was encased in a bubble of serenity. It was an escape from the overly political and economic complications of the modern world. It was how the world was supposed to be before the pestilence of human gluttony and selfishness; before the infesting plague of corporations and the false sense of entitlement, before the desire for power and control over the world's natural resources. Frank couldn't help but feel somewhat responsible for the raider invasion. As part of the project, he played a small role in the media's publicising of the island. He wondered whether the human race was capable of exchanging mutual respect with the environment; taking only what was necessary as opposed to hoarding for profit. The raiders were taking something that didn't belong to them only because they knew there was no true leadership or control to stop them. They wanted to take what they believed to be their right to freedom and keep it for themselves. This is where Frank's opinion differed to Javier Paraíso.

Javier believed that Autark was their land, the people who travelled to start a new life or play a part in the government funded study. In Frank's eyes, Javier was naive. To him, there was a difference between claiming ownership over a property, and ownership over a nation. It was a difficult argument to uphold, seeing as there was no evidence to suggest that people once did live on this undiscovered land. He had heard rumours in the past, fluttering from the mouths of the merchants of Merribank Market, but he chose to believe those as they were, rumours.

Later that afternoon, they followed the river upstream and by evening they pitched a camp along the riverbank, beneath the curtain of hanging willow branches. It was too dim and gloomy to progress through the night. The darkness of the forest was always something of which to be wary. Raiders aside, the chances of getting lost or running into a natural predator were at a dangerous high. Bears and wolves were known to reside in Autark's forests, especially on the eastern front. It was best to wait until first light and continue with the clear aid of daylight. Carlos made some alterations to the shift patterns. They would be taken in pairs, hundred metres along the riverbank at either ends of the camp. Carlos and Derek did exactly that, sitting opposite ends of the camp by the tree line. They found spots which gave them a clear view of the clearing and the river. Following the river was safer than the open fields and valleys surrounding the northern road to the military base. In the meantime, the Grand River would also provide some sense of direction.

Back at the camp, the group had built multiple fires to give the impression that their numbers were larger. It was an otherwise clever ploy, tarnished by the fact that the raiders enslaved hundreds to be at their disposal. Raiders didn't care about their soldiers. Their soldiers were slaves, bands of pirates and brainwashed children forced to believe that what they were doing was for the greater good. They would strike without hesitation, regardless of how many people there were in the group. Frank wanted to speak with Barry about what happened to his home. He had overheard Tracy speak with him back at the cabin and knew that there was no apology that would suffice. Nothing he said could wind back the clock. He watched his old friend, sitting alone in the dancing shadows of a campfire.

Frank listened in on John and Mike talking around the campfire.

"...I studied at the University of Eastern Colorado before enlisting in the marines," Mike explained.

"You were a marine?"

"Yes sir, two tours in Afghanistan."

"But not anymore?"

"No sir," Mike replied. John didn't respond. He stared intently into the enticing flames of the campfire.

"What about yourself, what did you do?" asked Mike.

"Well nothing as eventful as you... I did different things, different places. Spent some time up in Wyoming as a national forest fire marshal."

"Sounds interesting."

"Was boring as hell..."

John continued to prod the burning fire with a stick. The burning light highlighted his brash moustache, his features more eccentric under the fire's luminescence. Mike laughed quietly at the old man's lack of enthusiasm. He was about to speak until John lifted his head for the first time.

"Why you out here, boy?"

"What do you mean?"

"Well look at you – you're still young – still got all your teeth and then some. Just trying to figure you out is all."

"There's nothing to figure out."

"No? Then why are you fighting here? Thought you said you was a marine?"

"I was, but not anymore. After my last tour they allowed me to retire due to… unexpected circumstances."

"Unexpected circumstances," John mumbled to himself, his attention back on the hypnotic flames between them. "What happened?"

"John," said Annie. She had also been eavesdropping but was more understanding toward Mike's privacy and lack of detail.

"No, it's alright," Mike insisted. He hesitated for a moment. John could see the cogs rotating in his mind to prepare himself for what he was about to say.

"I was on the last week of a six month tour. I'd received word that my wife and daughter had been in an accident. Wasn't her fault, other driver pulled out without looking, sent them both into hospital."

Annie and Kara sat up straight, all attention on Mike.

"I was immediately granted leave and got the first flight back home. By the time I got to the hospital, they were already gone."

"I'm so sorry," said Annie.

"It's okay. Was a long time ago." He waved it off but she sensed the unwanted burden of his past. He stammered briefly, refusing to look either her or John in the eye as he continued.

"I wasn't happy back home anymore, and fighting was the only thing I was good at. Thought this would be the perfect opportunity to start fresh, clean slate."

"Well we appreciate your help," said Annie.

"That we do," John awkwardly trailed off. A wave of guilt showered over him for asking the man to dig up his past.

"Hell, if you hadn't shown up back there, we probably wouldn't be here right now." They nodded. Kara turned back over and tucked herself into her bedroll. The crackling of burning twigs was all that remained to fill the silence.

John's last statement stuck with Frank. His mind conjured up repulsive examples of what the raiders might have done to them had Mike not been there. The rest of the group spoke very little that night. They hadn't eaten throughout the day and Frank felt himself drift in and out of consciousness. The temptation of the fire's warmth lured him into a false sense of security. They were never safe.

Sam hadn't put the book down since they left the cabin. He was sat on a log near Annie and scribbled away. The blunt pencil in his hand was engraved with tiny teeth marks that caused the wood to peel at the top.

"Can I see?" Annie asked. She moved closer to Sam to sneak a quick peek but the boy resisted.

"It's not finished."

"That's okay," she insisted, leaning in for a closer look.

"No!" Sam cried. He snatched the book away. He stuck out his lower lip and his eyes drew deeper with sadness. Annie held up her hands and scooted back over a foot or two. It was the first time she had seen him behave this way. He spoke openly around her now. She dismissed his outburst and allowed him to return to his drawing. Silence lingered over them for some time and soon enough, Annie's curiosity got the better of her.

"Sam?" Annie said. "Can I ask you a question?" The boy looked up and nodded. He shut the book and placed it beside him.

"How do you come up with your drawings?"

"I don't come up with them by myself."

"No? Where do they come from?"

"I don't know."

"But you said you don't come up with them by yourself. Where else do they come from?"

"They said I can't tell you."

"Who did?"

Sam didn't answer her. He lowered his head sheepishly, eyes darting from side to side as if to check nobody was listening around them.

"Who told you not to tell me, Sam?" Annie persisted. She noticed the palm of his hand gently stroke the surface of the book. He turned away, hopped off the log and wandered over to Tracy with the book clamped in his grasp. As he approached her, he stared back with bold eyes that glued to Annie. She let him be. They had only known each other for a couple of weeks and she didn't want to jeopardise his trust. She found his behaviour most peculiar and had never encountered a child quite like him before. She thought about the scars on his back, the experiences he must have endured during his captivity at the military base. The children were scarred. That audacious glare in his eyes exemplified the deprivation from his past. His life before the raiders was most likely a short one at that. This was all he knew. Whatever there was before, if anything at all, he had most certainly forgotten now. The raiders had drained his mind, only to fill it with their sadistic ideology.

Annie felt sick just thinking about it. She could hear the river about a hundred yards from the camp. The rushing flow of the current only worsened her feeling of nausea. She looked beside her and noticed Frank; eyelids drifting down and shooting back open in a repetitive cycle. He looked exhausted. The hairs of his beard had grown longer and scruffier. The bags under his eyes had formed multiple layers, his skin far paler than she once recognised. She gently placed her hand on his shoulder. His head jolted up, startled.

"Let's get some rest," she said. He nodded in agreement and the couple slipped into their bedrolls, lying side by side next to the dying fire. They listened to the river, and the distant hysteria of a wild coyote that howled through the night. Annie took one last look up at the starry spectacle in the sky before drifting off into a soundless slumber.

The following morning Frank was woken by the prodding of a blunt object into his gut. He opened his eyes and saw Kara kneeling over him. She held Frank's shotgun and nudged him with the stock. "Time to move."

She extended her arm and pushed the shotgun into Frank's grasp. Frank was suddenly aware of the gnawing hunger in the pit of his stomach. He felt it rumble and churn as he rose. The lack of food was straining the group and draining morale. He noticed the others beginning to become short tempered over the littlest things. The previous night he briefly overheard Kara and Derek have a small altercation about the schedule. Derek felt they were way behind whereas Kara took the hindrances into consideration. Frank was too tired to get involved, but the real truth was that he just didn't want to.

He packed his bedroll along with his knapsack. They had already boiled water that morning to take with them for the day. Derek stamped his heavy boot into the last burning embers. The ball of his foot pivoted from side to side and the burnt firewood crunched and flattened down into the cold ash.

Barry and Tracy led the way at the front of the group. Derek took it upon himself to watch the rear, keeping his distance from the others. He took every opportunity he had to avoid Frank and Annie. Frank questioned his own actions back at the cabin. For a long time he felt uncomfortable with what he had done, knowing that in that moment he was not in full control of his actions; but as time passed, he couldn't help but feel what he did was justified. He was protecting his wife, at least that's how he saw it. He separated the man he saw as a threat from the woman he loved. He could have killed the man, but he didn't. Was that only because Carlos had stopped him? Only now did he understand the perils of his impulsive actions that day. He was haunted by the possibilities of what he might be capable of doing. Had it been somebody else that stood between them, somebody he cared about? He could never live with himself.

A single burst of fire rang out through the woodland. It sounded far off and reverberated out across the pines in static layers. The group stopped and looked at one another for reassurance.

"Could be Carlos," said John.

"Better fucking hope its Carlos," said Derek.

Throughout the course of the morning they had been following the trail that Carlos had left behind. Although Barry needed glasses to see, he was very astute with his observations. He picked up on things Frank never even thought to consider. It wasn't just about footprints. He picked up on everything. Muddy depressions in the trail served as a treasure trove of information. As they pushed on, he explained how tracking humans was easier than animals. Animals were unpredictable; more inclined to be influenced by their surroundings and changed their course at the first indication of danger. Humans on the other hand, walk in a deliberate and predictable fashion, they don't always pick up on everything. It wasn't enough to just find a set of spoors. He looked at the depth of the imprint to judge the weight of the person. He observed the imprint's pattern, the distance between each spore to estimate the speed in which the person was travelling. He also looked at disturbances in nature; trampled grass, snapped branches. If he knew them, Barry would put himself in the mind of the person he was tracking. *Where am I going? Why am I going this way?* They could hear him mumbling his thoughts out loud. Settlers around the island had travelled to him in the past to ask for help in the event of a missing person and Barry was more than willing to offer his services.

Max's nose was down in the mud, sniffing vigorously at a newfound discovery. Barry knelt down beside the dog and ran his fingers across the damp surface. He lifted his hand and rubbed the fresh material between two fingers. His face transcended into a puzzled expression. He leaned in closer and allowed the substance to touch his tongue.

"Blood." He spat back over his shoulder.

"What? Are you sure?" Tracy questioned.

"Let's not panic. Might not be his," said Mike.

A thick scent hit the group all at once, bitter to the nostrils. It was a musky burning smell, an abomination to the natural air of the forest. They peered ahead and above the not too distant pines raised a single pillar of charcoal grey smoke. The more they pushed onwards, the larger the quantity of blood. Panicked thoughts rushed through Frank's mind. *Was it Carlos?* Late afternoon had approached and they usually caught up with him around midday. He wondered if the raiders had got to him, if the smoke was coming from a raider camp. He had never fired a gun at another human being before. He didn't know if he could step up to the plate when the time would call for it and he hoped that he would never have to.

Max let out a low, abrasive bark. The group's attention snapped up ahead in sync. They peered through the abundance of pine trees, squinting their eyes for a better look. Max stopped just in front of them, arms and legs spread out in anticipation. He was staring dead ahead. Within seconds he was gone, darting off into the woodland. Frank ran ahead of the others to follow him. He pushed his body through the natural obstacles in his way, ignoring the prickly pine needles that slapped across his face as he passed. He was right on Max's heels. The dog dived through the heavy undergrowth and Frank followed suit without a second thought. He felt the thorns pierce his skin and snag his waterproof poncho. They broke through to the other side and reached the gorge of the steep valley. The ground dipped low and the flourishing pines towered over it, blocking out any natural light. The smell of damp moss wafted in his general direction. Sitting in the gorge was the charred remains of a burnt out jeep. A stream of faint smoke rose from the gaps in the dented bonnet. Max's growl rumbled through the atmosphere. Frank raised the shotgun. The shady outline of a figure leaned inside the back of the jeep.

"Don't move!" he shouted.

The figure stopped what he was doing and took two steps back, his hand reaching out behind the jeep.

"I said don't move!" Frank repeated firmly. He felt the adrenaline flood his veins, his finger itching on the trigger. The figure raised his hands slowly, leaning in to peer through the contrasting brightness.

"Frank?" the voice called out from the darkness. He recognised the accent.

"Carlos?"

The figure stepped into the light. The prominent beam waved over to reveal a doeskin tunic. A lifeless rabbit dangled by a noose around Carlos' waistband. Frank sighed in relief. He lowered the shotgun and closed his eyes. His hand trembled. He stuffed it into his pocket to conceal his anxiety.

"Jesus Christ..." he muttered.

Carlos wiped the sweat from his brow and leaned against the bare trunk of a wilting pine. "For a second there, I thought you were going to take my head off with that thing." Max sniffed the motionless animal dangling from Carlos' waist. The rest of the group piled into the gorge.

"Oh thank God," said Kara. "Thought something had happened to you."

"Sorry, found this and got carried away," Carlos replied, inspecting the wrecked open-topped jeep.

The smell of smoke had now been replaced with reeking gasoline. There was another disturbing aroma, a pungent odour that lingered the surrounding air. Carlos led them closer to the vehicle for further inspection. The ground surrounding it was doused in oil. The entire left side of the jeep was littered with bullet holes. The engine and petrol tank had been shot up and the last remaining drops of fuel seeped out and dripped onto the forest floor. Carlos revealed the body sitting in the driver's seat. A dented helmet concealed his face, his head dropped to one side with a disfigured neck. Frank stared curiously, his eyes drifted lower. A single wooden arrow protruded the centre of the man's chest. It had penetrated his breast plate, deep enough to pierce his heart. His torso was covered in blood.

"Oh my God," whispered Tracy. Annie turned away, shielding Sam's eyes from the carnage. She knew he had already seen worse but she would do anything to prevent him from seeing more. Carlos retrieved his rifle leaning up against the rear of the jeep.

"I already checked it, nothing of use to us."

John gazed up the valley through the pinewood palings.

"Must be a road up there."

The door of the passenger side was already left ajar. Derek leaned in and picked something up from the seat. He lifted it up slowly to show the others. Another helmet. Streams of dry blood coated the chipped Kevlar exterior. Derek looked down to his feet and realised he was standing in a trail of blood. He dropped the helmet immediately and hopped back. Mike circled the vehicle and scanned it up and down.

"This is an LPA jeep."

"How can you tell?" asked Carlos.

"Same uniform." He gently tilted the head of the driver up into the light. "Don't recognise him though, must be with another company."

"Poor bastard," muttered John.

"Where do you think that trail leads?"

Mike followed the trail of blood with his eyes. They were faint and scattered but the dark shade of red was distinctive upon close inspection.

"Barry, how far is the nearest settlement?"

"Um, I-I'd say about three miles."

"Which way?"

"Up that way," he said, pointing in the direction of the blood stained trail.

They followed the trail up the hillside and discovered a narrow dirt trail. The blood had coagulated in the mud and overlapped the thick tyre tracks that veered off the road into the direction they had just come from.

"We shouldn't be on the roads," Derek grumbled.

"N-n-nobody comes around these parts anymore."

"Well somebody did," said Frank.

Tracking the blood became more difficult as time went on. The distance and frequency in the occurrence of blood droplets decreased over time and they were veering further and further from the river's path. Barry insisted that the river slithered back round to the direction they were heading but they had yet to find out.

The trail had gone cold. The blood stopped abruptly and so did the footprints. There were no signs of disturbances to suggest the person had collapsed or fallen from loss of blood. The tracks just vanished. Carlos stared down into the vacant muddy road.

"How is that even possible?"

"Look," said Annie, pointing far ahead into the distance.

The group peered through the misty atmosphere. Frank was taken aback by the masked structure up ahead. Its dull grey outlining was camouflaged against the dreary sky. He would have probably never even noticed it had she not pointed it out. Situated on the horizon far off down the road was the towering composition of a concrete wall.

'It can't be,' he thought. 'Wolvendale?'

# ELEVEN

The initiation of winter's first snowfall interrupted the night sky. The group had set up camp up a mound away from the road that was mostly concealed by the forest. Tracy and Kara had built more sound traps with the leftover twine and some of the men dug through the earth with their bare hands to prepare a pit fire to conceal the flames. Finding dry wood to burn was near impossible. The relentless rainfall over the past month had smothered the island, leaving a damp residue that would soon freeze as the temperature dropped. Frank had chopped branches to size with his machete. He compressed the limbs and stuffed them down into the pit. Carlos took the flint from his satchel and struck the serrated jaw of his knife against it. Chipped sparks bounced across the shallow pit but nothing followed.

"We should have collected some of that gas."

"We didn't have anything to put it in. Try again."

Frank used his hands to shelter the branches from the wind and Carlos struck the flint once more. The snap of the spreading embers crackled to life and gave birth to a small fire. Frank snatched more branches he had already severed and pitched them up against the burning wood. The dampness of the kindling sent heaps of smoke up into the air. It rose high up above the trees and into the murky sky. John piled rocks and stones around the edge of the pit to further conceal the flames.

The group sat huddled in a circle around the fire. They were less than a mile from what they believed to be the abandoned town of Wolvendale. Frank saw that everybody was agitated. Eyes darted off into the pitch black darkness at that faintest of sounds. Even if there was no sound, their minds played tricks on them that sent them into a state of paranoia.

A single rabbit was not enough to go around ten people and a dog. They shared the miniscule scraps of meat with wild asparagus that they had found along the way to accompany it. Eating such small portions only made Frank's hunger worsen.

He craved for more but it was enough to get him through the night. They had also collected a bunch of nettles which Annie brewed in a pot of boiling water. Lacking the luxury of cups, she let the pot cool and passed it around the camp for everyone to share.

Carlos and Mike took first watch. The camp was a lot smaller than their previous locations. They had set up beyond the grassy knoll of the roadside and burrowed deeper into the forest for the night. It wasn't the most secure of locations but they didn't want to be any closer to a potential settlement than they already were.

"We going through there?" Derek asked the others.

"Where?" John replied. He seemed irritated and short tempered by the lack of description.

"Wolvendale."

"I thought it was abandoned?" Tracy asked.

"It is. Has been f-f-for nearly three years now," said Barry.

"Three years?"

"I heard the stories," said John. "Just never believed them."

Frank sat up curiously. He felt an irritating itch at the base of his scalp and scratched it with his filthy nails. "How is that even possible? Isn't Wolvendale the most populated place in Autark?"

"It was. N-nobody really knows what happened to the p-p-people there. Some say raiders took them, others say they just vanished."

"What a load of shit," said Derek. "Raiders probably got it and people are just blowing the whole thing up."

"What about the arrow?" Annie asked.

"So they got a couple sticks with string, who gives a shit?"

"We really ought to know more before staggering in there," said John. "Carlos will no doubt want to scout it out at first light. We need to get past it to get round the base of the mountains."

Barry's head shot up. "Mountains? Oh, no. Y-y-you don't wanna go there."

"Why not?"

"That's Beothuk territory. 'Grey Wolves.' We should be heading north."

"Can't go north, its swarming with raiders," said John.

"Wait- grey wolves?" Tracy asked.

"Yeah."

The others remained silent, confused as to what Barry was babbling on about, but he continued anyway. "You mean you d-d-don't know? That's where that arrow came from. Not from the r-r-raiders, it's the grey wolves. They say they went e-e-extinct back in 1829 or something. I know a frontiersman down s-south, said he lost his h-hunting party up there; said they were attacked by men and women in caribou furs with wolves. He says the wolves ripped the calves of his g-group and the tribe folk finished them off with harpoons and bows."

"They tamed the wolves?" Tracy asked, leaning in with curiosity. Barry nodded. "Not just any wolves. N-n-newfoundland wolves."

"So?"

"They're also s-said to be extinct."

The camp fell silent once again; unsure of how to respond to Barry's tall tales of entire species resurrecting from extinction. Kara quickly shifted the conversation to food. Frank was passed the pot of nettle tea and brought the rim up to his dry, cracked lips. He tilted the pot and sipped its contents. The taste was bitter but he took pleasure in the warmth of the liquid flowing down his throat. He savoured each sip of the tea and let the hot air flow up into his freezing face. He passed it on to Tracy and caught sight of Annie feeding the boy.

Sam sat on her lap and she fed him the tiny shreds of rabbit meat. He had caught a fever the night before. His skin was pale against the reflection of the fire and his scrawny body withered behind the fraying rags. The people of Elkford had been kind enough to spare a small fur garment for him but it was drying by the fire. Annie was engrossed in the activity. Frank was worried about her. He noticed the bags under her eyes. She was slouched over the boy. It irritated him. Her caring nature had become an obsession. She began tending to him so much that she forgot to care for herself. The boy was more than capable of feeding himself, but she insisted on helping him anyway. She took pity on him. Frank approached Annie and discreetly asked to speak with her in private.

"Hang on, just got these last bits," she replied, referring to the finely cut scraps of meat in her hand.

"Kara, can you watch Sam for a minute?" Frank asked.

His eyes never strayed from his wife and she was surprised by his persistence. Annie let the boy down to his feet and placed the rest of the scraps into his tiny hands. "Go on, I won't be long." The boy wandered over to Kara and sat by her side. Frank helped Annie up to her feet and guided her off to one side, far enough away from the others so that they could speak in private.

Frank and Annie stood together in absolute darkness. They were just out of earshot from the others. He glanced back through the black columns. He caught glimpses of the group between the trees and checked to make sure nobody was listening.

"What is it, Frank?"

"I'm worried about you."

"I'm fine."

"No, you're not. You're exhausted."

"We're all exhausted."

"I just don't want you to feel like you're solely responsible for Sam. The others can take care of him just as much as you can."

"He's more comfortable around me."

"I don't care. He's just going to have to get used to the others."

"Why is this bothering you so much?"

"Because-" he paused unexpectedly, his feelings stifled his words. He stopped for a moment and leaned his hand against the rough bark of a nearby tree. Disregarding the indecision, he just came out and said it. "I think you're getting too attached to him."

Annie stared back then looked off to one side. She shook her head and glanced out into the night.

"I can see it in your eyes," he continued. "It's the same look you have whenever you hand him over to me or Tracy."

"What are you talking about?"

"Look, I get it."

"What?"

"I know we tried for a lot of years after we got married but-"

"Frank," she stopped him firmly. Her attention snapped back immediately, her beaming eyes cold and vulnerable.

"Don't even go there."

"He doesn't belong to us."

"He said it himself, he doesn't know where his parents are."

"That doesn't mean they aren't out there. Our plan was to find someplace safe for him to stay."

"Look around us, Frank. There are no safe places. For

God's sake, we're sitting in our own filth out here. He's safe with us. You said it yourself, 'as long as we're together, everything will be okay."

He felt the tension rile up inside of him. They argued back and forth, every defying response added another layer to his burning emotions. "You know we can't keep him."

"We can take care of him."

"No. Annie-"

"He needs us."

Frank slammed his hand against the tree. "He's not our son!"

Annie jerked back at the sound of his booming voice. The adrenaline coursed through his body. He was shaking. A cool sweat formed in the pores of his face and bonded the hairs of his brow. He glared over to the camp and noticed the turning heads but he chose to ignore them. Annie stared back at him, eyes glazed with fear. She stood distanced, her posture frail. She turned her back on him and walked with haste back over to the camp.

He tried to call out to her but his voice was besieged by the overdose of raw adrenaline. "Annie..." he choked. It was all that he could muster.

Frank rested on his side in the still of the night. He stared across at the burnt out pit that had withered, cold and bare. The last remnants of smoke wafted out and were snatched up by the passing wind. The snow drifted down slowly and settled on the forest floor. A vacant patch was left by the pit where the ground was still somewhat warmer. He tucked his knees up into his torso and huddled to stop the heat from escaping the encased bedroll.

He was shattered, but he could not sleep. All he could think about was Annie. He was overwhelmed with regret; the way he reacted, the things he said. The image of her staring back at him in fear permanently stamped across his mind. He felt embarrassed. He had never acted that way in all the years they had been together. He was starting to become terrified of himself. Terrified of the things he had done since they left the gates of Elkford. *What am I becoming?*

Hours had passed and Frank was still lying in the freezing cold. He looked up at the sky through the wilting branches and listened to the nightlife around him. He found himself constantly lifting his head to the faintest of sounds. His eyes had adjusted to the darkness and he found it a lot easier to see further now that the fire was extinguished. A harsh snap caused him to spin around. It was close by, not too far out of the camp. It sounded like a branch or twig. He sat up in the darkness and listened closely. His heart pounded in his chest. He thought about waking the others, but he didn't want to be held responsible if it was nothing but his mind playing tricks on him. He heard the faltered shuffling of leaves draw nearer. It was the rhythmic pattern of footsteps. He was sure of it. He peered out into the shade of the forest and caught sight of something. It was blacked out, a disfigured silhouette hat approached ever so slowly. Frank felt the pins and needles engulf his entire body. He could not move, no matter how hard he tried. He fell onto his back and could only manage to lift his head enough to see the approaching figure. The crunching of undergrowth grew louder with each hobbling step. The shadow stepped out of the tree line and into the moonlight.

It was a person. A man smothered in wretched blood. He limped slowly. One foot dragged behind the other, moving closer and closer to Frank. He tried to call out but his lungs tightened up and seized his vocal chords. He caught sight of the man's face. Thick, fresh blood drained his eyes like a leaking fountain. A gaping hole centred his forehead. His neck leaned to one side and divulged the exposed wound, blown out at the back of his skull. Strands of brain and flesh dangled to the side. The man reached Frank's feet. He reached out, staring directly into Frank's eyes. Frank stared in horror. The figure's skin began to melt in front of him - oozing over him in a tar-like substance - and leaving only flesh and bone to remain. He wanted to close his eyes, to turn away, but his body would not let him. The monster mounted Frank slowly. The fleshy remains of the figure wrapped its cold bony hands around his throat. Icy fingertips surfaced the back of his neck. They brushed against each individual hair that stood up straight. It began to squeeze, choking him. Putrid bile rushed out from its gullet. Frank felt the acidic liquid smother his face. It reeked of rotting flesh and the damp forest. The skeleton slowly released its grip on Frank's throat and glided its hands down his back. A tingling sensation shivered down his spine. The creature's deadly eye sockets tracked in towards his face. The tingling stopped all at once. It paused, its face inches away from his own, staring. A rupturing pain pierced Frank. He felt the razor-sharp dagger plundering his spine.

Frank's eyes burst open. He jerked up. His back arched at the intense stinging that inflamed his spine. He gritted his teeth through the pain, emitting as little sound as possible. He fell back and rolled the small of his back in a circular motion, rubbing it against the skin of his bedroll in an attempt to erase the pain. The figure was nowhere to be seen. He could hear his fluffy companion rushing to his aid. Max pushed his head into Frank's neck and brushed it up against his face. He placed his arm around the dog and took a handful of Max's hair between his fingers. He felt it clumped in his hand before gently releasing and stroking it neatly back into place. He took a deep breath, closed his eyes, and blew a lengthy gust of breath up into the air.

Frank opened his eyes once more. Dawn was approaching but the darkness had not faded just yet. He stood up and scanned the surroundings of the camp and imagined the demon in his nightmare spying on him behind every tree he laid eyes on. He shook his head and the absurd notion away and noticed a white arrow on a nearby tree drawn in chalk. It was Carlos' signal. He had left one each morning to indicate the direction he was travelling when scouting ahead. The group would erase it upon departure to leave no clues behind for any raiders pursuing their tail. Frank dug his hand into his jacket pocket.

He rummaged around its contents and pulled out the antique wooden cigar box.

First light was usually the purest sight of each day. Normally Frank could admire such a sight, but the tender pastel shades of this morning sky could not be appreciated. Instead, they were replaced with nothing but the trepidation and melancholy of his endeavour. He sat beside Max under the branches of a tall pine on the edge of the hilltop. It overlooked the nearby settlement and was now clearer without the haze of the previous day. He placed one of the remaining cigarillos between his lips and struck a match across the piece of flint. The small flame illuminated his face. He glared hypnotically at its intensity before touching it to the end of the cigarillo. He watched the tip of the cigarillo burn red with every puff. The flame crawled down the matchstick, its tip blackened and melted into a scrunched, deoxidised clump of ash. Frank blew out the flame before it touched his fingertips and held the smoke between his cheeks. The cigarillo sat loosely between his fingers. Max curiously sniffed around the hill and eagerly lifted his leg to mark his territory on a nearby tree. Frank tossed the match down and watched its smoky outline fade amidst the undergrowth.

He closed his eyes and when he opened them again he was greeted by Max's tongue scraping up the side of his face. The sky was mildly lighter. He had fallen asleep again, this time only for a shorter period of time. He rubbed the sleep from his eyes and noticed the cigarillo still sitting between his fingers, shrivelled to an inch and cold as stone. It dropped from his grip and rolled gently to a halt. He stretched outward, arching his back and groaned in relief. The pink sky glazed over the valleys and the very top of the sun peered over the distant walls of Wolvendale.

"Morning," said Barry from behind. Frank turned to greet him and noticed the hunting rifle in his hands. A sharp metallic clank indicated the bolt securing a round into the chamber.

"Want t-t-to join me?" asked Barry. He offered Frank a helping hand up to his feet which Frank gratefully accepted. "Carlos is already out there, isn't he?"

"I was s-s-supposed to go with him."

"What about the others?"

"They'll catch up."

"You sure?"

"Yeah, we'll be b-back before they know it."

"Alright."

They needed food. There was no question about it. He knew a measly rabbit to feed just under a dozen people would not suffice. The discomfort from the previous night's events was enough to encourage him to accompany Barry on his scavenge. Annie was with her sister. He trusted Tracy with Annie's life and knew they would do anything for each other. He just hoped that in time, sooner rather than later, he could find the courage to apologise for the things he had said.

# TWELVE

A thin layer of wet snow settled over the deserted road. It appeared more tranquil in the early hours than it had the night before. Frank and Barry followed it in search of food. The gigantic concrete wall became clearer with every step. Crows taunted them from above. They cackled like witches on either side of the road. Max dug his nose into the slush as they moved, sniffing vigorously for anything out of the ordinary.

"Y-you think Carlos is around?" Barry asked hesitantly.

"Maybe, he might already be inside for all we know."

Max let off a low growl. It was barely audible. He stared dead ahead. Frank followed the dog's eye-line toward the distant front gates of Wolvendale. Rustling bushes caught hold of their attention. They raised their weapons at the ready, only to discover a flock of pigeons burst out from the concealment of wilting pines. They scattered up into the air and flew back west.

Frank sighed. Sweat dripped down the side of his temple and intertwined between the hairs in his grey beard. As he studied the dog, he noticed the stains in the wet trail below. He knelt down for closer examination and dipped his fingers into the material. It was blood. A metallic rattling echoed off by the gates. Their attention snapped up. Max's growl grew louder and more menacing. Frank gently placed his hand on the back of the agitated dog. He peered ahead and spotted thin vertical objects sticking out of the ground outside the gate that was left ajar. A thick metal chain that was too long to hold it shut rattled as the wind blew against it. It slammed hard and reverberated back open as far as the chain would let it. It was only then that Frank knew what the objects were. They were spikes. There were at least eight of them embedded in the ground at offset angles, stained in dry blood and dirt. Pinned to the top of their sharp tips were the heads of the dead; a frieze of deterrence. Some eroded skulls; others still decaying, flesh dangling from their gaping necks. They sat lifelessly atop the spikes with taut grins and gaping sockets. The sparseness of remaining hairs tangled around their fragile skulls, split ends blowing out to the wind. He observed a single raven flap its wings and perch itself on one of the impaled heads. Its monotonous caw lingered along the enclosed trail and resonated deep within him. It cawed again, louder this time, as if to deter them from this ghastly place. Frank looked back at Barry over his shoulder.

"We need to get off the road..."

"Sh-sh-should we get the others?"

"Yeah. Whatever food that might be behind those walls can't be worth the risk," he replied. "I thought you said you've been here before."

"I-I-I have. It was never like this."

"When was the last time you were here?"

"I-I.. I don't remember," Barry stammered.

"Barry…"

Barry hung his head in embarrassment. "Okay. Three years." He then caught sight of something. His eyes instantly transcended to a wider, more shocking realisation.

"M-m-max!"

Frank spun around. Max had darted off up the road. The dog hollered wildly. He sprinted past the spikes and slotted himself through the gap between the towering iron gates.

"Shit!" Frank exploded back up to his feet in pursuit.

Barry trailed behind, doing all he could to keep up. Frank felt the adrenaline pump through his veins. His legs drove forward in a burst of adrenaline. *Shit... Shit... Shit...* He sprinted through the clearing, no regard for what may have been lying in wait. He heard Barry calling out from behind but all he could do was run after Max. He shoved passed the menacing deterrents, accidentally knocking down one of the wooden spikes in the process. The skull slammed to the ground and tumbled away from the spike into the soggy dirt. Frank reached the gate and desperately tried to heave his body through but the gap proved narrower than he anticipated. He tugged hard on the thick metal chain in a burst of frustration.

"Hold it open!" he ordered Barry who was close on his tail. Barry slung his rifle over his shoulder and held the doors as wide apart as they would let him. Frank knelt beneath the chain again and forced his body through. He felt his chest scrape past the rusty metal and heard the harsh tear of his waterproof. He staggered through and caught a glimpse of Max dashing around a corner up the street. Frank pushed the gate as wide as possible but there was no way Barry was going to fit. Barry stepped back, staring Frank directly in the eye.

"You go on ahead, I'll find another way."

"Barry, wait!" He reached through the gap and snatched for him but he was already gone. For a second he truly believed Barry would return. "Barry?" He whispered through the gap. No response. He quickly turned and was greeted by the overwhelming construction that was Wolvendale.

His eyes scanned every window for any signs of movement. He broke away from the centre of the T-junction and took cover behind a spilling dumpster on the street corner. He peered out from behind the dumpster. His mind flooded with endless outcomes and none of them were positive. The buildings on either side of the road were four stories high; all industrial warehouses with large steel shutters, some open, others bolted shut. The windows were smashed to pieces and the rusting metal left stains of mouldy orange and brown across their exterior. Waste and other material flowed freely in the street along with boxes, shoes, glass and one thing that stood out in particular, an overturned cargo truck.

The truck itself had burnt to a charred crisp. Its once white metallic sheen had now deteriorated to a flaky matte finish. Frank cautiously stepped out from behind the dumpster and stalked through the central strip. He reached the toppled cargo carrier lying flat on its side in the middle of the road and leaned against it. He shimmied along the cargo towards the rear, his back hugging the wall. He felt an intense vibration against his back and quickly backed off. The cargo came alive. Rumbling steel echoed out through the street. He moved outward, side-stepping closer to the rear of the cargo, the shotgun firmly in his grasp. Like a mirage or illusion, a wave of black matter poured from the rear hatch. At first Frank thought it was oil, tons of it spilling out onto the streets, but the flowing movement soon split into multiple pieces. He looked more closely and trained his sight on the disgusting reality. It was rats, hundreds and hundreds of rats. Masses of large black sewer rats poured out into the street, scurrying in all directions, toppling and climbing over one another. They dispersed and scampered away, squeezing their damp disease ridden bodies into every gaping crevice of the rubble. One whiff was enough to make him puke. He stood legs apart, dry heaving what little contents he contained in his empty stomach. A diminutive portion of vomit splashed to the ground.

Franked snatched the rag from his back pocket and held it in front of his face. It smelt of his own sweat and the clammy forest but he didn't care. It was better than the reeking stench from within the cargo. He leaned inside and peered into the shadows of the cargo. A swarm of buzzing flies circled the interior. He leant the shotgun against the side of the crate. With his free hand, he took out a match and struck it against the box and held it up to the darkness, the flame dancing in his grasp. With every baby step the smell grew more pungent. He took one more step and felt a wet, slippery material squish beneath his boot. Moving his foot away, he lowered the match to reveal what was underneath.

Rotten flesh. He panned the flame along and discovered a heaped pile of shredded pig carcasses. The meat was slimy, pale and bunched together. Thousands of wriggling maggots burrowed deep into the decomposed pork. He gagged at the thought of eating the rancid flesh. He felt empty. There was so much meat, enough to feed everyone, yet it was all wasted.

A distant bark muffled from outside and the match singed the tips of his fingers. His hand instinctively jerked back in a spasm and he cursed bitterly beneath his breath. He snatched the shotgun, leaped back outside and ran in the direction he'd thought he heard Max's call. All he could think about was Max's safety. Up ahead on the top of the mound was a squared off farming area. On the opposite side of the road was what appeared to be an abandoned hardware depot. Frank took in his surroundings. He leaned against the wooden fence and observed the bales of hay stacked beside rows of wooden coops surrounded by chicken wire. Listening closely, he could hear the clucking of hens, alive and nesting. *Someone must be tending to them.* He knelt down and brushed away the earth below. It was tough and compact like wet clay. Even the weeds struggled to grow here.

Another faint bark startled him from behind. The depot's front entrance was bolted shut. The doors were tight and sturdy, chains latched tight in loops around them. God only knew what was being kept sealed on the other side. There was a reason it was locked.

Frank hesitated. He knew Max was inside but feared what else might potentially reside from within. For Max to act in such an unpredictable way was unheard of. Frank felt light headed. The pressure and conditions were now getting to him.

He had seen and done things that he knew he would never do given other circumstances. He had eaten very little in the past three days and what he had eaten he had just regurgitated. He felt weak. Tired. He moved to the side of the depot and discovered the emergency fire door, propped open ever so slightly by a brushless broom handle.

"*Max?*" he whispered through the shady hallway. On one side of the isle were rows of offices. Papers and other assorted stationary sprawled the floors. The once pristine brass plaques on the doors were now faded and chiselled away. More documents spilled out into the hallway. On the other side from the waist up, was a transparent acrylic window looking out into the depot. The tall isles had been cast aside to make room for this internal allotment. Heat lamps hung low from beams and down lit tables filled with potted herbs and vegetables. Their harsh exposure juxtaposed the pitch black shadows around them.

Frank could hear the jangling of chains. He peered through the scratched dusty window and scanned the depot. There was no sign of Max. Just as he was about to move on, he saw some movement. A pair of hands emerged into the light. Dirty fingernails dragged through the soil on a nearby table. A disturbed groan echoed through the tall structure.

He was not alone.

He tried to see beyond the light but it was too intense. He moved away from the window and continued round into the open. Silhouetted figures shuffled and clanked across the concave strips of light. The lack of windows and harsh lighting caused a musky heat to circulate the room. Frank moved in closer, scurrying silently through the darkness. The humidity was unbearable, the smell of sweat foul. He felt the air stick to his sweating body. More chains rattled and rumbled in unison. The prehistoric grunts echoed nearby. He squinted into the light. Glimpses of a figure emerged from the darkness and into the work station of a tomato patch. His skin was filthy, a sickly shade of grey and he wore little clothes to shelter his body. The meat on his bones was scarce. His posture hunched over, a permanent hurt expression plastered across his frail face. In an instant the man slapped the side of his head with an open palm and barked vocals of a gibberish tongue.

*Christ...*

Light shimmered off the thick chain-link shackles binding his ankles. They were thick, heavy chains, similar to that of those at the front gate. Frank stared in utter disbelief. The man's sanity in submission, a forfeit to the darkness.

*What the hell is this place?*

The light reflected off the tables and illuminated the steel cross grid catwalks above. The sounds of heavy boots marched overhead, the outline of a figure watched over the workers. Frank couldn't understand. He didn't want to understand. A stir of commotion snatched his attention. The skinny man screamed in a panicked frenzy. His arms flailed wildly. Frank spotted black and white fur track past the light. The border collie whimpered in the shadows.

Frank broke away from the cover of stacked crates. He ran forward and leaped over the work station. He could hear the emerging cries of others drawing in. The rustling of chains clanked viciously and more rapidly, louder and louder with every passing second. Frank pulled Max away from the man who was now in full perspective. The man leaned back, his eyes bugged wide and shelves of bags hung beneath his eyelids. The cruel light reflected off the top of his bald, wrinkled scalp. His mouth gaped open to reveal rotten loose teeth. He cried out inconceivable words.

He lunged forward. Frank held the shotgun up horizontally as a barrier. The man latched on. His bony hands felt cold against Frank's knuckles. A hot flush of sweat overwhelmed his senses. He struggled against the man's surprising hold on the weapon. The shotgun shook in his hands, pivoting from left to right with every ounce of relentless strength. The man bellowed sinisterly into his face. Strings of saliva flew from the man's mouth and elasticised back into his filthy beard. Frank knocked the shotgun up into his jaw. The man's grip released. His lower back slammed into the table. He jerked back, teeth gritting as he cried out into the depot.

"Max!" Frank hollered. Together they dashed back out from the isle. The tormented cries and jangling chains were all too close. Within seconds more deranged bodies emerged from the gloom of the depot.

Frank slowly backed away, a bubbling sickness set in the pit of his stomach. Men and women stared back, their bare bodies closing in from all directions. They looked starved, malnourished, the bare minimum. He could just about make out the slightest of utterances.

*"Help us..."*

They shambled toward him in rattling shackles, arms raised in a semblance of revenants. They groaned, screamed, voices cracking under the strain on their throats. A bright torch flickered from side to side on the catwalk above. The figure called out but Frank could not hear over the cries of those around him. One of the men lunged for him. The shackles buckled from the overstretched strain. The man fell at Frank's feet, his scrawny palms clutching at his ankles. A sea of hands clasped out for him from all sides. He waved them off frantically and used the shotgun to shove their feeble bodies aside. He tripped over his feet through the masses and made a break for the fire door.

The light shone through the gap in the open door. He could hear the sound of rattling chains and bare feet slapping against the floor. Bated breaths on the back of his neck. Max dove through the fire escape and completely wiped out the broom handle. Frank reached out but the door slammed shut in his face. The light faded along with it. The bodies shoved into him from behind and pushed his body weight into the release bar. All at once they ruptured out from the depot and into the light.

Frank slammed hard into the rubble. The gritty scraps of tarmac daggered speckled imprints into the palms of his hands.

He turned over and shuffled back. Their grazed hands reached out for him. They clutched his jeans and pulled themselves closer, caving in on him. Their eyes squinted, deprived of natural light for so long. Frank struggled, he could feel clenched fists bashing down against his thighs. Max bit down on one of their ankles. The slave thrashed back like a fish out of water. His foot caught Max in the collarbone and the dog squealed back into the rubble. All at once they stopped. Their eyes opened wide, staring beyond. Frank listened. A single rumbling engine revved fiercely. Together the slaved bodies shot up and scampered out into the open; their legs straight, pumping like a steam locomotive. Frank looked up, dazed and confused. They ignored his presence. He scooped the shotgun back up into his arms and ran across the hilltop.

Frank burst through the wooden gate head over heels. He managed to regain his balance just in time. He ran through the spacious open plain that diverged from the rest of Wolvendale. Hundreds of crows flocked up from the bursting gate and cawed wickedly as they flew away. He looked down to check Max was still by his side and felt something snatch a handful of his jacket. The force of the grip yanked him back down into the dirt. Frank rolled over onto his side and caught sight of the opposing force. A ragged woman stood over him. She had long black hair and wore tattered clothes. Frank's hands shot up in surrender. He noticed her faintly tanned skin and gleaming green eyes.

"Hide," said the ragged woman. Max growled ferociously and stood between Frank and the woman. Her glance darted back and forth between Frank and the depot. Frank turned back to where he had just come from.

On the other side of the road, a raider stormed out from the depot with an assault rifle at the ready. He snatched up the first fleeing slave he could lay his hands on and shoved him headfirst into the dirt. The crack of the rifle boomed the desolate streets of Wolvendale. A single shot into the back of the head. Nearby slaves stopped running. They fell to the ground in surrender while others tried their luck for a shot at freedom. The raider fired in bursts at the feet of those fleeing.

The ragged woman ushered Frank and Max back into a narrow gap between two of the chicken coops. He could see the woman wasn't a threat and called for Max to stand down.

"Get back here!" a booming voice hollered from the open road. More gunshots. Frank stared through the narrow slit in the coop's wooden panels. There were chickens inside, alive and nesting. He held the dog close to him and felt his paw throb meticulously. He shushed silently over Max's wheezing, eyes back on the ragged woman who stood out in wait.

A hostile revving engine sounded up toward the hilltop. It was a black motorcycle. A second, shorter raider dismounted the bike, sub-machine gun in hand. The brutish raider rounded up the runaways and lined them up by the wooden fence. The woman stood completely still, frightened that if she moved she too would suffer the ultimate price. Like the others, she also was bound with shackles, but unlike the others; hers were bound on one ankle only. It was a longer chain, the other end latched to the concrete wall of the grocery store next door. The shorter raider kicked open the gate and marched toward the ragged woman.

"What the fuck happened here?"

"I-I did not see," she replied.

"Bullshit. I just got here and I saw a lot of things."

"I was tending to the chickens. I heard the shots and came out just now."

Frank's fingertips touched the shotgun. He slowly pulled it closer, his finger shaking only inches from the trigger. He laid still, glimpses of black leather boots paced by the chicken coop. A single gunshot blared out in the distance. The raider swung around in a panicked sweep. He turned back and marched toward the woman and slapped her to the ground with the back of his hand. He was now in perfect view. Frank eyed up the short greasy man between the confined gaps of the chicken coops. He stood dominantly over the ragged woman. She groaned and held her hand to her cheek which had now turned red and raw in the cold.

"How many are there?!" he screamed down to her.

"I don't know what you're talking about."

Frank rose to his feet and aimed the shotgun. He pushed the stock back into the pocket of his shoulder, lining the sights. His finger itched the trigger; his body taut, shaking with fear. The raider noticed him from the corner of his eye. He turned and faced him with a menacing stare that shocked him still. Frank flinched and jerked back. He heard a sharp hollow thud slam into the raider. He opened his eyes. A long wooden shaft embedded the raider's neck. His eyes widened into a thousand yard stare that penetrated Frank's soul. He stood for as long as he could until his limp body dropped and folded onto the ground. Frank stared at the man, then back to the ragged woman.

"Look out!" she cried. Frank turned fast, so caught up in the moment that he had forgotten about the other raider. The raider raised his rifle. Frank felt the rifle's trained sights lock onto him and he shied away from the impending shot. The awaited sound of a gunshot was replaced with that same swift thud of contact. Frank peered back up past his cowering eyelids. The rifle clattered against the debris below. Another arrow, this time piercing the raider's chest. He dropped to his knees and the blood soaked through his green shirt in wide spread. Frank stared blankly. Another arrow zipped past, this time only inches away from his head. He felt the air wisp past and it snapped him back to life. He returned to the ragged woman, lying down in the hay-littered dirt, the shackle still bound to her ankle.

"Look away," he uttered, his body shaking. He kicked the chain out in front of him and the shotgun blasted in his hands. The steel pellets ripped through the metal chain and split it free. She got to her feet and shoved a bundle of something wrapped in fastened rags into his pocket. Frank stared back. "Run."

The woman nodded and turned her back. She ran out into the street with the others and they dispersed in all directions.

Another arrow pierced the wood of the chicken coop and vibrated to a halt. Frank dived back to cover. He waited behind the coop, the raider's dead body beside him. His shaking stopped. He stared down into the oozing pool of blood that soaked into the hay around him. He would wait for the next shot and then he would have an opening. The zip of the arrow faded into play and struck the inert raider once more. Frank shot up to his feet and made a break into the open.

Frank and Max darted out of the gate and rushed back down towards the strip. He ran as fast as he could. He turned the corner of the toppled cargo and felt his body crash into something blocking his path. He flew back and slammed down into the dusty debris. Barry yanked him back up to his feet and the others followed close behind. Annie emerged from the group and wrapped her arms around him. He looked around and acknowledged the others. "How did you get in?"

"There was no other way," Barry said. He gestured to the front gate down the street and it was now wide open. Frank counted the numbers and realised somebody was missing.

"Where's Carlos?"

"We were gonna ask you the same thing," replied John.

The low growl of engines faded towards Wolvendale from beyond the wall. All eyes were now on the front gate. They stared without a sound. The first truck came into view. There were at least two more behind it. Raider foot-soldiers jogged along either side of them, firing their weapons. Together they dived down into the jagged rubble behind the cargo carrier. The sound of bullets pinging steel resonated the street. Frank peered out from the cargo and saw the flurry of arrows rain down against the pale sky. The front tyre of the first truck burst wide open. The tyre burst and echoed through the street. The front of the truck dipped to one side and bright orange sparks chucked up from the friction. The truck screeched and swerved before crashing straight through a concrete pillar.

More arrows whizzed by from all directions. He spotted a group of people emerge from the broken windows of the abandoned buildings. They scaled down with immense speed and acrobat skill. Their skin was tanned and their clothes crafted from the pelts of caribou. A red chalky substance decorated their faces in patterns that summoned visions of ancient tribal tradition. The men and woman hollered and whooped as they touched ground. They closed in from all sides, the raiders completely off guard. The first one down used a harpoon forged from iron as a spear and plunged it straight into the heart of a raider. The others formed together, firing flocks of arrows at both raiders and the group. Frank stared in both horror and intrigue. It couldn't be. It wasn't possible.

*The Grey Wolves?*

John dropped to one knee. He roared to the top of his lungs. Frank turned back and saw the arrow sticking out from his calf. Derek and Mike returned fire. Frank and Barry placed John's arms around their shoulders and heaved him up onto his one good leg. His left leg was in shock, paralysed from the knee down. Kara stuffed Sam into Annie's arms and dragged her along with her. "Run... Run!"

The group sprinted deeper into the backstreets of Wolvendale, weaving in and out of toppled vehicles and obstacles that crossed their path. The inaccurate flurry of bullets and arrows rained over the tops of their heads. Kara stayed close to Annie and Tracy. A makeshift arrow burrowed straight down in front of her feet and ricocheted out across the tarmac. She lifted her head and tracked the trajectory back to a furry figure perched high up a rusty old crane. Without hesitation she emptied the twin barrels of her sawn off shotgun up towards the figure. The bow fell first and shook against the ground. The body followed shortly after, thudding hard face first into the dirt below.

"Which way?" Derek barked over the gunshots. Barry led them to the farthest corner of the settlement. They bolted inside a storage facility in a flustered shambles.

"Shut the door!" yelled Frank. Mike and Kara pushed the sliding shutter doors together and slammed them shut. Pinging snaps of gunfire ricocheted off the rusted steel compound. This facility was also dim. The only source of light was the strip of skylight above.

"Where we headed, Barry?" Frank pestered. He could hear John trying to suppress his pain through faint grunts and groans.

"H-h-hold on, let me think."

Mike looked around for something to hold the door shut. All that surrounded them were industrial wooden crates too large to carry.

"That way," the soft voice piped up from Annie's arms.

Sam hopped down and wandered off towards the back of the facility. Max followed close behind him. The others shared a series of thought provoking glances.

"We're not seriously following a damn kid, are we?" said Derek. His arms shot out, questioning whether he was the only sane one among them. Kara led the others to pursue the child.

"We haven't got many options left."

It was the sad truth. The others grabbed their gear and followed the boy through the tall isles of crates. With Kara and Max by his side, Sam edged open the flimsy corrugated iron door at the back. It juddered back on its hinges and Kara checked the narrow alley both ways. It was clear. Sam guided them along the damp, slanted pathway, hidden away behind more industrial structures. They were at the very edge of the Wolvendale. Frank flinched at every gunshot they heard, he listened to the weak defenceless slaves cry out in agony. Sam seemed unfazed. He was somehow able to block it all out. He was so focused on escaping, he didn't allow anything get in his way. Rubble and debris slanted up at a forty-five degree angle against the town's concrete perimeter. Sam pointed down the path and the others caught sight of his finding. A large pipe stuck horizontally out the side of the angled slope.

"Jesus..." Barry murmured. "I c-c-complete forgot about this." He ran ahead with a spring in his step. The discovery invigorated a sudden burst of enthusiasm in the plump man.

"What is it?" asked Kara.

"S-s-sewer system."

"Gross."

"No, it's n-n-new. They were going to install this right before the town went down. I rem-m-member seeing the trucks import the piping that day."

The pipe's circumference was made of thick iron. A collection of materials and tools gathered dust in a littered pile nearby. Kara squatted down with one hand resting on top of the pipe. She starred down the gloomy tunnel and held her nose at the foul stench ahead. It wasn't the scent of human excrement; but rather the damp and feral stench of rodent droppings.

"How far do you think it goes?" said Kara, squinting down through the eternal abyss. Mike knelt down beside her, hunching his shoulders to fit into the pipeline.

"Only one way to find out."

The group piled in, crouching low. They took baby steps through the cramped tunnel. Mike took point and Derek covered the rear. Frank stayed close behind Annie and Sam. He could feel Barry's heavy breathing on the back of his neck. His sweat settled into the hairs of his eyebrows. A thin puddle of murky green water trailed along the centre of the pipe and occasional rat dropping stuck to their shoes. They pressed onwards, squatting awkwardly through the enclosed space.

Frank began to feel lightheaded. Nauseous. His vision blurred. He was certain the pipe's diameter was shrinking and closing in on him. A firm pressure compressed around his ribcage and lungs. The further he delved into the confined passageway, the more pressure he felt suffocating the life out of him. The sound of gunfire echoed behind them through the narrow tunnel. Frank felt the vibrations in his hand that pressed against the side of the pipe. His lungs were going to burst. He tried to call out but words could not escape him. The last tiny breaths of air left his body. His vision became more disorientated. He could still control his limbs but it looked as though they were beyond the pipe's boundaries. It closed in further. His eyes deceived his mind and spatial awareness. His eyelids grew heavier; he could no longer keep them open. Everything stopped at once; he dropped forward, his consciousness lost. He landed face first into the back of Annie and slid down into the foul substances beneath.

# THIRTEEN

An entire day had passed. The events that took place in Wolvendale were only just beginning to settle in. There was still a long journey ahead of them. Their original route to the military base had now been compromised. Word spread through the grapevine of the raider outposts running back to the military base and now their security was tighter than ever along the Grand River. Now the group were forced to do what they feared most, there was no alternative. They would have to take a detour through the mountains.

The mountains of Autark were a sensitive subject among settlers. Although the south eastern highlands had been swept during the construction of a radio tower with stronger signalling capabilities, the search was not thorough. The mountains were considered uncharted territory. Rumours soon started to spread. Whispers of incidents about missing people fluttered among the surrounding settlements, leaving settlers with an array of tall tales and nightmares to share.

The group set off in the early hours of the morning. They found themselves over-encumbered in conditions where the snow showed no signs of letting up. What few ounces of strength some possessed were used to carry the weak or injured. The mountains were far too steep along their western face so they would have to go around them from the south. For every mile they ascended, the temperature dropped by two degrees. The wind was brutal and relentless. It kicked the snow up from the ground, its texture like flaky grains of sand in their eyelashes. Their list of fears only seemed to increase the more they went on. How could they go on when catching pneumonia from the cold was the least of their worries? The weather and lack of food cut their travel time in half. More stops meant more time without food. They discovered space surrounded by a tree line of thick pines and split up in search for consumables.

Two fishing tackles drifted beneath the depths of a narrow stream. Up above the surface, the water's current remained calm and steady. Gusts of wind disturbed its serenity, rippling outward in perfectly parallel form. On the other end of the fishing rods sat Derek and Carlos across the riverbank.

"You ready to call it a day?" asked Carlos. "Been out here two hours now." He tightened his posture to shield from the cold and rubbed his thumbs together over the handle of the fishing rod.

"What are we doing?" said Derek, deflated. His eyes remained fixed on the rippling water beneath.

"Well I told you there would be no fish here."

"No. I mean what are *we* doing?" Derek gestured between Carlos and himself. "Out here, wasting our time and risking our lives for some little shit."

"He found you a way out of that mess, didn't he?"

"So what? That mean he's Jesus now?"

"I'm not saying that. Look, you didn't have to agree to this. You chose to do this."

"What the hell do you know about me?" Derek grumbled.

"I owed Javier a favour. Now that I'm actually out in this mess, I'm thinking this return is worth way more than what he did for me."

They were left encompassed in a moment of silence. Carlos focused on the phenomenal snow-capped mountains above; the dreary sky clouded their peaks and the snow on the pines grew thicker the higher he looked. He could still feel Derek's vibes. More questions, a calculative gaze over the water.

"I told Barry not to go in there," said Carlos.

"What, Wolvendale?"

"Yes."

"Then why did he?"

"I don't know. The man is unstable. I told him, 'it's too dangerous.' I said to go around the eastern wall and meet me on the other side."

"You think he's dangerous?"

"I think he is a liability. He says one thing and does another."

"So what are you saying?" asked Derek.

"We need to be more careful. I don't know how well we can trust these people. It was not difficult to track you down with what you left behind. It could have just as easily been raiders stumbling across those tracks, or worse, those other people you spoke of."

Derek nodded his head, humming in agreement. "Least he was right about something."

Carlos stood up and reeled in his line. He was unsurprised to discover nothing latched to the other end. "Come on, we better get back. They'll probably start wondering where we are." Derek stood and watched, he tossed the fishing rod over his shoulder, balancing the bottom of the grip in the palm of his hand. He stuffed his other hand into his pocket, grabbed a handful of chewing tobacco and packed it into his mouth. Flakes of tobacco dropped from his mouth and buried themselves amongst the black and grey hairs in his beard. Carlos started hiking back up the riverbank.

"Oi, Carlos," said Derek. He hobbled up the trail and caught up with the scout. "What's your angle in all this?"

Carlos's eyes wandered over to the river and then back to Derek. He shrugged his shoulders, his upper lip sticking out to one side. "I guess sometimes people have to stop thinking for themselves and start focusing on what's best for everybody." Derek stared at him for some time, his eyes squinting, reflecting on the response. Derek rolled his eyes and continued ahead.

"What?" Carlos asked.

"You're full of shit, mate."

Barry sat alone against a lonesome willow; basked in a collection of decayed wildflowers that shrivelled and curled up over the ridge like crumpled spiders. He looked down over the edge at the stream that flowed on past the concealment of the forest. He reached into the knapsack beside him and pulled out his canteen. He slowly unscrewed the cap and took a swig of its contents. The colour of his cheeks transitioned to a warm glow. He took another swig, heavier this time. He seemed drained, exhausted. He didn't even bother to wipe the spilling drops gliding through his white beard. He pushed his spectacles further up the bridge of his nose and sat limply against the tree.

"Barry?" a voice called out to him.

He lifted his head and saw Tracy standing over him. She too looked drained. Her dry brunette hair was tied back in a loose bun. Her arms hung loosely by her sides. The pungent aroma of whiskey masked the air. Tracy snatched the canteen from Barry's hands. He barely put up any sort of fight to take it back. She leaned in and sniffed his contents.

"What are you doing?"

"Oh, l-l-leave me alone."

"It isn't safe out here, and you're drinking?"

"I don't care anymore, alright? I j-just don't care."

His head hung low, his words strung together with an intoxicated slur. Tracy knelt down beside him. She held the canteen out in her hand, staring temptingly into the dark abyss. She brought the brim to her dry, pursed lips and knocked back a gulp of its contents. She winced at once and the bitter alcohol singed her throat.

"You made this?"

"Yeah."

"Tastes awful." She screwed the cap back on and set it aside. Barry remained silent, encapsulated in a bubble of his own little world.

"Look I know you're scared. We all are."

"I lost everything."

"I understand. Our home got raided too."

"I'm n-n-not just talking about that," he replied.

"Everything before... my job, m-my house... my wife."

"You were married?"

He nodded.

"I'm sorry."

Barry waved her apology aside. "When I c-c-came out here, I thought I could have a fresh start, you know? Seems like trouble follows me wherever I go."

Tracy stared at him, studying every detail of his round face. She felt pity on him, but there was something more. There was sympathy, an attribute of common ground.

"You can't give up."

"What difference does it make? Y-y-you started this thing without me, you can finish it without me."

"I can't do this without you, Barry." He turned to her, perplexed.

"We've both dealt with our fair share of loss. The past few weeks I've been trying to figure out what the hell this is all for. Why I'm here. I feel like a spectator watching the world carry on without me and no matter how hard I try to contribute, I can't help but feel worthless."

"Don't you see, I n-n-nearly got Frank killed back there."

"You came back, didn't you? That is not on you. You've got to stop blaming yourself for everything Barry. Without you this group wouldn't have even known about Wolvendale. You prepared them for that. Everything else was completely out of your hands." She moved in closer to draw his attention but his eyes only stayed with what was left of autumn's dying foliage. He picked what remained of a withered blue flax flower and began plucking the petals away, one by one, then scattered them to the wind and watched them land only a few feet away.

"Listen," Tracy continued. "Having you here, knowing now especially, that you- *we*, have both had our losses... Knowing that you can still go on is the only thing keeping me going right now."

Barry looked up at her for the first time. His haggard eyes stared back at her through his thick bottle-rimmed specs. His rosy cheeks intensified. He stuttered briefly, unsure of how to respond. She shuffled closer to him and rested her head upon his shoulder. He froze rigidly. He didn't understand, he wasn't used to it. He felt her bundled hair brush against his neck. It tingled and sent a shiver up his spine. It felt good. It wasn't cold. It was intense, like the spark of an electric current. He felt something he hadn't felt for a long time. He loosened his shoulders and allowed the warmth to consume him. He leaned back against the tree and together they sat in silence, watching the plants dance and sway in the breeze.

Frank's eyelids peered open. A thin layer of moisture blurred his vision. All he could see was the cloudy sky and branches above. The pines rustled violently. For a moment he thought they were going to topple over and crush him. Freezing gusts of wind blew over his body. He shut his eyes and felt the moisture escape and roll down by his ears. His lips felt dry and cracked. His stomach bellowed and churned. A cracking pain engulfed his mind like an axe to the back of the skull.

He sat up slowly and took in the sight of the campsite around him. Scattered bags and bedrolls piled around a dying fire. He brushed the snow on him away with his hands. There was no feeling in his fingertips. They had transformed to a pale white. John sat nearby, closer to the fire. He tried to call out to him but his throat was bone dry. John heard the desiccated utterances escape him.

"You're awake. I was starting to get worried about you, friend."

Frank wiggled up out of the bedroll and flipped it around his body like a blanket. He hobbled over to John and took a seat on the ground beside him. "Water."

John pointed behind him. "Your bag's there." Frank turned and rummaged through his belongings. He snatched the canteen from his knapsack and chugged the water down quickly. The icy water overwhelmed his insides, his heart encased in a layer of frozen glass.

"I'm afraid we ate those eggs of yours," said John.

"What eggs?"

"The ones you had in your pocket there."

The ragged woman sprung to mind. He wondered if she had made it out of Wolvendale alive.

"How long I been out?"

"About a day. Here, eat this." John served up a piece of grilled beaver into the empty cooking pot and handed it to Frank. He took it and immediately began to wolf it down. The meat triggered memories of Wolvendale and sparked pestering odours of the toppled cargo crate. Frank gagged profusely, almost choking on the meat. He coughed up a piece and spat it back over his shoulder.

"Take it easy. Chew your food," said John. "Carlos bagged us that beaver this morning; would hate to see it go to waste."

"Where's Annie?"

"She's down by the creek collecting water with some of the others. I gotta tell you, your wife is one tough lady. She wouldn't leave your side the whole time. Took her a lot of convincing from Kara to get her away, clear her head, you know?"

"What the hell happened back there?"

"The shit hit the fan, that's what." John lifted the leg of his blood soaked jeans and revealed his wound, a green strip of cross-threaded stitches. Thick clumps of dry blood sat burrowed between each suture. "All they had was a spare fishing line."

"Does it hurt?"

"Hurt like shit when she did it."

"Who were those people?"

"From the looks of things, seems to me like your friend was right all along. Quite frankly, that angers me a little bit."

"Because he was right?"

"No. Because it means that ungodly asshole that sent us on this suicide mission never filled out a full investigation of this place before this project began."

"It wasn't down to Javier. It was Bullon's job."

"They're both nuts, and we're all nuts for coming out here in the first place."

"So there really are natives to this land?"

"Sure looks that way."

Frank took in a deep breath and went in for another bite of the beaver meat. He took smaller bites but he couldn't help but attack it. The meat was cold and dry but at least it was food. He washed it down with more water and immediately regretted eating so quickly. Short bursts of cramps kicked him in the stomach. He slowed down and took a moment to breath.

"You mind if I ask you something?" Frank asked.

"Shoot."

"Back at the cabin, when that man entered and you... you know. Was it easy?"

"You mean to kill him?"

"Yeah."

"No. Some say it gets easier the more you do it, but for me, it's never easy."

"But you didn't even hesitate."

"That was different. I was paid to do a job and unfortunately, that's part of the job. I'm a man of my word."

"I don't know if I could ever go through with it, pulling the trigger on someone."

"Want my advice? Don't think about it so much. It'll drive you crazy and worse yet, it'll get you killed."

"Not sure I can ever stop thinking about it."

John began cleaning his wound with a wet rag and wiped the dirt away to reduce his chances of infection. He took the rag and wringed it out to the side before tipping more water into it and running it across his leathery face.

"There's something I've been meaning to get off my chest," he continued.

"Of course," replied Frank.

"I'd like to thank you - and Barry - for helping me out of that mess back there. You didn't have to do what you did."

"You're risking your life to help us. Even if it is just for the payoff, you're a part of this group."

"You know, at first it was for the reward. I don't think I would have taken this job without one. But after all this, meeting you folks and seeing that boy come outta his shell like that... It ain't just for the payoff anymore."

Frank's head gently nodded along with the older man. He could see John eyeing him up and down, analysing him in any way possible. "That says a lot about a man, Frank. I think you're more equipped for this journey than you realise."

"What do you mean?"

"The last thing I expected when that arrow hit me was for someone to haul me out of there. This group is full of people doing it cuz' they're expecting something in return. Some do it for possessions, others do it because they want change in the wider spectrum of things."

"How can you tell which one I am?"

"The one doing it for the reward wouldn't have done what you did. They'd have left me back there for dead and made something up to cover their tracks. If you ask me, I don't completely trust all the people here in this group, but I know I can trust you because of what you did, you follow?"

"I think you're forgetting that I'm part of that materialistic category you mentioned. I'm only doing this so I can rebuild my home."

"No you're not. You're doing it for more than that, friend."

"How so?"

"It could just be for the materials, but from where I'm sitting; looks to me like you're making sure what's yours remains yours, that this land is safe enough for you and that wife of yours to live in."

Frank's eyebrows rose unexpectedly. "I never thought about it that way."

"Sometimes good men do bad things, doesn't make em' bad people. We're good men in a shit awful situation."

Frank felt the corners of his lips curve into a smile. The old man cursed in a way that only exemplified his years of wisdom. John's words were reassuring to hear. He'd finally been given some perspective that wasn't conjured by the limitations of his own thoughts. He took another bite out of the tasteless meat and chomped down past the gristly fat. As he bit down again he heard the chilling snap of a twig down through a tapered gap in the pines. He froze up, eyes wide and cheeks stuffed with beaver meat. John popped open the flap on his holster and brought the revolver up within seconds. They sat without a sound. The insipid cuttings of meat sat stuffed inside Frank's mouth, congealing in his saliva. He feared to make even the slightest of sounds. He daren't to even swallow in case he swallowed too loudly. They heard whispers of impatient inflections. Frank watched John closely in the corner of his eye. His eyes piercing the pines like a hawk. His thumb slowly rose from the grip of revolver. He gradually pulled back on the hammer, cocking the weapon. It clicked into place. His attempt to be silent only seemed to amplify the noise in Frank's mind. They heard the sound of shuffling foliage draw nearer, brushing past the millions of fallen pine needles.

"Someone's out there."

Mike lay on his side at the edge of the flowing stream. He held the canteen at a forty-five degree angle and allowed the fresh clean water to fill it. Once full, he shut it tight and moved his mouth in place. The cold water trickled past his lips and flung up, splashing against his cheeks. He sucked in his cheeks and slurped the water. He could hear rhythmic taps against the water's surface behind him and turned to discover Max, lapping up the water with his tongue. The dog lifted his head and licked his lips contently. His glossy brown eyes gazed back at him over the water and his head tilted curiously to one side.

"That should be enough for now," said Annie. She felt a brief tug on her coat. It was Sam. He held the black leather book up for her without a word. She smiled and took the book, reviewing the open page he had left for her. The pages were more stained and crumpled than before. A new sketch displayed a lying figure surrounded by dogs of a larger scale. *Wolves?*

"Who is that?" she asked, pointing down at the stick figure in the drawing.

"I couldn't see," he murmured softly.

"What do you mean?"

"It was snowy."

She finally understood. The sketches resembled predictions or visions of the future. He had established that to them time and time again, but now she understood where they came from. It was as though he could actually visualise them in his head and see them unfold before him. The sketches were direct illustrations from his visions.

"I done another one," he said. He reached up on his tiptoes to show her and turned to the next page. Annie examined the drawing; a smaller stick figure holding hands with two larger figures.

"Is that you?" she asked. Sam nodded his head and smiled. Her attention tilted up to the other two figures in the drawing. She knelt down and allowed him to see where she was pointing. "And who are these people?"

"That's you." Sam's tiny finger slid across the page to the figure holding his other hand. "And that one is Frank." Annie couldn't help but smile at the child's purity. She began to well up. How could a child so sweet and full of innocence exist in this cruel and unforgiving time? She thought about Frank and how they hadn't had time to talk things out. His words had cut through her like a knife but she knew he didn't mean what he said. Frank had been used to it just being the two of them for so long. He feared change, feared responsibility. He'd acted differently ever since they departed from Elkford. Frank didn't hate other people, he had just gotten used to the idea of them growing old together, and only together. She hoped that he could adapt to others, hoped that they could work this all out, and most of all, she hoped that they could both restore their lives to what it was before.

She closed the book and wrapped her arms around the small boy. He hugged her back and when she pulled away he tipped his head curiously to one side. "Why are you crying?"

"I'm not crying. It's a lovely drawing."

Annie returned the book to Sam. "We'll be there soon, Sam. This will all be over soon." She knew it would be difficult. The settlers of Autark had barely scratched the surface with the mountains. The route following the Grand River from Wolvendale to the military base was infested with raiders. Carlos had barely made it out alive from investigating and managed to cover his tracks upon returning to the group. There had been a brief overview of the mountains but as far as she knew, they would be the first of their people to truly scour the highlands of Autark.

"Annie?" Kara called out. She stood distanced from the others and gestured Annie over discreetly. Annie asked Mike to watch over Sam and Max. She saw Sam sit by the water's edge, Max beside him with his chin rested upon the child's leg. She joined Kara by the edge of the forest. "Everything okay?"

"Do you think we can do this?" she whispered.

"I do."

"How do you know?"

"I don't, but I have to believe it. That boy sitting there has something special, we've all seen it. If there's anyone that can help the people take back this land, its him."

"I came to this island to get away from everything that went wrong back home. I wanted a fresh start. Now that this is all happening, I'm starting to wonder if I made a mistake."

"We've all been thinking that. You can still turn a new leaf Kara. I truly believe that I discovered that boy for a reason. I think he can help us do this."

"What will we do when we get there?"

"Let's cross that bridge when we get to it, shall we? Let Carlos worry about that. For now, let's just focus on getting there."

"You're right..."

Annie leaned in and gently embraced the young woman. "You may not believe it, but I think this journey has brought out the best in you. I appreciate what you're doing, even if it is for a reward." Kara caught sight of Mike glancing over. She cleared her throat and shied away from his gaze.

"We should head back," said Kara. Annie took hold of Sam's hand and helped him up to his feet. "Come on boy." Max circled the two of them and followed her back towards the camp.

Kara and Mike followed closely behind. She felt intimidated by his athlete physique. She had always been independent. She had to take care of herself her whole life, and whenever someone tried to get close she would turn them away; but for some reason, whenever she caught sight of Mike, the high barrier she built was extinguished. She stared at his toned biceps flexing through his jumper. She felt his gaze once more, he'd caught her looking. She turned away. The more she tried to repel, the more obvious it came across. She didn't look back at him but listened to his quiet words.

"Everything alright?"

She struggled to express her true feelings. She shrugged them aside and focused on the reality. She didn't know this man well enough. She couldn't let him in, not yet anyway.

"Yeah, all good," she replied bluntly. She didn't look back. Instead she caught up with Annie and walked by her side.

A booming gunshot rumbled through the forest around them. Pigeons shot up from the pines and flocked into the misty atmosphere above. Annie flinched at the sound and dropped the pot of water. It crashed to the ground and spilled out into the snow.

"Frank?"

# FOURTEEN

Mike and Kara hurtled past the surrounding pines and into the secluded campsite. He held the AK-47 close to his chest and raised the barrel outwards as he turned into the camp. He could feel Kara's presence sweeping round behind him, covering the other side with her shotgun drawn. The place had been ransacked. Sheets of tarp and bedrolls lay overturned into piles, bags rifled through, their contents spilled out into the snow. Mike moved forward one step at a time, the rifle an extension of his body. He scanned the woodland around them. Over by the tree line, his eyes drew to where the snow turned a deep shade of burgundy. Beside the spilling colour was a sheet of tarpaulin. He looked closer to see the dark hairs sticking out beneath it, a head, face-down in the snow. Mike turned back to Kara. Her eyes stared down into the pool of blood.

"Keep her away," he whispered.

Kara stepped back and held out her hand to signal for Annie to wait in hiding. Max scampered around the camp, sniffing everything in sight. He chewed away at the leftover beaver meat, abandoned in the snow. Mike got down on one knee. He pinched the edge of the tarp and peeled it away. It was the body of a man. He wore olive cargos and a black hooded coat. His arms were tucked and bent beneath his chest, the stiff grip of a knife in his frozen fist. Mike sighed, relieved. He turned back to Kara and shook his head before pulling the tarp completely over the body and bloody mess around it.

Kara guardedly led Annie and Sam through to the camp. Annie stopped at the sight of the mess. She breathed heavily in and out. "Frank... Where's Frank?"

"We'll find him," Kara reassured. "They couldn't have gone far."

A figure stepped out into the opening of the campsite. Mike shot up and trained the rifle's sights on its position. "H-h-hold your fire," Barry called out, hands raised above his head. Carlos, Derek and Tracy  stepped out from the trees behind him. Mike lowered his weapon and shook his head. "This sneaking up on each other has got to stop."

"Apologies," said Carlos. "What happened?"

"Frank and John are missing. Place has been looted."

"Damn."

Tracy came to Annie's aid. She put her hands on either shoulder and sat her down on the trunk of a fallen pine. Bent splinters of wood snapped at the base of the trunk, still partially connected to the stump. Annie caught sight of Frank's double barrel shotgun left deserted up against his abandoned bedroll. She began to hyperventilate, her lungs kicked into overdrive.

"Somebody get her some water," Carlos ordered. Kara picked an enamel mug off the ground. She washed it out with a splash of water from her canteen then filled it and handed it to Annie. The mug shook in Annie's hands as she guided it up to her lips.

A chilling undertone froze every member of the group in the camp. The whispers of another language reverberated off the enfolding pines. They could have been no more than fifty metres away down the ridge's drained basin. There were multiple voices, each calling out to one another on their approach up to the camp. Max's attention broke away from the meat. He stared through the trees, completely focused. Derek and Carlos grabbed what they could from the ground. Kara snatched Sam up into her arms. Tracy pulled Annie up to her feet. The mug dropped from her grasp and clanked against the fallen tree.

"Go. Go," Carlos hissed.

Mike stood closest to the approaching party and peered down through the snow-glazed branches. There was no visual but he could still hear them, their voices raised in response to the clanging mug. The others scrambled together. Mike shuffled back, the AK at the ready. The voices closed in, riled and bloodthirsty. He turned at the camp's edge and darted through the pines

They pushed up and over the ridge, aching chests and blurry sight. All they could hear was the low tenor of the environment around them and the rhythm of their boots crunching through the snow. It could have been raiders, or the grey wolves, but whoever it was, they weren't sticking around to find out. They didn't stop moving. They just kept running.

The fog thickened with every step. The first signs of a blizzard brewed in the high altitude of Autark's eastern mountains. Annie held Tracy's hand tightly. She would never let go. Together they followed Kara through the mist and didn't look back. The wind flushed in from the side and swept Annie's hair in front of her face. She scratched it away with her fingertips. Her eyes squinted through the wind. She could see the vapour from her dry mouth thrive with ever breath. Tracy looked around her, her head shot back and forth in a panicked flurry.

She stopped dead in her tracks. "Barry?" Annie's arm locked straight and jerked back to halt.

"We need to keep moving," said Kara.

"But where's Barry? He was right behind me."

"They'll catch up, come on."

"Barry!" she yelled through the mist. Kara dived back and clamped her free hand over Tracy's mouth. "Be quiet." Tracy pulled herself away. Her eye's scanned the area around them. The wind grew more aggressive with every passing second. They could barely see further than ten feet in front of them. There was nobody there. Not Carlos, not Derek, nobody. They stood in the middle of the storm, panting heavily to catch their breath.

"We have to go," said Annie. She herself was desperate to find Frank. It was all she could think about. She needed to see him, to be with him. She looked down. Max was no longer by her side.

Hollering voices returned. Their followers were fast approaching, closing in like a pack of starving hounds. Tracy panicked. They were gaining on them. The dreary contour of faded figures came into view further behind them. Her eyes caught sight of the orange grip sticking out from the back of Kara's waistband. That was it. It was her answer to everything. Tunnel vision consumed her, finding Barry was her only intention. In that moment nothing else mattered. She lunged forward and snatched the flare gun from Kara's belt. Annie's jaw dropped, her eyes widened. "Tracy, no!"

The course of the blizzard was now in full effect. Frank held John's arm over his shoulder for support. They held their hands up in front of their faces to shield their eyes from the snow. They struggled to even place one foot in front of the other against the ruthless winds.

"We have to find the others," yelled Frank.

"What?" John's croaked voice muffled back through the blistering gales.

"We have to find the others," he repeated, much louder this time.

They had reached the edge of a mound. Frank stood and looked down at the sloped white canvas. The snow thickened in the air. Clumps of white materialised against his jacket. The wind rammed into him at incredible speed. He could feel the cold press through his clothes and wrap around his thinning body. A burst of air muffled from behind. They both heard it and together they turned to face it. It sizzled like the ignition of a firework fuse. A stream of orange light shot vertically up in the distance. Its vibrant glow illuminated through the mist and intensified once it reached its peak. It remained motionless in the air for a moment. The cracking of gunfire in the distance dampened through the storm.

"What the hell is that?" said John.

They stood still, side by side, awestruck by the flickering orange light that burned a hole in the sky. Frank was drawn, like a moth to a flame. The roaring screams faded through the violent wind. He saw them sprint through the thick fog, at least three of them and one charged him. There was no time to react. He tightened his body and absorbed the oncoming blow. The man gored Frank's gut. It knocked him straight off his feet and sent the pair of them tumbling down the sloped mound. Frank's vision blurred into streaks of horizontal stripes. His body tightened up even more, the raider's arms wrapped firmly around his torso. Their combined weight caused them to fall faster. Frank's body flipped up, his left shoulder slammed into the trunk of a bare pine and flung them further down the slope. He could hear the raider's heaving breaths of hostility puffing through the haze of motion. Their bodies crashed against the snow-padded rock and gunshots echoed above.

The tangled pair plunged down into a stone crevice that backed onto a narrow stream. The raider pushed Frank's tangled body aside. He raised the rusty dagger high in the air and drove it down into the flesh of Frank's outer thigh. Frank's spine coiled back. He lifted his jaw, gritting his teeth in agony. The muscles in his leg seized up, a pulsing cramp. He flung his arms, swinging at anything in reach. The man absorbed the feeble hits and brushed them aside as though they were nothing. Frank's arms jolted back. The raider towered over him and was on him in seconds. Frank thrashed his body to shake him off but the man was far stronger. Their bodies lashed out in an inelegant burst of desperation. He felt the raider's filth ridden fingernails rake repeatedly across his face and eyes.

Frank nabbed him by the wrist, digging his claws into the man's skin. The raider's other hand clamped down on Frank's face, his thumb plummeting down into the socket of his left eye. His eyeball pulsated under the suffocating pressure and he could feel the tearing of his corneal. He imagined the horror of the man's thumb wriggling around inside of his head. He felt the sting of fresh grazes across his eye. Frank's fist balled tight. He swung up, crashing against the raider's temple and knocking him into the shallow stream.

The vision on his left side had disappeared and the skin around his eye had swollen and grazed along the surface. He felt the blood drip down his face; the throbbing pain in his eye. His right leg went numb from the waist down, and when he looked over he saw the rusty blade still protruding from his thigh. His hand brushed limply across his waist and the machete filled his grasp. The raider lifted his groggy head and slowly rose back to his feet. With every ounce of strength left in his body, Frank unhitched the machete and drew it from its sheath. He stabbed the blade into the earth below and used it to lift himself to his knees. The raider swung around, only metres away. His eyes burned with absolute rage. He lunged back for more. Frank yanked the machete up and felt the weight of the raider plunge into him. The raider shoved him back onto his shoulders and landed right on top of him. He heard steel tear through flesh. The raider's body stiffened, his pale eyes staring only inches away from Frank. The entire weight of the man rested in Frank's grasp. The thick red substance trickled down the machete over his taut fist. More blood gurgled in the raider's mouth and poured down his chin. Frank watched intensely, his eyes focused on nothing but the man's suffering. He gasped for breath and choked on his own blood. Frank stared until the man's suffering had ended. He shoved the lifeless body aside and ripped the blade from the man's spilling guts.

He lay still; half of his body in the snow, the other half in the stream. The stream's sub-zero waters brushed up against his jeans and soaked through to his legs. Pebbled stones dug into his back. Everything on his left side had softened to black. His body squirmed at the squelching of his eyeball. All he could see was the swirl of grey and white whirlwinds above. Nature's relentless storm encapsulated his body. He closed his eye - the other now permanently shut - and listened to the droning current of the stream. Although the furious blizzard perpetuated his fear, the continuous humming of the wind filled him with a sense of tranquillity like no other. He knew he had to do something or else he would surely die, if not to the storm, then to the hands of the raiders. He tried to fight it, tried to lift himself, but there was nothing left in him. He just laid there, still. He didn't move.

Carlos peered directly down through the branches of the dead tree. He was perched high. The arches of his feet gripped the branch like the claws of an eagle. He held the bolt action rifle in his hands and leaned against the trunk by his shoulder. All he could see was white through the hairs dangling in front of his face. The group had been pushed further up into the mountains than they had planned, losing one another to the storm. He thought he saw something pass below, a moving shape that faded up ahead. He heard muffled cries followed by two faint rounds popping off. Two sharp flashes of amber. He waited for a moment. Nothing. Branch by branch, he descended the tree and made his way out from the cover of the pines. He lowered his posture, bent at the knees. He lifted the bolt on his rifle and cocked it back. Five rounds. He cocked it back into place and held it up. The wind's current rattled against the barrel, his aim swaying through the blizzard. He tightened his muscles to keep it under control, his heart racing. The faded shape returned to view. He could not make out any details, a matte grey silhouette flat against the wild snow. He stopped and stared down the barrel of the rifle, sights lining up to the tall shape ten feet ahead of him. He exhaled slowly and squeezed the trigger. The gunpowder ignited and sparked a jagged burst of smoke at the muzzle. The rifle kicked back in his arms, a deafening crack of a single shot contained itself in the bubble of the storm. The shape dropped instantly. Carlos cocked the rifle. The empty casing spun out from the chamber and was lost to the snow. He pushed the bolt back into place and moved toward the charcoal figure, the rifle still raised in his arms. As he got closer, two more folded bodies came into view, lying still in the rising snow.

Carlos approached the closest, the one he had shot. The snow began to fall quicker now, settling atop the dead man's leather trench coat. He had a masculine build, face down in the snow. Blood stained the snow around him. Carlos edged his foot forward and kicked the body over to face him. The body rolled, arms rigid and lagging behind. It already began to stiffen, joints clicking as it moved. Carlos tossed his rifle and satchel down. The dead man's mouth gaped open and blood poured from his chest and stained his shirt.

Carlos stared, no expression. He moved in closer to the other bodies. Two raiders. He lifted one of the deceased raiders, a middle-aged female, and dragged her through the snow. He dumped her body over the man's motionless body then placed the second one, a teenage boy, next to them. His legs brushed rapidly back and forth to cover the trail left behind in the snow. He wiped the cold moisture from his red nose and took one last glance at the stack of bodies. There, it was done. He was never there. He wondered how long the blizzard was going to last, if it could last long enough to engulf the scene entirely. He would do it himself but there was no time. The temperature dropped suddenly. He felt a hot flush in the pores of his forehead from lugging the lifeless corpses. He needed to go and find the others. What would he tell them? The distant howl of wolves pierced the air around him. He'd have to figure that out along the way. His eyes shot up, darting ahead and back over his shoulder. He snatched the rifle and stumbled back through pines. He needed to go, right now.

# FIFTEEN

Frank felt the roughness of coarse sandpaper graze his nose and lips. He opened his eye and saw Max, too close to focus. The dog wheezed silently, licking Frank over and over. The blizzard had seized but the snow continued to fall. How long had he been out? The dreary white sky had descended into darker shades of grey. Day's cycle was drawing to a close and he was losing light fast. He felt faint and light-headed. A small puddle of blood had formed in the bowl of his left eye and when he turned onto his side it rolled down his face and into the snow. He could still feel the eyeball. It was intact but had settled farther back into the socket. He looked up and around but there was no one to accompany his companion. Max wheezed and hopped over Frank. He brought the dog in and embraced. He brushed the snow from Max's coat and ruffled the fur beneath his chin. His fingers were numb and felt as though they were going to snap off at any moment. He curled them into a ball to his lips and blew the warmth from his body onto them. As he sat up, a sharp, digging pain reminded him of the knife embedding his leg. He inhaled a single deep breath through gritted teeth and turned away.

There it was again. *That damn raven...* The monotonous caw mocked him. He turned to its call and spotted it sat upon the lowest branch of a nearby tree. His attention drifted down to the dangling object hanging at the branch's edge. It was his knapsack, hanging by a single strap to the tree he had hit on the way down. The flap was open and its contents had spilled out into the snow at the base of the steep mound. He tried to stand up. It was no use. Instead, he used both his hands. He dug his claws into the dirt and dragged his battered body through the snow. Max followed. He seemed unsettled, tilting his head to one side. The dog had never seen his master move in this way before.

Frank had always been soft with Max in the past. He remembered the first night he brought him home as a pup. It was a rainy night back home and when Annie locked him in his cage for the night he wouldn't stop crying. He knew you weren't supposed to go down for the first night but he couldn't help it. He loved Max and always mollycoddled him when and where possible. Annie always told him off for feeding Max cheese but he did it anyway. What was the point in having a dog if you couldn't spoil it? That's the way Frank saw it anyway. He trained Max to be obedient and in return he'd shower the dog with unconditional affection. But now more than ever he'd noticed changes in both himself and the dog.

The blood flowed quicker now and left a messy red trail in his tracks. He stopped under the tree for a moment and gazed up the mound. It struck memories of falling across its jagged edges that looped over and over again in his mind. Max's ears shot up. Something caught his attention through the white fog above. Three figures stood. Two older men either side of a woman. Frank spotted their familiar fur garments that cloaked their bodies. They watched him, studying his every movement. They were still, calm and collected. Frank noticed Max's unaggressive poise; he seemed unbothered by the party of three watching from above. The two men were dressed in caribou furs, similar to that of the men and women he had seen in

Wolvendale. The woman's attire, however, was concealed by a long black cloak, layered with the feathers of a raven. She had long black hair and her skin was tanned like the others. Frank squinted through the mist. He tried to call out to them but his throat seized. His cough was sickening, and when he looked back up, they had already turned their backs on him and retreated beyond the mound. Something landed just a few feet away and rolled toward him through the snow. He couldn't believe his eyes and had to touch it to make sure. He snatched the chunk of meat with both hands. Frank looked back up to the mound but nobody was there. He brushed the snow away and attacked the meal ravenously. Although it was raw, it was packed with nutrition. He recognised the taste. *Caribou.* He rarely saw them in the west but they were well known to roam the fields of the eastern coastline. He wandered if they took pity on him, or if they believed he would die down there by that stream. All he could do was be grateful that they spared him, and more gratefully so, fed him. In that brief moment, he had prepared for a swift death, but he couldn't give up, not now. In his spur of desperation, he felt complete and utterly ashamed. Max's eyes stared lustfully at the glorious meat. Frank took one last bite and tossed the rest to the dog who attacked it with the same instinct that he had just displayed himself.

He remembered the gunshots from before. *John.* Could he have fended the other raiders off? There was no way he was making it back up there in his condition. He looked down into the snow and recognised some of his equipment; a canteen of water, blanket, saucepan, matches, socks, a fishing hook. Something was missing. He stared up at the knapsack, hanging loosely by a single strap. He took a sip from his canteen then stretched up with both arms. The corroded dagger scraped against his muscles at the slightest of actions. Max sat in front of him and stared with those pearlescent eyes. They say it's harder to watch the person in pain than to be the person in pain, but Frank would much rather be in Max's position any given day. He pulled the rag from his back pocket and tore it at the corner to lengthen the material. His palms suddenly became drenched in sweat. His heart pounded in his chest, desperate to flee his body. He balled the rag into a bundle and held it between his teeth before gripping the handle of the blade. He counted to three in his head. Slow and steady.

*One...* *Two...* *Three...*

He chickened out and looked away. "Come on you bastard," he uttered to himself. He closed his eye, his breath faltered. Adrenaline coursed through his veins. He gripped the handle and gave it one great pull. He cringed at the sound of steel exiting his body. He fell immediately and his teeth sank into the soaking rag.

Max came to him. The dog's cold wet nose pressed against him and blew spouts of cold air into his face. The blood began to flow quicker now. He pulled the rag from his mouth and unbuckled his jeans to reveal the jagged puncture in his thigh, clotting it with a fistful of snow. The feeling was lost, frozen without sensation. He wrapped the rag around the wound and weaved it into a tight knot. Using the tree for support, he rose to his feet and tugged the knapsack from the supple branch. It buckled up and he tugged it once more, this time harder. The branch flung up and the bag released along with a white mist of snow. Frank crashed onto his right side. He felt the roaring sensation, as though his thigh had been struck with a hammer. He cried out but there was no one there, no one to hear him. More of the bag's contents had spilled out. Shotgun shells, an empty bottle of antiseptic and a roll on bandages left from Barry's supply. The antiseptic had soaked into the damp bandages. He took the bandage roll and squeezed it above his eye. The sting engulfed the entirety of his left eye socket. His voice box rumbled under the pressure of his strenuous cry. He unravelled the drenched bandage and wrapped it diagonally around his head to cover his eye. The stinging didn't stop.

His attention returned to the puncture in his leg. The blood continued to soak through his jeans. He had just removed four inches of a six inch blade from the inside of his leg. He knew that a pile of snow wasn't going to cut it. His eye drew to the vibrant red of the shotgun casings. He untied the rag, the snow now an icy pile of cherry slush. He reached for the knife in one hand and took a shotgun shell in the other. Sitting up against the tree, he cut a surgical incision into the shotgun casing, careful to keep as far away from the primer as possible. The last thing he needed was a lethal blast of lead erupting in his hands. He dropped the blade; poured the contents of the cartridge into his bloody palm and separated the pellets and wad from the gunpowder. The gunpowder was all he needed, and more of it. He did the same with two more shells. He poured water over the wound and dabbed it dry with the rag. He took the gunpowder and pressed it into the burning wound. He needed to hurry. The blood was already pouring out between his fingertips. He could feel his body weaken from the loss of blood. He struck a match from the pack, igniting the phosphorous. The flame juddered in his shaking hands. Ever so slowly, he edged the flame closer to the abrasion. A bright spark flashed from the side of his leg. The match fell from his grasp, extinguishing in the snow below. His throat and eyes tightened. The spark's pallid sapphire outline flashed across the black canvas of his closed eyelid. Max's panicked call became distant and faded. The shock took hold of his body. It seized up, shoulders hunched. Possessed. He had no control. No control.

Night had fallen. Frank's battered body lay rigid in the snow. He lifted his head and the bristles of his eyelashes flickered to shake the cluster of snow. He saw her standing over him. Strands of long hair fluttered out from the hood of her waterproof in the wind. Her warm moonlit smile filled him with life. He tried to get up but his legs wouldn't permit him; and when he looked back up to see her, she was gone.

"Annie?" he called. He took in his surroundings and saw the moon, round and full. Its light reflected rhombus waves off the face of the water. She wasn't there. His mind had deceived him once again, but it had been so clear, so vivid. He pleaded with himself to believe it wasn't true. Max sat beside him, covered in a layer of snow. Frank brushed the snow away, eyes drifting up to where the stream curved out of sight. It was a start. He thought it might lead him on a path at least. He needed shelter and warmth, but most of all, he needed to find Annie. If she made it out- *no*. She had made it out. She had to. She must have been ahead of him. He prayed the others were there to watch over her and the boy. *Sam*. He realised now that his decisions were selfish. He wanted to make amends for his cruel words. The last remnants of his dying embers re-lit and struck the fire inside him. The wound had stopped bleeding but movement could change that and without proper treatment, it was exposed to the risk of infection. He tied the rag around it and wrapped the blanket around his freezing body. He shuddered. Frosty breath caused him to squint against the cold. Max was up, watching him stuff the rest of his equipment back into the knapsack before placing his arms through the loops.

Frank began to crawl.

His shuffling body created a metric percussion that blended with the forest's fervent nightlife. He heard the distant screams of wildlife; an orchestra of foxes, jackals, deer and the chilling howl of a wolf pack. He worried they would pick up his scent, especially with all the blood, but he couldn't let that stop him. If anything, it pushed him on farther. Max stopped every few feet and stared into the darkness. Frank continued on upwards and slowly made his way round to a clear opening layered with untouched snow. He found himself lost to the darkness. He was beyond the stream now. It had drifted off into the cracks of a large boulder formation. There was nothing left to follow. He crossed the open plain, leaving behind a single sluggish trail. He saw a gap separating the tree line ahead and decided to go through it. The trees cast strong prickly shadows in the snow. He noticed Max's pace quickened. The dog moved briskly into the shadows to investigate. Max came to him bearing a gift. He settled it down by Frank and brushed it closer to him with his nose. Frank picked it up for a closer look. It was a brass bullet casing. He didn't know what size. He had no knowledge of ballistics. It was larger still, perhaps for a rifle. He took it as a sign to keep going. He was on the right track.

The moonlight shone through the branches and bounced off the tangled pile in his way. He crawled closer. The thick blanket of snow concealed whatever was beneath. He brushed it away with pale fingers and felt the cracked frozen leather on the other side. Something heavy lay before him; the entire pile had stiffened in the cold. He lit a match to gain a better view. The flame revealed an arm, then a torso. Piece by piece the image came together through the dim orange flame. He used the pile of bodies to lift himself onto one knee. He didn't recognise the young boy on top, or the woman on the other side. He nudged the frozen corpse aside and it rolled over in one solid block onto the deceased woman. When he brought the match back over he saw the face of the body beneath.

John's deadpan stare penetrated his soul. The man gawked with dry, dilated pupils. Beneath that magnificent moustache, his mouth gaped open with cracked lips. His wrinkled skin had surpassed the most colourless of tones. A painful expression. Frank's skin began to crawl. Spurted breaths struggled to escape him. His lungs felt tight across his ribcage and the fading flame drew inward to the dying match. A tiny puff of smoke rose up and vanished into the shadows.

Frank knelt over John's body in the dark. He continued to stare; the lit image in his head came to the forefront of his mind through the darkness. He wiped his face with rattling fingers and took the renowned revolver from John's holster and stuffed it into his belt. He moved round to the other side and leaned back across the other two bodies. Rummaging through the belongings of the dead, he discovered a single satchel that held few items. He tossed the useless belongings aside and found a small, shrivelled apple; brown with wrinkled skin. Beside it, a scrunched piece of paper. It was stained with dirt and folded into quarters. He opened it up and discovered handwritten words. It was a letter. He rested the note onto his lap and struck another match, biting into the tasteless fruit as he read. His eyes panned across each line. He frowned at the scorned words, eyes darting back quickly with every new line. He read faster and faster. The note consumed him. Dread and anger. Each word resembled a stabbing dagger in his back that dug deeper and deeper as he read on. The bottom of the letter was torn but his eyes carried on in disbelief, pleading for more. There must have been more.

Frank scrunched the letter into a crumpled ball and tossed it aside. He looked up and spotted a faint blinking light in the distance. A red glow flickered on and off. It called to him like a beacon of hope. He knew that wherever he was, the signal would guide him and lead him back to where he needed to be. He used the support of the bodies to lift himself to his feet and he began limping. One foot dragged behind the other, abandoning the pile of frozen corpses in the bitter cold night. The decayed apple core barely protruded the snow. The top of the note was still visible. A gust of wind flapped the paper's rigid corner and bloody fingerprints stained the first line.

*Carlos...*

# SIXTEEN

The mountains of Autark fell silent under the fall of night. Derek marched with high knees up the steep incline. An ungodly amount of snow had fallen over the past week. It settled up to his shins. Every step took twice the effort of the one before it and the snow stuck to his clothes like clumps of icing sugar. He carried the .38 tight in one hand and gazed at the intermittent glow of red light up ahead. As he got closer, vertical and diagonal pillars of grey formed a dim structure against the black sky. A haze of dreary clouds glided overhead. He moved toward it and soon realised it was the structure of a watchtower. He began ascending the steel steps that wrapped its pillars. His boots thumped with every step. A droning clatter of metal. When he reached the top, he noticed the busted padlock and chain lying at the base of the door. He peered through the double-glazed windows but it was too dark and masked with snow to make out any detail. He thought about wiping the frost away but the element of surprise was still in his favour.

Derek clamped down on the door handle and barged through with his shoulder. He stormed inside, the .38 up at the ready. A petrified face turned from the radio terminal against the far wall of the boxed room. Barry stared back. His beady eyes quivered behind his round spectacles.

"What the hell are you doing?" Derek barked. His tone was impatient, desperate for a response. Barry's stutter droned for a lifetime. He stared down the barrel of the gun pointed directly at him. He stood up with hands raised, either side of his chest and backed away from the terminal.

"I-I-I was j-j-just trying to g-get a signal."

"Oh yeah? What you panicking for?"

"...Y-you're pointing a gun at me."

"No. Don't even go there. Feels like I've caught you in the act, caught you doing something you shouldn't be doing."

"Wh-what are you talking about?" Barry replied. Derek paused, as did everything else inside the cramped watchtower. The only movement was that of the snow fluttering across the window like tiny grains of sand. Derek shot Barry a quizzical frown. He tilted his head to one side, calculating and back-tracking the entire journey from Elkford in his mind. It felt like it had been months, maybe years. Then he stopped. His head tilted back up with piercing eyes that clocked onto Barry and nothing else. It was a specific expression, something rarely seen. It was as though he'd cracked an impossible code, or the world's most unsolvable of riddles. "Oh my God," he hushed. "It's been you all along, hasn't it?"

Barry's eyes widened. He shook his head in confusion. He wasn't up to speed in the slightest.

"You've been working with them all along," Derek concluded. "You slimy fucker."

"Wh-what?"

"Admit it. It all makes sense. Who better to work for raiders than the bastard who was in a deal with them in the first place."

"That w-wasn't up to me. They threatened to k-k-kill me."

"Enough shit. You tell the truth right fucking now or I put a bullet through your skull." Derek slammed back on the hammer. Now that is was primed to fire, the gun felt heavier in his hands. He held it straight out in front of him, aimed at Barry who stood only four metres away. Barry continued to shake and blabber. He leaned back and flinched at the clicking mechanics of the revolver.

"Tell the truth!" Derek barked.

"I didn't do anything," Barry shouted back. Derek turned away and sighed heavily through his nose. He looked back. His finger slowly twitched on the trigger. A sudden force drove him away, a raw strength of flesh and bone that gored him from the side. His hip jerked first and the rest of his body followed suit. He felt the gun go off in his hand but by that point it was way off target. A bright flash of light filled the room and the deafening gunshot reverberated off the four walls.

Mike tackled Derek to the ground. He clamped his grip on the hand with the gun and pinned it out of harm's way. Derek thrashed back in a tumbling mess. They scuffled and swung for one another in a battle for restraint. Barry fumbled for his rifle leaning up against the wall. Mike ripped the pistol from

Derek's hand and pushed himself away from the oaf. "Don't get up," he demanded. He held the sights of the .38 trained on Derek who laid flat on his stomach. Barry snatched his rifle with shaky hands and spun back round to face the frantic skirmish. Before he could even raise it, he felt an overwhelming sense of dread devour his actions. The mechanical slide of a bolt action rifle cocking into place turned everybody's attention to the door. Carlos took one step inside, his rifle immediately aimed at Mike. Barry panicked. He lifted the rifle with pathetic delay and chose to hold the weapon's attention on Carlos.

The four men froze in the confined space of the watchtower in the fashion of a Mexican standoff. Each man sealed with intense pressure, the fate of another at their reign. All it took was the slightest pull of the trigger. Barry was the only one without a weapon aimed at him, yet he seemed the most nervous. His body shook so much that his spectacles danced down the bridge of his nose. He thought about pushing them back up but didn't want to risk taking his finger away the trigger, not even for a second.

"Let's all just take it down a notch," said Carlos. His voice was gruff and sinister. "Now. Barry," he continued.

"First thing I want you to do is turn off that beacon."

"B-but what about the others?"

"I said switch it off," he demanded. Barry didn't rebel.

"The others with you?" asked Derek, still lying on the floor below.

"No, haven't seen them," Carlos replied, calmer this time.

Barry backed up to the terminal. He flicked a switch on a separate circuit panel and the red intermittent glow was extinguished at once. Carlos saw him do so in the corner of his eye and let out a sigh of content. "Good." His eyes returned to Mike. "Now, may I ask why you're pointing that thing at Derek?"

"He was gonna shoot him," Mike replied, gesturing over to Barry.

"He's a traitor. He's working with the raiders," Derek called out from the floor.

"Nobody is a traitor," said Mike.

"What about you?" Carlos interrupted. "We don't know you. I mean we don't *really* know you."

"I've put my life on the line for you people more than once."

"It certainly seems that way. Would be a good way to get us to put our guard down though."

"What the hell are you talking about?"

"Maybe you're not working with the raiders. Maybe you're working for yourself. I mean what do the LPA really want? Why would a man from another nation put his life on the line for a newfound country that he has no ties to."

"I have my own reasons, those that are my own on a personal level."

"Sounds pretty suspicious to me. What do you think, Derek?"

"Sounds like a load of horse shit."

"Stop," Barry cried. He held the rifle even tighter. "Just stop this, p-please."

"There's no need to get upset, Barry," said Carlos. "We're only humouring the man. After all, we all know you were the one who made a deal with those men in the first place."

"I had no choice."

"Sorry Barry." Carlos swung the rifle round to Barry.

*Clank.        Clank.        Clank.*

He stopped. They all did. The robotic footsteps echoed outside. They clambered up the steps of the watchtower, growing louder with every step. All eyes were on the door, their weapons still aimed at each other. Nobody dared to make any sudden movements. The footsteps grew more frequent, overlapping one another in an unorganized fashion and then they realised, there were multiple footsteps. Mike and Barry stared at Carlos; a man whose intention to take the life of another was interrupted by an oncoming party of strangers. Even though they stood in sub-zero temperatures, droplets of sweat glided down the sides of their heads in a hot flush. The footsteps had now reached the top landing. The three men glanced out of the window but could only make out faded figures through frosted glass. *Clank. Clank.* The figures made their way around the landing ever so slowly. The one in front turned and stood in the doorway unarmed and lifted her head. It was Kara. The moonlight glistened off the roots of her crimson hair. She held an ominous stare; her face and clothes doused in trickled trails of blood. Carlos stared back over his shoulder. "What happened to you?"

She didn't reply. Her eyes dropped to the floor in exhaustion. Tracy peered inside and noticed the standoff. She shoved between Kara and the doorframe and placed herself directly in front of Barry.

"What the hell is going on in here?"

"That bastard behind you is working with the raiders," said Derek.

"What?" she repeated.

"The man is a traitor," Carlos agreed. The ladies' presence caused him to become nervous and agitated. He was now the centre of attention. Barry was still in shock. He lowered the rifle and struggled to make eye contact. "Y-y-you were going to shoot me."

"You what?!" cried Tracy. Her eyes shot Carlos piercing daggers, her fists clenched tight.

"Nobody's a traitor," said Mike. "Let's all just calm down."

"He's right," Annie called out from behind Kara with Sam in her arms. "This storms been messing with our heads." Kara stepped inside and caught Carlos off guard. She lunged forward and forced Carlos' shooting arm down with a swift chop. She grabbed hold of the rifle and disarmed him, tugging the rifle back. She jammed the stock into his chest and knocked him back against the wall. She held the rifle from the barrel to appear as no threat and proceeded to hold out her hand for the .38 revolver. Mike stood in silence, stunned by her rapid actions. He handed over the weapon immediately. She moved the guns into one corner of the room and did the same with Barry who put up no effort to hold onto his own. She turned to face the group and began unloading the weapons as she spoke.

"Here's how this is going to work. The nights are colder. The blizzard has died down but the snow is still falling. We wait it out here for the night and wait for Frank and John. Whoever fired that shot is a dumbass to say the least, but the raiders won't go after it in this weather, not at night anyway. We found you because of that beacon, but we can't leave it on because raiders might come for it."

"What about our weapons?" Derek asked as he rose to his feet and dusted himself off.

"No weapons. Not for you guys anyway. We got about four hours till dawn. I'll keep watch. Think you can hold off from killing each other till then?"

The men shared a disheartening look. It was more embarrassment than anything else.

"What makes you so trustworthy?" Derek questioned.

"After what she did for us out there, I owe her my life," Annie replied. Mike studied the blood-soaked Kara. She stared blankly; Annie's words reminded her of her actions. He tried to catch her attention to comfort her but she was lost in the swarm of her own memory.

"You expect us to sleep through the night out here with unloaded weapons?" said Carlos, indulging in his own rhetoric. Kara snapped back from the burdening trance. "I never said you had to sleep. But we've got a long day ahead of us so I suggest you use this time to rest up."

Later that night, Annie and Sam sat side by side in one of the four corners of the cramped watchtower. She wrapped the single remaining blanket around them and pulled it in tight to trap their bodies from the cold. The wind moaned like indignant phantoms against the steel structure of the watchtower. After the confrontation, Mike attempted to find a signal but the radio equipment had been rendered useless. They would have to go it alone and hope that reinforcements from Elkford would reach the base before them. Kara sat on the only chair. It was propped beside the closed door so that she could hear of any unwanted intruders. She arched her back against the chair and stretched her arms out wide. The others lay still on the cold hard floor. The desire to sleep was trumped by the sore conditions.

"Annie?" the boy whispered softly.

"Yes, Sam?" she replied.

"What's a traitor?"

She paused for a moment, trying to find a definition that would best cater to his understanding. "It's when someone says they are your friend but they lie, or they say they will help you but they don't."

"Oh. That's not good, is it?"

"No, it's not."

"Do you think we will be okay?"

"I hope so."

"Me too." He rested his head upon her thigh and yawned.

"Where is Frank?" he whispered.

"I don't know."

"Do you think he is safe?"

"...I don't know." She knew he didn't mean to worry her but it was only natural. Her heart sank when she first entered the tower, only to discover the absence of her husband.

"I want to see him, and Max," Sam continued.

"Me too, Sam," she replied. She placed her hand over his head and stroked his hair over and over. His purity overwhelmed her. She lifted her head and peered out of the window. The snow encapsulated the surrounding area. It was tough to make out anything in the snowfall. Through the darkness she spotted a collection of dotted lights far off in the distance. The miniscule specks of light seemed like an eternity away. Was it the military base? Her faint, troubled glance broke away from the mystery and returned to the boy. She would have to wait until morning to find out. For now all she could do was rest but she couldn't without him beside her. *Where are you, Frank?* Her heart crawled up into her throat. She sat consumed by her own damned imagination, hoping for his return yet dreading the worst all at the same time.

Tracy woke lying on her side. It was still dark out. The mist of clouds concealed the moon and it was now darker than before. She listened to Barry and Derek's gargled snoring symphony. Even Kara had dozed off. The silhouette outline of her head hung loosely and she sat leaning to one side of the chair. Tracy listened to the shuffling sounds of movement only metres away. The amalgam of experiences over the course of their endeavour had scarred her. She felt like she was afraid of everything. She kept her eyes still but watched the room around her through the corner of her eye. A shadowed figure stood up from the scatter of sleeping bodies. She peered through the darkness but couldn't make out the individual. All she could gather was the male physique. He stood completely still. She thought he was staring, watching her. It intimidated her and her heart pounded like a beating drum. He stood there for a whole minute and soon after he silently moved closer to her side of the room. She shut her eyes. The thought of being trapped inside a room with people on the edge of their minds petrified her. The man moved away from her view to the corner of the room. She heard faint shuffles but daren't to look. He returned to view shortly after and paced himself across to the door with a bundle of something in his arms. The man took one last glance at Kara who sat fast asleep beside the door and opened the door as quietly as possible before slipping out into the wilderness.

Tracy stood up in the middle of the room. She panicked, wondering if she should wake her younger sister or Barry. '*No. This is it,*' she thought. She saw it as a sign; her time to step up and contribute, to discover and prove her worth. She waited, knowing he would take his time to descend the steel steps to avoid the noise. Doing as he did, she slipped out onto the landing as quietly as possible and checked back through the frosted window to check she hadn't caused a stir. She feared the monotonous breeze. It held a shrilling undertone that she thought might wake the others. All was quiet. She was in the clear. Peering out over the railing, she caught a birds-eye view of the man stepping out from beneath the watchtower. Tracy began her descent. She treated every step with care and kept her eye on the man moving further out into the clearing. When she reached the bottom, there was nothing left for her to hide behind. All that stood between them was the punctured mantle of snow, disturbed by his heavyset tracks. She followed his lead but he soon stopped in a beam of moonlight. She paused in the shade behind him. Her heart sank and fear took hold of her once more. The man's significant features now came to light. His long straggly hair dangled over his hide ensemble. His head hung low, listening out behind him. Carlos turned around. She stared at him from across the clearing and neither of them spoke a single word. The sleeping boy rested amidst the bundled blanket in his arms. A delicate gasp escaped her. Carlos turned his back on Tracy and continued on his way. She couldn't move. No matter how much she wanted to go after him, her body wouldn't let her. All she could do was watch and she hated herself for it. It was as though her mind had split into two alternate realities. Her heart said, '*go for it*,' but her mind said, '*I can't.*' The more distance he covered, the less she saw. She tried to do it. Tried to force herself to pursue; but before she could conquer her fears, he had already faded beyond the snowfall and disappeared through a crack in the tree line. He was gone, and so was Sam.

Tracy stood alone outside the watchtower. The isolation only enhanced her feeling of regret. There were only a few hours left until dawn and the raider search parties would start looking for them again soon. A single tear glided down the inside of her cheek and dripped down into her coat. She heard shuffling in the snow and a final thud caused her to turn and face it. Frank knelt before her. His arms hung loosely by his sides, his head low, gasping for breath. Max darted up to Tracy with his front paws on her thighs. She gasped, pulled back from her lament trance and rushed to his aid. "Oh my God. Frank."

She knelt beside him and lifted his head. He stared ahead into the vast wilderness. He seemed lost, his mind astray from the situation. Pigments of snow materialised in his thick grey beard, his face an unsettling shade of purple. The blood-soaked bandage around his eye rendered her speechless. Without padded compress, it was doing little to stop the bleeding.

Unspoken words retreated further from her lips. The snow had glued his good eye near shut. A film of moisture coated its surface. She helped him up to his feet and remembered what she had just let happen. Her face churned in guilt. She became a sobbing wreck.

"Where is he?" It was all he could muster through the pain.

"He took him," she cried. "He took Sam."

"Which way?"

"Frank, your eye…"

"Which way?!"

She gestured up over the hill, her hand landing directly onto the crack in the tree line. "He just left. I tried, Frank. I tried but I couldn't do it."

"Annie. Is she okay? Where are the others?"

"Up there," she replied, eyes on the watchtower above. He pushed passed her and persisted on with his endeavour.

"Go and get them. Now."

"Frank, wait-"

"Just go," he repeated without looking back. Max sensed the others nearby and dashed up the steps of the watchtower.

Frank didn't stop. The thought of Carlos handing Sam over to the raiders sent adrenaline coursing through his veins.

Although he was injured, his determination drove him. Everything else was scattered. Single frames of past memories flashed to the forefront of his mind. He remembered the day they first discovered Sam in the back of the cart. It seemed so long ago; his quiet self, cowering in the corner with that enigmatic book in his little hands. There in that moment of pursuit, a wave of reconciliation crashed over him. He knew that he would do anything for Annie, so would the boy for that matter. Having Sam around made her happy. That was all that mattered, nothing else. Sam had grown on him. That was the truth. He pushed away for so long in fear. Fear of attachment, fear of dependence and responsibility. He battled with his selfish ways for so long that he'd lost sight of what really mattered.

"Hold on, Sam."

He pushed through the small collection of pines that led to an open stretch of snow. The immediate discovery of prominent footprints guided him. *Carlos*. They must have been his. The dim grey of morning's first light enhanced his view. Snow built up in every crevice of the steep mountain's charcoal surface. They rose over him to the left beyond another collection of dying pines. What sounded like a crack of thunder struck his focus. The sound generated from a dip between two peaks. The distant rumble shook the ground beneath his feet. He watched the avalanche plummet down the face of the mountain and crash into the basin. The snow erupted into a cloud of white dust and devoured the surrounding forest. Its distance generated a melancholic beauty that distracted him from everything wrong in the world. The flooding of a grand mass that enticed those who witnessed its great force.

Frank continued to follow the tracks. He crossed the stretch of snow that arched around the trees. The outline of the man came into view. A shuffling figure hobbled ahead of him. He needed to get closer. His leg slowed him down, just the same as the boy slowed Carlos. He lunged his left foot forward with every broad step and dragged the other behind him. He was closing in. Deep, grunting breaths helped him to absorb the pain. His nose ran in the cold but there was no time to wipe it. There he was, ten metres in front of him. He trudged after him through the snow. It was a sluggish and harrowing ordeal. If it wasn't for the fact that one was pursuing the other, it could barely be defined as a chase. Frank had enough. He pulled the revolver from his belt and aimed it up at the wolf in elk's clothing. Carlos had already heard him following and knew there was nowhere to run. He stopped dead in his tracks. There was no alternative. End of the line. Frank peered through his flickering eyelid. He blinked to rid the built up moisture and felt the icy droplet glide down his punished face. Carlos turned with Sam in his arms.

The boy's eyes lit up in terror. He squirmed but it only made things worse. Carlos squeezed his arm tighter and held the boy up as a shield.

"Let him go," Frank grumbled through his desiccated throat. Carlos said nothing. Together the men used the opportunity to catch their breath. The wind entwined the branches of the nearby forest. A dull whistling surrounded them as they stood in the open. Vapour rose past tired breaths. Carlos lowered his stance and pulled the hunting knife from his belt. He held it up to the boy's throat with shivering hands.

"Get out of here, Frank."

"I'm not leaving without him."

"You take a single step forward and I slit his throat."

"You're not going to do that."

Carlos stared back, edgy, but intrigued.

"You need him alive," Frank continued. "You show up without him and the raiders will kill you themselves." Carlos' eyes bugged wide. There was nothing discreet about it; an overt, shocking realisation that Frank knew more than he bargained for. He'd surpassed anger altogether and his exhausted lungs projected a roaring battle cry. He sprinted toward Frank, Sam and the knife still up in his grasp. His shoulders pivoted up and down with every jolting stride. He pelted forward, closer and closer. Frank aimed down at the scout's legs. He wanted to shoot but the risk of hitting Sam stopped him from pulling the trigger. It was too late. Carlos tossed Sam up at Frank's face. The force of the throw knocked Frank back. Sam flew over his head and skimmed across the snow.

Carlos was already over him, ready with the knife. Frank felt disorientated. There was no time for hesitation. He slammed down on his back and his head jolted along with it. His finger tugged back on the trigger as he fell. The crisp gunshot echoed throughout the clearing. With his limited vision; he saw Carlos standing over him, the knife still raised high above his head. An expanding patch of red oozed from his gaping belly. Frank stared in bewilderment. Another gunshot fired from behind. This time it penetrated Carlos' lungs. The man dropped to his knees.

Frank turned and saw the smoking barrel of the assault rifle. Mike stood at the other end of the rifle. He lowered his aim and together they turned their attention back to Carlos. The knife dropped from his grasp and penetrated the snow. He folded in towards his wounds. He rolled back and forth, writhing in agony. Frank edged backwards. He looked back over his shoulder and saw the boy run to him. He embraced the child with his free hand and pulled him in close. He felt the weeping suction of Sam's gasping breaths against his chest. He'd never witnessed him like this. The fiasco with Derek back at the cabin was bad but this was something else. There was a subtlety to the trauma, a prolonged side effect. This was no sight for a child. No sight for anyone. Sam sobbed into his chest, eyes shut tight. Frank watched Carlos squirm in a puddle of his own blood and paused momentarily. Beyond the gruesome spectacle, something caught his attention. His focus racked beyond the traitor and over to the forest wall where the land dipped into a natural ditch.

He heard them immediately.

A series of low growls reverberated into the open. Four beasts emerged from the depths of the forest. A pack of wolves. They seemed agitated, shoulders broad and legs spread. They were not large, a slender-skulled species with white pelts and furs of grey and brown. It was only then that Frank realised he had laid eyes on a rare and true phenomenon. They were Newfoundland wolves, a subspecies of the grey wolf. Barry was right. This was real, they were right there in front of him. He knew that he was one of the few people in the world to ever see such a magnificent creature and he only wished that he could do so with both his eyes. He was so engrossed, so intrigued by their presence that he almost forgot the severity and danger they were truly in. It was clear from their scrawny bodies that they had not eaten in some time. They approached with caution, staring wickedly into the eyes of their prey. Beyond the malice and resentment, there was desperation, an undying will to survive. It was all an act to obscure their thriving hunger. Frank felt Mike's hand on his shoulder.

"No sudden movements," he whispered.

The former U.S. marine lifted him up to his feet and they slowly backed away. They didn't run. Frank knew better than to even attempt to outrun a pack of wolves. Instead, he broadened his stance and created enough distance between him and the wounded man. The wolves moved in closer, circling him. They snarled and revealed their grim set of canines. Frank held the boy even tighter. They broke Carlos from the group, leaving him to fend for himself against the oncoming slaughter. They lost interest in Frank and Mike and turned their backs on them. He knew what was coming. If they didn't leave now they might never have another chance. They turned their back on Carlos and began walking. Mike stayed by Frank's side, standing in support of his injured leg. Frank covered Sam's head with his hand and held it against his chest. "Don't look." The viscous growls grew louder and more ferocious. Tormented screams cried out from the dying man's throat. He could hear flesh shred and tear. The panicked screams drowned beneath the booming howls of the hungry beasts. Crows flocked from nearby trees and congregated high above the slaughtering grounds. They cawed in anticipation, a deadly synchronised spiral, patiently awaiting their opportunity for the leftover pickings.

"He's gone now," Frank whispered to Sam over the isolated screams. "He's gone."


They followed Mike's tracks all the way back to the watchtower. It felt twice as long as it did before to get there.

They hauled through the last collection of thick pines and pushed into the open. Frank's vision was limited but he could still see Annie gasp through the tender snowfall. She dropped her bag and trudged through the snow with high knees to get to him. The group were already there, spilling out of the watchtower in a cluster of confusion. They frantically passed their belongings down to one another; equipment bags and weapons that sprawled in a piled mess at the base of the staircase. They were carrying more than they could handle. Frank could hold himself up no longer, and when she finally reached him, he slumped forward into her arms. She caught him and placed her icy palms on either cheek. Mike leaned in and relieved him of carrying the child. Frank fell to his knees and Annie fell with him.

"Frank..." she whispered with bated breath. He couldn't look at her. His head dropped, ashamed and exhausted. He felt the others gaze upon his tarnished eye from afar. He felt her pull him closer and she held his weary head in her arms. He found the strength to hold her, clutching the sleeves of her jacket.

"I'm so sorry," he murmured. "I'm so sorry."

# SEVENTEEN

The group's detour into the mountains had been longer than anticipated. They had packed their belongings and abandoned the watchtower that morning. The tower's radio equipment had suffered damages to the harsh conditions and the group didn't know how much longer they could last in the cold. For once the sun was shining. They had begun to make their way down the other side of the mountain. The route was still densely covered in snow but at least the wind had died down. Frank rested his exhausted body on the bark of a decayed tree stump. A moment of rest had been long overdue and the others took a minute to stretch their tired limbs.

"Barry, I need those supplies," said Kara. Even though she had washed most the blood away, particles and faint trails still layered the pores of her skin. Barry was one of the few that managed to recover his supplies from the raid. He tossed his bag over to her and she knelt beside Frank, rummaging through its contents.

"How's it holding up?" she asked.

"Still stings like hell."

"Well it might sting a little more in a sec."

She pulled out Barry's medical kit and noticed Frank's uncomfortable glance. She knew he didn't want the others to see. He had gone out of his way to change the bandage in seclusion the last time. She felt the other's inquisitive eyes on them and decided to turn him away. Annie was by his side, holding his hand in support. Kara began working away on checking the wound. He didn't want Annie to see. She had seen the first time and the deprived look in her eyes filled him with guilt.

"We haven't had a chance to talk," he said.

"We haven't even had a chance to catch our breath," Annie replied.

"I'm sorry about what I said."

"I know you didn't mean it that way," she replied. "But you were right."

"No. I was wrong. He may not be our boy, but what we're doing for him; we're going to do it until we know for sure that he's safe. If that means taking care of him while he's still young then that's what we'll do."

Kara was distracted by his words. She paused for a moment but didn't want to interrupt and continued on changing his bandages. Annie's smile warmed his heart. He could feel her hand squeeze his own and he gently circled his thumb across the top of her hand.

"Are you going to tell them what you told us?" said Kara.

"Yeah. They deserve to know."

Mike used the time to polish the weapons at hand. The beauty of the AK-47 was in its simplicity. At first, most men who joined the Autark movement from the western world were against its representation. They saw it as a rebellious symbol throughout history. Sure it was arguably less accurate due to its heavier build, less adaptable and ergonomic, but the recruits didn't fully understand the genius in its employment. Its parts weren't small and dainty, they were big and robust and that reflected in its operation. The LPA had a limited budget for resources. They took to the AK for its reliability and economic advantage. It was a weapon that fired and very rarely jammed. One thing the grunts didn't take on board was the fact that the LPA operatives had done their research. The raiders themselves used the same exact models, the idea being that ammunition costs could be cut and used elsewhere. The LPA were encouraged to scavenge up the ammunition necessary from their fallen enemies. They let the raiders supply the ammunition for them.

Mike glanced over to Kara who was finishing up on replacing Frank's bandages. He couldn't see the wound as Frank was faced away but his attention was all on Kara. She was calm and collected. Her head was in the right place and that was a rare sight in dark times like these. His discreet glance had turned into a more indiscreet gawp. She caught sight of him and he snapped back down to his task at hand. He moved on to the bolt action rifle; Carlos' Mosin Nagant. Cocking the bolt back, he began examining the inside of the chamber. He thought about the scout, a deceptive liar that led them out into the wilderness for all that time. How could he have not seen it? Mike was a man who valued honour and the valiant acts of the loyal. In his eyes, a man of Carlos' stature didn't deserve to carry a rifle with such a profound historical legacy. Its multiple variations over the years had made appearances in thirty seven wars, including both world wars. Frustrated, he slammed the bolt back into place and overlooked the path ahead.

Barry and Tracy sat together in the middle of the trail. Barry held Max's weary head in his hands and scratched beneath his chin and down around his belly.

"You ever own a dog?" asked Tracy.

"I-I-I did once. Was a long time ago though."

"Can we get one for ourselves when this is all over?"

He smiled and looked into her eyes over his perfectly round lenses. He was intimidated by her candid approach. Like him, she was burdened with many fears, but behind all that she was a force of nature. "Sh-sure we can," he replied. "I know a breeder down south. We'll get an English setter."

"Part of the fun is choosing the dog. You're going to take that away from me?"

"I-I-I am, yeah, but I'll let you name it."

"Hmm. I don't think so, I'm awful. I mean I almost named Sam, 'Phil'."

"Phil?" Barry said in a burst of laughter. "S-s-sounds like a middle-aged plasterer." They laughed together in the middle of the snow-glazed trail. The sunlight shone over them through the branches of the naked pines. Barry watched Derek approach with hesitance. Derek could tell that his presence was unwanted but he did so anyway. He was awkwardly hunched and seemed to be burdened with the weight of the world on his shoulders.

"What do you want, Derek?" Tracy said abruptly. She scowled at him with squinted eyes. Barry felt her protective nature over him flourish. He felt safe with her and she acted differently around him. She was confident and brave, something he'd never seen before. Derek wringed the black beanie between his sausage fingers. "I shouldn't have been so quick to peg you," he said. "He got into my head."

"Let's just f-forget about it," replied Barry.

"I just want this shit to be done with so I can get out of here."

"Don't we all?" Tracy added. "You know what your problem is, Derek? You're a bully. If you spent more time helping us rather than moaning and losing your temper then maybe people would actually like you."

Derek scoffed at her remark. "Fuck all that. I'm not here for you people. Once I get what's coming to me I'll be off. This place is fucked."

"You still don't get it, do you?" said Tracy. She stood up tall and squared up to the ill-informed oaf. "Open your eyes. There's nothing coming to you because there's nothing left. The raiders are invading every settlement we know. For all we know, Elkford could be burned to a crisp and Javier Paraíso along with it."

Derek didn't reply. He looked away, unable to hold her intense stare of judgement. He wringed the beanie even harder before stretching it out and stuffing it back over his balding head.

"Guys, Frank wants to say something," Kara announced.

Frank stepped forward. All eyes were on him. Barry thought Kara's interruption came at a good time. It probably defused things before they needlessly escalated any further. Annie stood supportively by Frank's side. He observed the others. The group was drained. They stood hunched, weary from their travels. Charisma wasn't his strong suit, but they needed to hear something to keep them going. He looked into the eyes of every single one of them as he spoke.

"Carlos wasn't who we thought he was. The truth is that the raiders made him an offer. An offer filled with empty promises. They poisoned his mind the same way they poisoned the minds of their captives. They've got that whole area locked off. We need to carry on, find a way through and make it to the harbour."

"How are we gonna do that?" Derek questioned. "There's got to be hundreds of them there and only seven of us, boy and mutt aside."

"Reinforcements should be there by then."

"But what if they aren't?"

Frank hesitated. That possibility terrified him. He would die before succumbing to the raider's sadistic will. Although pessimistic, Derek was being realistic. What were they going to do? If LPA reinforcements didn't show, that would mean that this small group of individuals were Autark's last hope.

"We'll cross that bridge when we get to it."

Mike's attention was elsewhere. Frank saw him pace up ahead, half listening to his somewhat meagre attempt to boost morale. He pushed himself up on his tiptoes and craned his neck over the bumpy trail ahead. "Guys, I see a fence or something up ahead."

The group followed Mike's lead to the symbol of potential inhabitants and structure. They discovered a barn and land surrounded by slant wooden fencing. The crops had died, shrivelled and wilting under the immense weight of the bitter snowfall. Winters in Autark had been most cruel over the past few years. Frank himself had missed out on a lot of trade due to the weather but usually managed to make up for it throughout the spring and summer. Kara and Mike volunteered to search the barn while the others waited by the gate. They walked side by side; rows of decrepit corn either side of their path, some completely flattened into the earth from where their stems had snapped in the storm.

The barn doors were wide open. Mike and Kara entered with caution. The floor was littered in hay. Frosted crystallised dew glazed over its surface. Piled sacks of manure collected dust in the corner and bales of hay lost their cubic form. The place had been abandoned for some time. There was no trace of life to be found.

"Check the hay loft," said Kara. Mike began climbing the wooden ladder without question. The beams creaked under pressure up above. She kept a vigilant watch by the door, scanning the surrounding crops. "Reckon we could defrost some of that corn?"

"Worth a shot," he called out to her from out of sight.

"Best check the rats and other critters haven't got to it first."

"I'll pick some on the way out," she replied. She could hear him rummaging around above. It was the distinct scraping of a burlap sack against the wooden floorboards above. A rough scratching noise. And then it stopped.

"Kara?" he called out to her once more.

"Yeah?"

"Where'd you learn to dress wounds like that?"

She smiled up through the floorboards even though she knew he couldn't see her. Her face tilted down at her feet in recollection. "I used to work with animals a lot back home."

"Like a vet?"

"Something like that. For the most part I was an inspector but I trained alongside a vet for two years. I spent a lot of time taking mistreated pets away from the incapable hands of their owners."

"Sounds like a headache."

"Believe me, it was."

"Heads up," he said even louder. She turned and noticed the object fall parallel to the ladder. It plopped to the ground, a frayed burlap sack that had seen better days. Mike descended the ladder and together they regrouped to the sack. Mike flipped his survival blade open and tore a hole in the top of the sack. He plunged his hand inside and lifted its contents.

"Corn seed," he grumbled.

"Hmm."

"It's better than nothing."

"When a person chooses to eat the seed rather than plant it for the future, you know they're desperate."

Mike scrunched the top of the sack closed and slung it over his shoulder. They returned outside and made their way back up towards the trail. The others were waiting in silence, anticipating the endless possibilities of their next meal. Mike didn't enjoy being the one to make their faces drop in disappointment.

Frank and Barry led the group along the trail and when they reached the top of the mound the view stunned them into silence. It was a breathtaking panorama of rolling hills coated in expansive forests. They could see a horizontal split between the forests where the serpentine arc of the Grand River ran out to the ocean.

"There it is," said Annie. Frank stared out to the patch of dreary concrete that stood out amongst the saturated foliage. A single radio tower peaked against the backdrop of the sky and a flock of birds glided leisurely across the landscape. It was maybe five miles or so away. They were getting closer. The more he watched, the more flaws he discovered in the view; pocketed areas masked with rising smoke, most likely raider outposts. The roads would be littered with convoys and patrols. Getting there undetected would be tough, but there was no way they'd last a minute in a fight. Frank could feel the others waiting on him. They now looked to him for direction. Frank was no leader. Never was. Yet he felt newly appointed as the man to guide them on the rest of this perilous journey. He was terrified, but he could never show it. He closed his eye and channelled the fear through taut fists. He squeezed tight and released. No turning back. One last stretch to their destination. Frank began to walk. He crossed the rocky path down the base of the mountain and the others followed his lead into the woodlands below.

# EIGHTEEN

The group had spoken little during their descent through the boreal forest. All Frank could think about were the many obstacles ahead. It kept him quiet, so he could only assume that it was also on everyone else's mind. They spent most of the day trekking north, away from the bitterness of the mountain's cold. Layers of snow gradually diminished over the course of their hike. They were out of the snow and back into the depths of the marsh forest.

Mike and Kara were always watching the perimeter. Ever since Carlos' demise Frank had noticed a change in her. She seemed more determined, more focused. She had always reported to Carlos throughout the journey and now there was no superior for her to call to. She seemed free, unbound from the shackles of hierarchy. She spent most of her time with Mike, learning new skills and absorbing the knowledge from his past experience of military service. They had worked out a schedule amongst themselves and figured out ways of communicating via calls and hand gestures.

Mike calculated the average distance to the Grand River from the vista they had feasted their eyes on back up the base of the mountain. The rest of the group followed just a few hundred metres behind. Frank lagged behind the others. His condition was worsening. His wretched thigh pounded with every step. He could feel the friction of flesh and bone rubbing together. He unscrewed the cap of his canteen and took small sips. There was not much left and their chance of finding clean water was beginning to look scarcer as the day went on. Barry caught up alongside him and placed his chubby hand upon his back.

"N-n-not far now," he said with reassurance.

Frank tightened the cap and slung the canteen back over his shoulder. He felt a pulsing sensation tighten in his muscles. His face churned to absorb the pain and he released a pathetic grunt. The shoulder was still sore from the plunge he took against the tree. Even the slightest of movement caused him masses of discomfort.

"You all right?" Barry asked.

"I'm fine. Just hurts a little."

"You know, I've b-been thinking," Barry continued.

"Once we're done with this, we can help each other s-s-start up again like before."

Frank continued walking alongside Barry, half listening to the stuttering man's wave of future prospect. He could see he was getting excited. His mind bounced from cloud to cloud in those dangerous heights above.

"We could even b-band together for the trade, help each other out, you know?"

"Barry," said Frank. He stopped him abruptly. Frank turned to face him. The others continued ahead. Their pace began to slow, listening over their shoulders yet still moving as to not make their eavesdropping so apparent.

"Look at this," said Frank, pointing up to the damaged eye wrapped in blood-stained bandages. "This is real, Barry," he said. "Please don't let your guard down on me. Not now. We're so close and I need you by my side so we can finish this."

Barry shook his head up and down in a burst of rapid movement. He looked away, trying his best not to make contact with the intimidating new feature around Frank's eye. Three sharp whistles brought his attention back to the group. They could have easily been mistaken for the call of a nightingale. Heads spun to its call and they stopped to listen. It was Mike's signal. All clear ahead. The sounds of flowing water came into earshot. *The Grand River.* It was close, maybe only a hundred metres away. Frank made his way to the front of the group with Max and together the group pushed their way through the forest ahead.

Frank began to see the outline of Mike through the brush. He faced away from him, watching the surrounding area ahead. They waited momentarily, lingering just outside the edge of the tree line. The first thing Frank noticed was the air. There was room to breathe. The forest beyond the boreal mountain was cold but its depths were suffocating and restrictive. The thick air of the mountain lingered down into the valleys below and now they were finally beginning to escape it. From where they stood the Grand River was far calmer than they had previously witnessed. Its waters flowed at a steady pace and it seemed wider than he had once remembered. Beyond the water was a strip of flat land, most likely a trail of some sort. Everybody stood at the edge of the tree line, frightened of stepping out too far into the open in fear that someone should see them. They scanned the area across the river but could only see brush and dirt. They stood there in silence for a minute. It felt like hours.

"We're going to have to cross," said Kara after some time.

"What about the current?" Mike asked.

"It's slow enough for us to withstand it." She stepped out into the open and approached the water's edge. "This area is shallower than the rest. Its narrow but it will do."

"That's a long stretch to cover, if we're caught out in the middle of that there will be nowhere to run," said Mike.

"Or worse, we could fall..." Derek added.

"How is that worse?" Tracy asked.

"I'll take a quick bullet to the head over drowning to death any day."

Frank ignored the comment. "Mike will take point, I'll cover the rear. We'll just have to be quick about it."

They were now closer to the sea and the Grand River was considerably wider. Their long and tiring journey had now brought them an end in sight, but getting there was going to be harder than ever. They began crossing the Grand River single-file where the water was shallow over smooth rock. Frank felt the freezing water flood his boots and weigh him down, squelching between his toes. It reached up to his shins and the rock below was layered with a slimy algae. It was slippery beneath the treads of his boots and provided little to no grip.

"Fucking cold…" Derek muttered through chattering teeth.

Frank knew that falling against even the slowest of currents could mean the difference between life and death. There was no way he could swim against the current in his condition. Even if they could, without any means of drying, the water's temperature would eventually kill them anyway.

"Mind your step," he said to Annie. She walked in front of him with arms out to her sides for balance. It reminded him of when they were young.

"I am minding my step," she replied. "I think I should be the one telling you to watch your step."

"Oh yeah? What is that supposed to mean?"

"Well I'm not the one who slipped into a ravine not too long ago."

"Fair point."

He smiled at her playful dig at his previous misfortunes. She was right in a lot of ways. Who was he to tell her to be so careful?

He remembered when they used to go for Sunday walks on summer days. There was a small stone wall that ran for miles across the edge of a field in the backcountry. Without fail, every week Annie would walk along that stone wall's narrow surface. She said she imagined herself as an acrobatic performer, treading across a tightrope suspended one hundred feet above the ground. She would sometimes fall and hurt herself, bruise a knee or twist and ankle, but that didn't stop her. He smiled at the memory and watched her tread lightly across the shallow rock. Then reality pulled him away from his past. He was committing the same crimes he had accused Barry of doing, only in this instance it was the past that tempted him away from the present. He knew that if they were to fall, the consequences would be far more dire than any bruised knee or twisted ankle.

Frank held Sam in his arms. He tilted his head so he could see the boy's face. Sam stared out into the water, resting his head upon Frank's shoulder. The trickling ripples reflected against the whites in his glassy eyes. He stared, fixated in the trance of the river's flow.

"Nearly there," Frank whispered to him. His toes seized up, stiff and without any feeling whatsoever. He saw Mike set foot on land at the other side. His boots felt heavier with every step and fighting the flowing mass of water grew increasingly difficult. He felt as though the river would sweep him from beneath the surface and chuck him along its course back west. All he could think of was the journey up towards Elkford and how he had survived such an experience beforehand. He couldn't let it happen again. He couldn't put Annie through anything like that ever again. Once was bad enough, let alone a second time. He had cheated death twice already along this journey. The thought of even tempting fate for a third chance was greedy and foolish. The others made it across without any problems. It was a small weight removed from Frank's aching shoulders, but a relief all the same. The roar of engines cut through the silence like a blaring gunshot. He hesitated, looking at Annie's abstract face. Fear settled around his heart, deep and dreadful. Together they turned, craning their necks towards the road to see what was approaching but it was too far to tell.

"Everyone down," Mike ordered. He dropped to the ground and pushed himself up against the few trees that separated them from the road. The others dropped in the thin patches of tall grass. There was no brush or foliage that could conceal them from the oncoming threat. Frank dropped and pulled Annie down with him. Together they shuffled through the dirt and hugged a nearby tree. He held her close with Sam between them. They breathed heavily, the nerves riling up inside of him. The mechanical beasts grew louder and nearer. Sam gasped. Frank held him tighter and softly shushed through jittering teeth. There was nowhere for them to run. The road was in front of them and the river behind. With his good eye, he peered past the edge of the tree and onto the road. Watching and waiting. The first tyre spun into view. His head jolted back to cover and he froze suddenly. He listened to the motors and could tell there was more than one vehicle. *Don't stop. Please don't stop.* The first vehicle soared past; it was travelling at great speed and had made distance from those behind it. Within seconds another roared by, this time slower. He heard the mechanical elements of their chassis. They shook and vibrated across the uneven terrain. A third vehicle approached. Its acceleration was far less aggressive than its predecessors. He heard it, right there on the road behind them. Frank held his breath without realising. His mouth gaped wide open and he stared back across the river. He could hear the tyres crunch over fallen twigs and sticks, snapping them to pieces as it dominated the road. The vehicle didn't stop. It carried on further up the road. They listened in complete silence until they could hear it no more. Frank shut his eyes and released the air from his tired lungs.

The roads were littered with raider patrols. The group had crossed to the other side and back into the concealment of the forest. Frank knew the raiders would be waiting for them. Those who had driven them up into the mountains had no doubt spread word through their camps to set up road blocks and routine patrols. He was surprised it had taken them this long to come across them. Maybe they had hoped they would not make it out of the harshness of the boreal mountains alive. They were safe for now. The raiders would not send more parties venturing into the depths of the forest. The roads sectioned off every square mile from the river to the military base.

Evening caught up with them and the rain had returned. There was no way they would make it there before tomorrow.

One more nights rest. It had only just begun to sink in. They had reached an area that was unlike any other in Autark. The earth had split open from earthquakes of the distant past. The forest floor was cracked open and revealed a whole new world of uncharted territory beneath. Roots of rotted trees protruded the damp soil and rock walls and further down into the darkness were aisles of muddy streams and caves. It was dark and wet but it would provide good cover for the night. They descended into the rock and took shelter from the rain on a bed of flat stone surrounded by walls of chalk and graphite. They were cold but it was too dangerous to build a fire so deep behind enemy lines. Frank thought about the firewood in this province. It would be too damp to burn and even if it did it would create masses of black smoke, sending a direct signal to their location. Even building a pit was impossible through such rough terrain. They would have to endure another night in the cold.

"How much water do we have left?" Kara asked. Frank rattled his canteen. It was light and he could hear the last drops of water shake against the steel interior. Barry checked his also, as did Mike and Tracy. "We've probably got a couple litres between us," said Tracy.

"Is that it?" said Derek.

Frank carefully removed the straps of his knapsack from his shoulders and dropped it to the rock below. The metal pot attached to it made a dull thudding noise as it landed. He let the others count provisions and sat himself down to rest. The others continued to debate and worry over the lack of water. It went on for much longer than he expected. His eyes drew to the cooking pot and he began to interject.

"We could build a rain catcher."

The others stopped and turned to Frank sitting up against the smooth dry rock beneath the shelter. "We can't," said Mike. "We lost the tarp back on the other side of the mountain."

"We'll use something else." Frank took the pot and got back up on his feet. He moved out from the shelter and knelt down into the dirt and placed the pot onto a flat wet boulder. "Barry, go find us some strong branches. Make sure they're long and thick, we'll need at least four." Barry nodded and took off without a word. He returned after twenty minutes, cradling thick birch branches in his arms. Frank took those he saw superior and began driving them down into the damp earth below. They stood firmly in the mud and he created a squared off section surrounding the pot. He turned to the collection of equipment under the shelter and studied each item carefully. *No good.* His attention drew to the single blanket they had left. Mike noticed his stare.

"It's too dirty," he said. "Material's no good either. It'll soak right through." Then he saw Annie, he stared through the hood over her head and into her concerned eyes.

"Come back under the shelter, Frank." She coughed as she spoke. She had been coughing ever since they left the mountain. Her eyes had sunken in a little and he knew she was coming down with something. He eyed up the poncho and remembered his own hanging over his head. It was perfect. He would make sure that Annie was warm that evening. The loss of a layer was a small price to pay for drinking water. He removed her poncho and tied it to his own at the hood. After tying each corner to a branch, the material naturally dipped at the knot and the rain began to glide into the cooking pot. Frank took the last remaining blanket and wrapped it around his wife.

Sam hadn't drawn anything for days.

Frank asked him before about them; about whether he saw them beforehand or created them himself. "They come in my dreams," Sam had said. His voice was opaque, a whisper of uncertainty.

It was dark and the others were resting. Tracy had offered to take first watch. She sat up upon a rock pile that led back to the forest, the Mosin Nagant slung over her shoulder. Frank and Sam sat together, backs against the chalky substance of a large boulder beneath the shelter. The moon was low that night and the light dipped in at an angle. Frank pulled the map from his jacket pocket and unfolded it for the boy to see. It was the map Javier had provided him before they set off from Elkford. The parchment was covered in stains and wrinkles from their journey. He held it out in the moonlight for the boy to see and watched his eyes scan across every line of detail.

"This is where we are?" Sam asked.

"That's right," Frank acknowledged. He panned his hand across the entire map. "This is all Autark."

"And that's where we are going?" he said, pointing to the circled spot on the far north-east corner.

"That's where we're heading, yes."

"Autark looks big."

"It is big," Frank replied. He found the child's naivety endearing, but it was also a prospect that saddened him deeply. Sam had rarely ventured far from the military base, especially unsupervised. He realised that he had never seen or known about the rest of the world. He was a slave child. A child soldier trapped in the confined bounds of the raiders. That was all he knew. But he wasn't like the others. It wasn't as most would think, not to Frank anyway. His ability to see into the future had nothing to do with the reason he was different. The thing that made him unique was the fact that no matter how much they punished and ridiculed him, he still continued to be who he was. He didn't let them take that away from him. He hadn't been desensitised, not completely. His reactions to the things they'd seen were different but he wasn't a killer like the others.

"Frank.."

"Yeah?"

"Why don't people remember when they are little? When they are really little."

"You mean like when you were a baby?"

"Yes."

"Well.. it's a bit complicated, but, your brain is still developing. It's still growing as you grow."

"..Do you remember your mum and dad?"

"I do."

"Were they nice?"

"They were nice enough. Firm but fair."

"What does that mean?"

"It means they were nice as long as I did what I was told."

Frank stared at the child's bleak face. He could read his mind like an open book, searching for answers to his own questions through the lives of others. "Sam, do you remember anything about your parents or the time before those people took you away?"

Sam shook his head, his lips dipped at either end. Disappointment. The boy craned his arm up over his head and began scratching his scalp like a chimp. He looked out into the trees. His nose twitched like a rabbit in that inquisitive way, searching through memories of his short past to find the answer he was looking for. In the end he gave up and returned his attention to the map as though he hadn't mentioned anything to begin with.

Frank rested his hands on his lap and felt the hardness of the revolver through his jacket. He pushed the material away and examined the weapon closely. By releasing the cylinder he realised a daunting discovery. Five bullets left. He slotted it back into place, kicking himself for forgetting to retrieve the bandolier of ammunition. He looked up at the beaming moon through the partition of land and thought about John - lying back there - his body frozen over in the bitter snow. The man had been good to him in the short time they had known each other but now he could do nothing to see him again. He couldn't think about it anymore. An unsettling discomfort set about his stomach and it reminded him that they had eaten nothing but corn seed for the past day. Barry set up snare traps around the perimeter earlier that evening, so they would have to wait until morning. For now all he could do was rest. He set the boy down to sleep and turned back over to his wife and spooned her. He held her close and pulled her in close to him. He could hear her sniffling nose and her body shook in his arms. He didn't want to catch anything off of her but even more so, he didn't want them to die in the cold.

Frank stared out into the open over Annie's shoulder. He listened to the raindrops tapping against the waterproof ponchos and heard them ping rhythmically against the cooking pot. The military base was only a few miles away. If they could make it past the raider patrols they would be there by tomorrow. He hoped that what he had read in that letter was true, that the LPA were sending reinforcements north-east. He wished that they would arrive tomorrow and by the time they arrived everything would be dealt with.

All he could do was hope, but hoping would do him no favours.

# NINETEEN

Frank woke in the middle of the night, his throat desiccated without any means of relief. He pushed his body up closer to Annie's in the darkness and clenched his teeth to stop shaking. The rain fell lighter than before but it was still going. He needed water. They all did. He carefully backed off from Annie and moved out into the open to check the pot. Half full. It was more than he had expected. He took the pot and returned to the shelter of the cavern. A short fire was worth the risk. He took the extra wood that Barry had collected and began building it away from the others.

He managed to stuff the tinder between a gap in the rocks and rest the cooking pot of water to boil from above. The twigs and snapped branches crackled and popped in the darkness. He turned and noticed some of the others stir in their sleep. He felt bad for disturbing them but they would thank him later. There were only a few hours left until dawn. The fire illuminated his surroundings, a dim orange of harsh shadows. He saw Barry get up and amble over into the light.

"Sorry, did I wake you?"

"Y-you did, but I need to get up anyway."

"Why?"

"G-gonna check those snares."

"Want me to come along?"

"No. Last time w-we ventured out together things didn't go too well."

"It's okay. We can leave Max here this time," he replied.

"I'll be alright."

"Okay."

Just as Barry was about to turn there was something inside of Frank that insisted he stopped.

"Barry, wait."

"What is it?"

"About yesterday, I didn't mean to have a go at you or anything. Things have just been so-"

"It's okay. I-I understand."

"I know, but-"

"I know, shut up." Barry smiled and seeing his smile made Frank laugh. "I'll be b-b-back in a little while," He swung his rifle over his shoulder and disappeared off into the shadows. Frank's attention returned to the bubbling water over the fire. He felt his eyelid dip, fighting to keep it open. Their journey had beaten him into the ground. He tried to recall everything but the truth was that he didn't know how long they had been out there. He didn't even know what day it was. It didn't matter. The only thing that mattered to him was getting them to safety; but before they could do that they would have to get past the harbour. He took the boiling pot off the heat and settled it to cool. He collected the other's canteens and slowly poured the water into each one, carful to disperse it evenly. He then scooped dirty water from a puddle and tipped it over the fire to douse the flames. He saw Annie's body shiver through the darkness. He lay beside her and held her close. It was still dark out and there was still time to rest. He closed his eyes and listened to the gentle patter of rain against the wet rock and mud in the open.

Later that morning, Frank woke to see Annie's shivering pale face. The bags under her eyes were more prominent and her nose a rosy complexion. Annie experienced a wave of changes, one minute she was freezing cold, the next her skin was layered with a cool sweat beneath the ragged blanket. She coughed as she drank the water he had boiled in the early hours of the morning. There was nothing he could do. They had no medicine or antibiotics. This area of the forest housed no natural herbs that could produce a curing remedy. The only option was to get to the harbour as soon as possible and hope that the fever would pass.

Just as Frank was about to help her up, Tracy ran beneath the shelter. She too was flushed with a cool sweat and her eyes targeted Frank in particular. "Have you seen Barry?" she asked. She breathed heavily as though she had been running for a while, huffing and puffing to regain her breath.

"He went out to check the snares this morning," Frank replied. "He not back yet?"

"No. He woke me before he left and said he'd be back by dawn."

"Okay calm down a second. I'm sure he's not far. Who was last on watch?"

"Derek."

"Then let's go talk to Derek."

Kara offered to tend to Annie and Sam. Frank kissed Annie on her forehead and told her to rest while he escorted Tracy in search of Derek. They lowered their heads as they left the shallow shelter and stepped out into the dipped inlet of split land that was now littered with dirty rainwater. The rain had stopped but the dark clouds still loomed over them in warning of its return. They climbed the steep stretch of rock to where Tracy was posted the previous evening. Derek was there. He sat with eyes shut, shoulders back into the comfortable groove of a smooth boulder. His fingers were interlocked and rested upon his bulging gut.

"Wake up," Frank said sternly. He nudged Derek's boot with his feet and repeated it once more. Derek grunted and took his time sitting up. "What?"

"What are you doing? This is how you take watch for everyone?"

"You're all awake, what's the problem?"

"Where's Barry?"

"How the hell should I know?"

There was no time for this. It may have been a good opportunity for a lecture but it was wasted on a man like Derek. Frank marched past him and Tracy followed him up into the forest. Tracy had helped him set the snare traps the previous evening. She knew the locations and together they visited them one by one to find him. There were three trapping locations. The first one was empty. The trap had sprung but there was no sign of any game or a trail to indicate otherwise. It had most likely sprung by accident in the wind of the night. The second trap was still primed. It was in an odd location. He hadn't used the surrounding foliage to funnel a route to the trap like the previous one. It was left close to a large rock formation. He thought Barry knew better. This wasn't his usual work. Maybe the conditions and lack of rest had clouded his judgement?

"Let's move on to the last," said Frank. Tracy guided him around the rock formation and together they circled back over the highlands above the cavern. They kept a close eye for cracks in the earth and on occasion they had to jump between gaps that would prove a nasty fall had they misjudged their steps. The last trap was located north of the camp on a narrow path where the dirt had eroded between the brush. The trap had sprung but not an animal in sight. Frank knelt in front of it and studied it carefully. The twigs were damp and tiny pigments of red coated their surfaces. The pigments of red spread out in specs across the tall grass nearby. It was blood.

"This one caught something..."

"Then where is it now?"

"I don't know, maybe a fox or something found it before we did?" Frank lifted his head and scanned the woodland around them. Nothing but more trees and grass. He stood up and began walking ahead of the snare trap.

"Maybe he-"

Something interrupted him. As he stepped forward, a sharp object crunched beneath his boot, the distinct shattering of glass. He lifted his boot and saw the object beneath. It had sunken into the dirt and the light shimmered off its surface. He squatted with broad knees and saw a short frame around the glass that he could raise it from. He lifted it and held it up for a better view. He heard Tracy gasp over his shoulder as she too witnessed what he had discovered. The frames were bent and the lenses had shattered. These were Barry's spectacles.

The group had packed up their limited provisions and regrouped where Frank and Tracy had discovered the glasses. Derek crouched down the same way Frank did and studied the area.

"No prints, you sure these are his?" he said.

"Of course they're his!" Tracy shouted from a distance.

Frank held her back and urged her to be quiet. Mike stepped up to the plate and began scouting the land around the trap. He strode with the assault rifle loosely in his grasp.

"There's prints."

"Where?" Derek asked.

"You're just not looking hard enough. See here, where the grass is trampled a little?" Mike kept low and tracked his finger along the newly discovered trail. "Hm. there's more than one set of tracks here," he continued.

"Think we can track them?" asked Frank.

"We can try."

"Hold on a minute," Derek interrupted. "We're already way behind schedule. We're so close to the harbour and you wanna go on a wild goose chase now?"

"He helped us get this far, we're not leaving him behind."

"Please. He's been a liability ever since we left the cabin."

"You shut your mouth." said Tracy. Frank could see her removing the rifle from over her shoulder. He quickly held it tight to stop her from doing anything she might regret.

"Easy there, love, you'll hurt yourself handling that thing."

"We're looking for him and that's final. Anyone who has a problem can take it up with me," Frank ordered. He marched right up to Derek, his face only inches away from the oaf's. He stared directly into his eyes. A brief moment of silence loomed over the two men as they stared off in the middle of the forest.

"Do we have a problem here Derek?"

Derek frowned, agitated. The tension between them over the journey had led to this. He could see his jaw clench through his skin. Derek grunted and turned his back on him.

"Let's get a move on," said Frank, his eyes never leaving Derek.

Annie breathed heavily. Her nose was blocked so the only way of breathing was through her mouth. Frank fiddled with the unlit cigarillo in his hands. *Where are you, Barry?* Autark wasn't safe anymore. He needed to get Annie off the island, Sam too. He imagined them sailing over the Atlantic towards Newfoundland and wondered if they could ever return, if things would ever go back to the way they were. He had moved his entire life to Autark. Leaving it all behind would be tough, he wasn't sure he could ever adjust to normal life again, but then again he may not have a choice. He took Sam's hand and they followed Mike's lead. Kara was by his side. He overheard Mike quietly teaching Kara of things to watch out for when tracking in the woods. He was glad that Mike was here. The man had saved his life on more than one occasion and he was certainly pulling his weight.

The trail led them straight to the edge of a ridge up ahead. They continued walking to the edge and Frank hacked away at the last layer of dense foliage with his machete. As he sliced into the brush, it split open like a gateway that revealed something spectacular; a grand vista of the north-eastern coastline. The drop over the edge could have been no more than fifty feet. He looked down into the remaining forest and tilted his head up. There it was, sitting comfortably between them and the Atlantic Ocean: The military base.

Sam sat down by the cliff's edge and began sketching in his book. His eyes were still, fixated on the base ahead. He didn't look down at his drawing at any point, only the base. The harbour was concealed by the forest but it should have been located on the other side of the base. Frank took Barry's binoculars from Tracy's belt and peered through them. One side was completely black and for a second he had forgotten about his eye. He ignored it and continued scoping out the base. "Seems quieter than I imagined..."

"What do you see?" asked Mike.

"A few guards posted at the gate, towers and perimeter. Don't see the slaves though. Wait." He looked closer at the gate. "There's a truck." The truck pulled up to the gate and the raiders waved it on through. It passed the gates and drove up the runway towards a concrete building at the other end. It stopped and two raiders exited on either side. The driver moved round to the rear and before he could open the tarp cover, another raider hopped out from the rear and pulled something out. It flopped down onto the concrete. It was Barry.

"Oh Christ..." he whispered to himself.

"What? What is it?"

"Barry..."

"What? Let me see," said Tracy, snatching the binoculars from his grasp. No more words escaped her. She may have wanted to talk but she couldn't.

"Don't worry, we're going to get him back," said Frank.

"And how we gonna do that?" asked Derek from behind. Frank faltered in his speech. He had to think hard about what he would say next. "We'll figure something out. We'll sneak in, I don't know yet. All I know is the harbour can wait. We're not leaving without him."

"The harbours just on the other side, we can find a way around. You sure you wanna risk your life for a bloody drunk?"

"We are doing this," Frank replied. Tracy lowered the binoculars and he felt her hand grip his forearm tightly. He turned to Annie who gave him a look that he had never seen before on her. It was doubt, there was no denying it. He didn't want to believe it of her but it was so obvious. It could not have been mistaken for anything else. He struggled to look away, so unexpected, but then he was distracted. He felt something tug his jeans and it took a while for it to really register.

Sam handed Frank his black book. He took it and studied the sketch. It was more detailed than his previous sketches, a complete layout of the base. Seeing it in the flesh must have struck something inside of him. "Can I rip this one out, Sam?" Frank asked politely. Sam nodded. He reached up and tucked the pencil back into Frank's knapsack. Frank ripped the page from the book and returned it to Sam. He handed the sketch to

Mike. "Can you work something out from this until we get there?"

"Will do," Mike replied.

They set off along the ridge's edge to find a way down to the forest below. Frank had hoped it wouldn't be like this. He wanted to go to the harbour as much as the others. He knew what they were doing was dangerous. The odds were against them and they had heard nothing from Javier or the LPA. It wasn't like he hadn't thought about it; leaving Barry behind. He could never do it though. The guilt and regret would rot him from the inside out for the rest of his life. Barry was his friend. Things were different now and he knew it. They would have to infiltrate the military base after all.

# TWENTY

"You people. You people come to this land from all corners of the earth. You come here - to the heart of this world - board its shores and claim it as your own. I have never seen such blissful ignorance or any such hypocrisy as I have these past few months. You discover such beauty, such wonderful land that has been untouched for centuries and what do you do? You wipe your arses with it as you do with every other country this world has known and then you have the audacity to point the finger at us? At least we are honest. That is partly why we are here after all. You think we are all that different? We conquer with force because we do to you as you did to those before you.

Autark... such ignorance from such filth.

You never stopped to think that maybe this land had a history of its own, that it had a name of its own and people of its own. You never once thought of that, did you? Well that is why we are here; to remind you of what it is like to have your entire life's work and legacy taken away from you in a matter of months. For thousands of years countries like yours invaded the world and sucked your own cocks at our doorsteps, ranting and raving about just how great you really were. If they didn't bend to your will you conquered them and claimed them as your own or at least polluted their culture with that of your own. Things are different now. Our ways may be cruel but at least we have respect for those who have walked the face of this repulsive world before us. We are merely thieves. We carry no legacy for ourselves but we deliver justice and irony to those who are too blind to see the error of their ways, and that is precisely what we are doing here today. We are taking something that was never yours to begin with. You have forgotten that true liberty - true freedom - comes at a price."

He listened carefully to the words under the confined darkness of the black burlap sack over his head. His breath was heavy and deep and he felt the meshed burlap rough against his lips as he inhaled. Footsteps circled him as the voice spoke. It was a man's voice; an articulate man with a chiselled foreign accent, Hispanic, Latin or otherwise. His wrists were bound behind him and the rigid posts were firm against his bruising biceps. The footsteps drew nearer. He felt the coiled rope around his neck loosen and the darkness was swiftly pulled away from him to unveil the bright light ahead.

Barry squinted at the spotlight suspended over him. Everything was soft, blurred edges that melted into each other like an abstract painting. His eyes would never focus with the absence of his spectacles. A striking black silhouette stood over him in the centre of the light. He blinked to adjust but nothing changed.

"Oh, I do apologise," said the man. He reached up for the lamp which sat on a swinging arm that pivoted in all angles. He pulled it low to the ground and aimed the light upward and in doing so the entire room transformed into a menacing nightmare of crooked shadows and bright pale eyes. "I almost forgot you struggle to see as it is."

In the corner of his eye, Barry saw the other figures standing in the wings, watching, observing their master perform before them. He was a little clearer now; a tanned individual with brown wavy hair, clean shaven and a distinct feature that caused his skin to crawl the moment he laid eyes on it. The entire right side of his face was marked with the remnants of a past disaster. The skin ashen and shrivelled, scarred from the burning of the flame. Barry probably wouldn't have noticed with his terrible vision but it was so prominent, particularly across his cheek and forehead.

"It's okay to stare, I get it every time I see a new face," he said, clocking onto Barry ogling eyes. "It happened when I was young and my village was raided by pirates. My father and I lived on a farm and had our fair few encounters with cattle rustlers. They put us down on our knees in the barn by the trough that the cows drank from and asked where we kept our savings. We didn't have much but my father was a stubborn man, he wasn't going to give them a penny. They took the brand iron from the furnace and God did it glow, that vibrant orange, like molten lava. In the end it was his stubbornness that did this to me. They questioned him again, this time with the iron only inches away from my face. I could feel the heat melting away at my skin before it even touched me. But yet again, my father refused to comply. They pressed the hot iron against me and dragged it down across my peeling face. I can still smell the burning today. They dunked my head into the water and held it there for some time, and when they pulled me out, my father was already dead." He stopped to watch Barry's reaction. He didn't react, just looked down and away, distancing himself from the horrendous tale.

Within seconds the burnt man helped himself into Barry's jacket pockets. He searched inside and out until he stumbled across a steel container close to his chest. He held it there in the pocket for a second, guessing what it could be before removing it and putting an end to his curious little game.

"Of course," he muttered aloud. He held the whiskey flask up into the light and bellowed out in laughter. He unscrewed the lid and shifted himself side on to Barry. Barry hollered at the sudden tugging. His captor clamped his clawed hand over Barry's bald head and yanked it back. All he could see was the warm yellow light against the dull ceiling. The burnt man wasted no time. As Barry's mouth gaped open in agony, he felt the burning sensation of alcohol flood down his gullet and windpipe. He choked and gagged but the liquid refused to stop flowing. He tried spitting it back up but the burnt man held his head firmly and there was nowhere for it to go. All he could do was swallow and endure the blazing inferno engulf his insides.

When it was finally down to the last drop, he was released. His head shot forward and he coughed the whiskey out onto the dusty concrete floor.

"You mustn't waste it," argued the burnt man. "You're supposed to savour your drink, enjoy it." Barry heard the flask clank into the shadows and before he knew it, a tightened fist pounded his gut and he thought his stomach would come rushing out of his mouth.

"What brings you so close to these parts?" asked the burnt man. Barry didn't reply. He sat with his head down, dry heaving at the floor like a regurgitating cat.

"When somebody asks you a question it is common courtesy to respond."

The burnt man stood in front of Barry and leaned in. He lifted Barry's head by his chin and looked into his eyes with a hypnotic gaze. "Do you know who I am?" Barry shut his eyes tight and pulled away. "Oh come on," the man continued. "It's not that bad. It doesn't matter, it isn't important. The real question is: Who are you?" There was a delay in his voice after every word, as though to contain his excitement. He began to circle Barry again as he spoke, his stride both elegant and leisurely. He was eloquent in his speech and did his best to articulate his cause, not that Barry took any notice. "You're not LPA, that's for certain... Are you with Paraíso's people? No that's right. I'm very sure we killed all of them already. Unless you managed to escape of course, but I doubt it." He glared closer on his second round and this time there was some semblance, a glint in his eye. "No. It can't be. The huntsman? Yes, I see it now. The man who brought me my meals- well, not directly of course but you killed them nevertheless."

Barry said nothing.

"Word around Autark is that you killed some of my scouts who came to collect the weekly share. That wasn't very nice."

"It wasn't me."

"Of course it wasn't you; look at you, but thank you for admitting that you're not alone out there. So come on now, who else is cowering out there in the woods?"

An uncomfortable silence lingered. The burnt man waited for some time before continuing.

"You're being very rude. Now I've spared your life, that is extraordinarily rare in dark times such as these. I've taken you in, offered you beverages and this is what I get in return? Personally I'm offended but I will take exception seeing as you have been out there for so long. I'm surprised you've made it this far. May I ask what has kept you going all this time?"

Barry kept his head down and his eyes shut. He didn't want to listen but he was bound with no alternative. The heat from the lamp settled a sticky sweat across his brow that dripped onto the bridge of his nose and glided down the insides of his cheeks.

"The drink? No, how ridiculous of me to say. More of that and you'd be off in a ditch somewhere dehydrating to death. Hope? No. You lost that some time ago, I can tell. Well what then, a woman?"

Barry opened his eyes without realising. He stared down into the harsh spotlight and his eyes began to sting. Moisture collected in the ducts of his eyes and every time he blinked he saw a silhouetted purple outline of Tracy's face stamp itself wherever he looked.

"No... a woman, really? Huntsman you rascal." The burnt man pushed playfully against Barry's collarbone and smirked. And then his eyes lit up. It was a horrific thing to witness. A genuine eureka moment that sent shivers down Barry's spine.

"Oh my goodness. Of course, how could I be so blind? Zero Two Seven..."

Barry lifted his head, his mind full of hatred. It conjured up things he could have never have imagined under normal circumstances. Evil things. Things that made him sick. He hated this man more than he'd ever hated anyone and he'd hated nobody.

"You don't know how happy it makes me that you are here in front of me today. You see, that boy belongs to me and I have been trying to get him back ever since he left my sight. He is a prophet and a glorious one yet. He will give me exclusive insight into the future. The more he does it and the more he grows the more descriptive and more detailed his visions become. I will be able to witness the future, fate and destiny and bend it to my will."

Barry's head slumped to one side and shot up unexpectedly. The whiskey was starting to kick in. His mind throbbed against his skull. He had drunk far too much in one go.

"What's the matter, Huntsman? Don't tell me it's got to your head already? We were just getting started. Ah well... Let's get this over with then, shall we?" The burnt man looked over to one of his onlookers in the shadows.

"The hammer please."

Barry struggled to focus and the sweat dripped down into his eyes. He could just about make out what was happening through the discomfort. A tall lanky teenage boy stepped out from the darkness. Held out in his hands was an offering of a steel claw hammer. The boy appeared frightened himself, as though he'd already seen what was about to follow. It was at that moment that Barry knew he wasn't the first person that had been interrogated in this very room. He began to shake uncontrollably. His jaw tightened. His shoulders knotted close to his neck. Something yanked him and the chair he sat on slid back. Within seconds more onlookers slid a wooden table between Barry and the man. The rope that bound his hands was cut with a blade and a brutish figure clamped his gigantic hands over Barry's wrists. The brute finally came into view, a behemoth as wide as he was tall. Barry tried to struggle but it was as though the rope had never been cut in the first place. The behemoth flared his nostrils like a raging bull and held Barry's right hand flat out onto the table while the others tied his left hand back behind the chair.

The hammer danced up and down in the burnt man's grasp. He juggled it loosely and then his clutch tightened around the wooden grip.

"I imagine you understand how this works? I tried to indulge you for a little while but you obviously couldn't cooperate under such circumstances, and quite frankly... this is much faster. I was planning on sparing you, you know, once I got what I needed. We could have always gone back to our original arrangements and your friends out there were to become my slaves. I think I've changed my- no, you've changed my mind. I think I'll kill them; but first I'll kill you. They can watch. I want to see their faces so that I can spot which one is the woman. It will be blindingly obvious of course. Terrible things will follow for her but that is just the way it is." He leaned one hand on the table, the other raised over Barry's hand with the hammer firmly in his grasp. He held it there, suspended high in the air, teasing him with what was to come. Barry felt his fingers rattle against the table. He murmured phrases of incomprehensible drivel but the burnt man ignored him.

"Now then... Where is Zero Two Seven?"

Barry stuttered like a broken record player. The valve released and the tears ran freely. Too late. The steel ball of the hammer crashed down onto his little finger. Barry cried out from the pit of his lungs. He felt the bone snap like a twig. He gawked down, his finger now bent out to one side. The burnt man raised the hammer again. Tears streamed and Barry became a sobbing wreck. He stared into the eyes of the burnt man who gazed back with that serpentine stare. The burnt man waved the hammer from above like a musical conductor. He rested it gently atop the next finger over, lining up his aim. He raised the hammer once more, high into the light and tried again, this time more sinister than before.

"Where. Is. Zero. Two. Seven?"

# TWENTY-ONE

A desolate field was all that stood between them and the military base. The wind shook tall blades of grass and delicate dandelions that formed a glorious wave across the open landscape. They could see more now, the base was more vivid and clear. Great meshed fences pointed with spiralling rolls of deadly barbed wire towered high above the ground. In such short time it had already gained the reputation of 'The Black Site' across the land of Autark. He had heard Javier mention it and he had also heard it numerous times uttered throughout the Merribank market without giving it any real thought. What once was a beacon of importation and protection had now succumbed to a prison.

Frank watched behind the comfort of the shaded pine. He could taste the ash against his dry tongue and it triggered a smell of burning in the air. The sun hibernated behind clouds of grey and it was difficult to pinpoint the time of day. He'd watched the single raider standing watch atop the tower for ten whole minutes. He held a cigarette in one hand and an AK-47 in the other. Max waited patiently by his side, up on all fours with his head low, also watching. He didn't growl or holler but instead he replicated the calculated vibe of his master. Frank heard the faint sounds of feet grazing over fallen pine needles. He leant against the tree with one hand and looked back into the cover of the forest.

Mike and Kara jogged up to his position. He noticed Kara's form; it was more pronounced, more disciplined. She had spent so much time with Mike that she was now beginning to move like a soldier, replicating his footing and the way he turned corners with a rifle. She glanced back and waved the others over with a snappy curved palm. Frank looked back up to the watchtower and sighed. "He's the only one."

"What, there are no others?" Kara asked. She seemed surprised and her voice rose unexpectedly.

"Not a single one."

"What about the slaves?"

"I saw some working over the garden but for a place that supposedly holds a few thousand slaves it seems a little quiet."

"You think they know we're coming?"

"Of course they know," Derek scoffed from behind them. Frank turned and frowned at the oaf standing with folded arms. Frank ignored him and made haste to change the subject. He turned to Mike with the map Sam had sketched in his hands.

"How many for the radio tower?"

"Just the one," he replied.

Derek's ears were burning, this was something new, something he knew nothing about. "Hang on a minute. What's this now?"

"We go in, find Barry and try to find a signal on the radio tower."

"I thought the plan was, 'go in, get Barry and get the fuck out of here.'"

"It still is, but without outside contact this island could be under raider control for a long time unless we do something about it. One of us just needs to get up there, get on the receiver and call out."

"We're two men and an entire bloody army short as it is and you want to split us up even more?"

"Less of us in there means less chance of detection," added Mike. "We sneak in."

"And how do you suppose we do that? Climb the fence and get pegged up on barbed wire?"

"No," said Frank, his eye moved right of the watchtower. Over where the field met gravel again, the stones and rock sloped upwards to form higher ground. It was littered with large boulders and the rock overhung the fence's perimeter. "We get in from there," he said finally, pointing a few hundred yards to the small cliff.

"We've got some rope but maybe not enough to reach down from there," Mike informed him.

"We'll see what we can do." Frank didn't look back. He was here now, nothing would deter him, not even a thousand of Derek's smug remarks. He felt this great aura inside of him that he had never felt so strongly before in his lifetime; a rush of adrenaline that seemed to elate his hands with pins and needles. He clenched his fists tight and opened them wide over and over again.

"You okay, Frank?" a voice startled him from behind, and for a brief moment his heart dropped like a dip in the road. He felt a comforting hand lightly place itself upon his shoulder. It was Kara. She stared him in the eye with a look of concern. She too had never seen him like this. She hadn't known him for long, but she knew him well enough by now.

"I'm fine," he said, trying his best not to look back at her. How could he do this? Take responsibility for the lives of many for the sake of one. He had grown fond of Kara, Mike too, Derek not so much but even so, he didn't know what he would do should worse come to worst. It was best not to think about it. They were here now and there was no one coming to get them, not if he didn't do something. They couldn't hide forever.

They retreated back into the forest and circled round to the incline. He stood back with Annie. The others clung to the large boulders that ran along the cliff's edge in wait of the perfect moment to infiltrate. Her face was still pale, her nose and cheeks red like a cherub. She had the blanket wrapped tightly around her body. "How are we going to find him?" she asked, her throat dry and gruff.

"We're not going to find him."

She looked up suddenly, puzzled by his response. "What do you mean?"

"I and they are going to find him. You are going with Tracy to take Sam to the harbour."

"What? No-"

"I've already talked Tracy into it."

"Frank."

"Annie, just listen to me. Sam is exactly what they want. We bring him in there and if they do find us then all of this will have been for nothing. You're not well and I need you to be there to get him to safety if things go south, okay?" "You can't leave me, not again. Please don't leave me, Frank." There was a sharp croak in her voice as she lunged forward and buried her head into his chest. The blanket fell slightly but was quickly caught between them as she embraced.

"I know," he replied. He hated seeing her cry and he too would soon start if she didn't stop. She lifted her head and looked up at him. "What about everything you said before? 'As long as we're together we can do anything.'"

"I meant it, every word, but this is just the same. We both have a job to do. I'm going to get Barry back." He turned and pointed to the young boy sitting close to Tracy who listened only a few metres away. "And you are going to keep him safe."

"Okay," she nodded, wiping away the few tears that soaked her weary face. "Just promise me you'll meet us there."

"I will meet you there," he said with regret.

Frank hated making empty promises, especially ones that he couldn't guarantee he could keep. How could someone promise such a thing? It was impossible to make that kind of promise but he didn't want to upset her at the risk of changing her mind. He was keeping her and the boy safe, her sister too, and that's all that mattered. Having them absent from the rescue was a gigantic weight lifted from his shoulders. Tracy's guilt and pressure to retrieve Barry only threw that weight back on.

"Head to the harbour," he said.

"Wait. How will I know when you are coming?"

It was a fair point. Of course if he was dead she would never find out, but he didn't want to dwell on that possibility.

"I'll think of something," he replied. It wasn't much but there wasn't much to give. "If you don't see or hear anything from us in two hours then just go. Get him to Newfoundland and don't come back."

"Frank, no-"

"Just be prepared," he said firmly. "Look... I don't want it to happen either, Annie. We've got to be realistic here. I just don't want you hanging around any longer than you need to be."

"I know."

"Thank you, and take Max with you. If it makes any difference..." he glanced over to Tracy then turned back to her and whispered, "your sister scares me a little. I also know she cares a great deal about Barry. If I can't do this then she'll tear through every raider in there just to kill me for herself."

She nodded again obediently and he caught a glimpse of her faint smile beneath the dread. He stroked her cheek softly with an open palm. He didn't like giving anyone orders, especially his wife, but sometimes things needed to be set in stone. He wouldn't put her in that position, not in her condition. She would do what she did best; nurture. He felt safe knowing that Sam was in good hands, the best of hands. There was nobody else more equipped to take him there. He didn't know what to think about leaving Tracy to protect them. His sister in-law was tough but her mind was elsewhere. Ever since Barry went missing she had been acting on impulse. He remembered her blank stare out over the military base from before. When they made their way toward it she had sometimes trailed behind, walking slowly and just staring, exactly as she did right now with the boy beside her. Sam stared up at her with squinted eyes. His mouth open, nostrils flared. He looked mesmerized, confused.

"What are you looking at?" he asked. She looked to him eventually as if her attention was being dragged away from her thoughts. "Uh, what?"

"What are you looking at?"

"Oh, nothing. Just thinking."

"Oh... are we going away from here?"

"Only for a little while," she reassured him.

"But we are coming back?"

"Hopefully."

"What is it like?"

"Away from here?"

"Yes."

"It's... it's not much different." Her heart sank as she said it. She wasn't sure if it was the right thing to do and she wondered if he could ever adjust to life in the real world. Getting his hopes up now would lead to a whole array of further questioning. She didn't know how long they would be gone for or if they could ever come back to Autark. She looked down at him sitting beside her and saw the disappointment in his eyes. He too now gazed down the dirt, fiddling with a twig in his hands. Some things were best kept in the dark for the time being.

The rope was tied around one of the boulders near the cliff's edge and given to Tracy. Since she was leaving, it made the most sense for her to support it as the others made their way down into the black site. Frank wished they had a winch of some sort to hold it but this would have to do. Kara peered out to the watchtower. The raider turned his back and leant across the railing on the other side. His arms were crossed one over the other and he set the assault rifle down. He dragged a long puff of smoke and hung his head, drained and fatigued.

"Now," she said abruptly.

Mike took hold of the longer end of the rope. He gave it a quick tug just to check it was tight and turned his back on the edge of the cliff. He took one step down against the cliff face, and then the other. He was now suspended twenty feet over the black site. He peered down over his shoulder and saw the rope dangling over the tall grass below. The rope was maybe halfway between him and the ground. He would have to fall some of the way. He stepped horizontally, one foot at a time down the face of the cliff until there was no more rock to lean on. The rock dipped back inland and the further he shimmied down the rope, the more he saw of the fence beneath the overhang. Reaching the rope's edge, he hung loosely with his arms fully extended and stared down into the brush below. He released his grip and fell the rest of the way. He bent his knees as he landed and rolled onto his side. He stretched his body out flat and kept as low to the ground as possible, lying in the cover of the grass, inching over to allow room for the next person. Derek descended next and then Frank. They pushed up against a large set of rocks that curved and backed onto what looked like a canteen shack. Kara was last to climb down, she did just as the others did but when she dropped she fell with great force. She landed awkwardly on her left foot, the right soon followed and sent her plummeting down to the ground. She let out a short grunting wince and held onto her ankle.

"Kara," Mike whispered. "You okay?"

"I'm fine, think I twisted my ankle."

His head snapped to the watchtower. The raider was still facing the other way. He darted out from cover, took hold of Kara's hand and hauled her back onto her feet. He tugged her by her hips and together they fell behind the concealment of rocks.

"Where's the radio tower?" Derek asked.

"By the side of the runway," Mike replied.

"Alright, see you guys later."

"Wait, what? Hold up. We can go together."

"You need to help these guys find the stuttering prick. If I gotta do this I'm gonna do it my way. I'd rather do the tower."

Mike shot a concerned glance at Frank for approval. Frank hesitated. The responsibility now back on him. "You know what you're looking for?" he asked Derek.

"I know what a radio transmitter looks like."

"Okay."

Derek pushed himself away from the rock and made a dash to the rear of the shack. Frank leant out one last time and saw the oaf slithering away in the grass.

"Derek," he called out in whispered tones. The oaf looked back over his shoulder.

"Be careful."

Derek nodded and returned to crawling before disappearing off behind the shack. Frank looked back to Mike who continued to watch out for any signs of movement.

"You should have let me go instead."

"I trust you with us more than I trust him. If he doesn't make it, we'll head there straight after." Mike was surprised at his lack of faith but they shared an understanding for the worst case scenario.

The sounds of joyous hollering and chanting rattled them from their gaze. The door to the shack swung back on its hinges. A drunken man stumbled out onto the wooden landing and was caught by the railing. He leant over it haphazardly and laughed hysterically at his own misfortune. Mike led Frank and Kara out from cover. They crawled the same way Derek had but this time they moved beneath the wooden structure that held the shack above ground. It was a basic configuration of wooden beams that were buried into the foundation below. They crawled through the dark and damp and when they reached the other side, they kept their eyes peeled for any signs of Barry.

They saw more of the black site now. Rows and rows of tents pitched up to one side. The wind rattled against their material that waved in the breeze. The base of the tents were filthy from where the rain had chucked mud and dirt up at them from the night before. There must have been at least a hundred of them. On the other side was the watchtower and beyond that they spotted a set of stairs that they would have never seen had nobody emerged from its obscure positioning. The steps descended underground. Frank saw raiders rise from the terrain and behind them followed a handful of men and women in tanned rags, bounded by thick rusty chains that struck him with the god-awful memories of Wolvendale.

"That must be where the slaves are kept," Kara whispered.

Frank nodded and awaited Mike's orders. They listened to the banging and pounding of riled up footsteps through the floorboards above. A sudden weight thumped into the mud to their right. Altogether their heads swung to face it. It was the raider. He had toppled over the railing and was lying back in the mud, staring up into the sky. They froze steady beneath the shack, watching him from a distance. His head tilted above and he let out a slur of intoxicated groans. Suddenly another wet thump sloshed into the mud beside him, a set of boots. A hand snatched the raider's shirt and lifted him by his chest with incredible strength. The strength was attached to a man with a deep and grizzled voice, the kind with a no nonsense attitude about him.

*"Get up you fool. Do you want him to take your head too?"*

Frank closed his eyes and tried his best not to think about who exactly the man might be talking about. He heard them clamber the steps into the canteen and the door slammed shut behind them.

The trio crawled out from beneath the shack and made a break for the tents. The cover would conceal them from the eyes on the watchtower. They stayed low, scurrying from one tent to the next, weaving in and out of the many rows ahead. He could hear the disgruntled snores on the other side of the tents' polyester coating; most likely raiders clocking off from night duty. A burning aroma of piss and rum lingered in the narrow alleys of this filth-ridden district. One of the tent flaps flipped open and a man exited with the wing of a chicken stuffed into his mouth and his hands fully occupied with the buckling of his belt. He looked up and stared death in the face as Kara's blade plunged up through his neck. He tried to scream but his cries were muffled through mouthfuls of chicken that were soon marinated by his own blood. She ripped the blade from his jugular and silently guided his body down to the ground.

Frank peeled back the flap and peered through the tent from which he came. He spotted a female slave, half clothed and sitting upon a roll of bedding. She stared back and released a faint gasp and proceeded to cover her breasts with the torn rags that wrapped her naked body. Frank shot his finger up to his lips and stared back at her. She nodded quickly, her chest full of air that she refused to leave her. He closed the tent and caught up with Mike and Kara who waited by the last row of tents backing onto the runway. Mike peered out and spotted a jeep with an open roof but his view was immediately obstructed. Something hit his face at great speed. Mike was knocked back into the dirt and when he looked up, a gigantic behemoth of a man stood before him. Kara raised her shotgun but it was too late.

They were surrounded.

More raiders emerged from all sides, their rifles drawn and aiming from every direction. Mike shot up and the three of them stood back to back. The raiders closed in on their prey. Frank clenched the revolver in his hand but he had fewer bullets than there were raiders.

"Drop your weapons," a voice commanded from behind the behemoth. From there a smaller man revealed himself, average height but smaller in comparison. The trio held onto their weapons, heads jolting back and forth with more targets than they could handle. Frank caught sight of the man and it was enough to make him stare. A burnt man. One possessed with a face tormented by scars that could only be created by evil. The brutish behemoth stepped aside to reveal a cowering plump man on his knees.

Barry knelt before them, his hands tied behind his back. His face doused in tears, his eyes bloodshot and dread plastered across his face. He looked defeated, as though they had taken his life and soul away from him. The group dropped their weapons and the burnt man paced back and forth. "To tell you the truth I am a little disappointed. I thought there would be more of you." Frank noticed the burnt man study him up and down and then his eyes landed on Kara.

"There's no way you're the one." He turned back to Barry.

"She is way out of your league, my friend." He laughed to himself and the behemoth released a deep, unsettling chuckle. Frank stared down the barrel of the assault rifle opposite him. The raider holding it snarled like a bloodthirsty hound and spat to one side, his eyes never leaving Frank. The burnt man stepped beside Barry and pulled a claw hammer from his belt.

"What is your name?" He gestured the hammer towards Mike but Mike remained silent, eyes scanning desperately for a way out.

"Very well," the burnt man continued. "Tell me, where is zero two seven?"

"His name is Sam," Kara muttered.

"What was that?"

"They named him," said the behemoth.

"Oh. How lovely. I tell you, that's going to make it harder for you when you hand him back over."

Frank pushed past both Mike and Kara. He was the eldest of the three and for some reason that made him feel obliged to take the fall. That was partly it. The other thing was the way the man spoke of Sam. Something riled up inside of him that wasn't there before. It prodded him in a way he never knew possible. "He's not yours to take, none of these people are." He held the ball of the hammer hard against Barry's temple. "Where is he?!" The burnt man's entire body quaked with aggression. The veins in his throat tensed up and a single strand of hair dropped down in front of his face.

A blaring gunshot deafened Frank from behind. He ducked down, both hands up over his ears. The burnt man's shoulder jerked back and the hammer dropped to the ground. Frank spun around and saw him standing there in the alley of tents. Derek's eyes bugged wide and the .38 shook in his hand. The behemoth shoved past the trio and charged for him, covering the distance in no time. Time seemed to slow down and the air was cut by a fine flying object. It wisped past them all and thudded hard against the behemoth's chest. Frank watched the brute jerk forward. He stared at the object protruding the behemoth and it soon became vivid. An arrow dressed with the feathers of a raven.

Mike and Kara scrambled for their weapons amidst the chaos. Derek let off another shot, this time penetrating the behemoth's skull and out the back of his head. The behemoth toppled over Derek and crushed his body against the wet mud. Frank dropped to the ground and stared up the runway. Mike unloaded the rifle all around them. Bullets whirled and the blast of Kara's shotgun followed shortly after. Bodies dropped like flies and the tents caved in under the dead weights crashing through them. Beyond Barry's panicked face was a sight that sent Frank's heart into arrhythmia. There they stood, mounted high upon the ridge on horseback, at least two hundred of them. Another fifty had already penetrated the fence with their tools and charged in on foot.

*The Grey Wolves.*

Barry's shoulder slammed into the mud, his hands still awkwardly tied behind him. Frank crawled forward and took hold of his friend's wrists. And then he felt them against his skin and he knew. He looked down and saw Barry's fingers, twisted and mangled in all directions. He hesitated for a moment but there was no time. They needed to go. He looked up and saw the burnt man retreating to the jeep. Only Frank saw him, the others too busy running and diving for cover. Frank felt himself rise through the anarchy. He felt possessed, driven by hatred and revenge. He pelted forward after the burnt man, after the one responsible for all that was lost.

# TWENTY-TWO

The burnt man dived into the jeep. The driver slammed his foot on the accelerator. Tyres screeched and rubber burned against the tarmac. Frank lunged forward and caught the spare tyre mounted on the rear. The jeep shot off and he felt the exhaust spew hot air against his ankle. The entire vehicle shook from left to right and back again, desperate to shake him off. The burnt man regained his balance and swung a right hook across Frank's jaw, his hand slipped and the rest of his body spun outward across the jeep. He saw the burnt man's balled fist coming down for another. The grey wolves howled as they rode by on their horses. Their arrows soared up over them and crashed across the tarmac. The jeep buckled and the burnt man was thrown back. His waist slammed into the spare tyre. Frank grabbed a handful of his clothes and used him to hoist himself up into the jeep. Before he could turn, a sharp elbow struck his nose. He sprawled back across the back seat, his upper body dangling out the side. His head drifted only inches from the runway that raced by at seventy miles per hour. He felt the burnt man on him, fist raised, ready to strike. His eyes lit up with those same flames that tormented his soul. The flames froze and so did his body and then Frank saw the evil in his eyes transcend into fear. Frank tilted his head back and he too saw it, whizzing by through the speeding blur.

The grey wolves circled across the open runway by the masses. They rode in unison, spiralling outward around the storming jeep like a deadly tornado. Another fist pounded Frank's jaw. His head dropped; his ear clipped the gravel and the blaze of carpet burn enflamed his ear. The wind rushed beneath him. Rocks and arrows hailed the jeep. He felt the burnt man's desperate clutches dig into the flesh of his injured thigh.

The jeep hauled up the runway. Frank held onto the burnt man for dear life. A burst of condensed air shot off nearby and they were tossed up into the cockpit. The jeep screeched in agony. Sparks chucked up alongside them and he caught a glimpse of the harpoon protruding the tyre. He looked up, the fence only thirty metres ahead. His head slammed against the dashboard, staring across into the driver's seat. The driver's neck shot back against the oncoming rock. His head thudded lifelessly against the steering wheel. The endless drone struck Frank's heart as the horn erupted. The engine roared, much louder this time. *Oh shit.*

He lifted his head but it was too late. The jeep cut through the fence like butter. The burnt man was torn from his grasp and their bodies were tossed up inside the jeep like ragdolls over the rough terrain. The car hurtled on, revving hard towards the edge of the cliff that overlooked the last remaining stretch of forest between them and the ocean. He felt the left tyre crash against something and the entire vehicle spun on its axis. It whirled round, skidding furiously across the gravel and as it took flight toward the edge, he felt his stomach leap up inside of him.

Derek shoved the behemoth off him. He spotted Kara and Mike diving for cover through the rushing fleet of raiders. He turned onto his stomach and crawled back through the alley of tents. It was narrower now, littered with collapsed tents and trampled possessions. He snatched the material of the tent in his path and chucked it up over his head. He kept going until he reached the open plain of the base and then he remembered his original task. *The radio tower.* It was just beside the runway, only a hundred metres away. He lunged up to his feet and ran straight towards it.

Slaves poured out from the underground, climbing over one another to escape the crowded stairwell. They spread outward across the base, hundreds of them shoving and tripping over each other. The crowd swallowed Derek whole. He heard the rattling gunfire overheard and bodies began to drop around him. The panic kicked up a notch, desperation blinded them. The shackles around their ankles buckled and snapped tight as they moved. Derek shoved past them and their bodies absorbed the slaughter of raider gunfire. He finally broke through and took the deepest breath he had ever taken.

The outer stairwell was just there. Four flights of steps. He didn't stop. The gunfire pinged off the steps behind him, chasing his feet. He dropped instantly and his jaw slammed hard into the third flight. He felt an odd sensation, a sharp nip of something that pinched his stomach. He looked down to find the gushing blood. The air seemed thicker now. The bitter taste of blood swirled around his mouth. He carried on; crawling, one step at a time, the door to the tower just around the corner.

Mike and Kara dragged Barry down with them into the dirt at cut him loose. They were pinned down. The gunfire chucked up rock and dust all around them. They had run across to the outskirts of the base and into a ditch that dipped against the high fence. Mike stared across to Kara, having never seen the fear in her eyes as he had this day. He had always seen her as a fearless woman, but now he saw it, something every living creature shared in common: the fear of death.

He lifted his head above the pebbled gravel and spotted the raider standing high in the watchtower. He had abandoned the AK and favoured the more intimidating RPG, a rocket propelled launcher that he lifted up over his shoulder. The raider wasn't looking at them. Mike's gaze panned across the battlefield to where the raider aimed. His throat tightened, muscles taut with anticipation. The radio tower. Derek dragged his body up the steel steps at a snail's pace, blood dripping down through the grated slits.

Mike pulled his rifle up over the mound and gripped it firmly. He aimed with precision at the raider high up in the watchtower. Taking a deep breath, he exhaled slowly through his mouth and squeezed the trigger. The rifle snapped like the crack of a whip. A cloud of dust kicked up behind the raider as he folded limply over the metal railing. The rocket took flight, a sharp hissing that pierced the battlefield. Mike's eyes widened. His head snapped back to the radio tower and he saw the last of Derek's trembling hand reaching for the tower door. The tower combusted into a flash of burning light and was swallowed by a toxic mushroom cloud of black smoke.

Mike's jaw dropped but nothing came from his mouth. He heard the horrific screech of the metallic stilts. They bent and snapped from the concrete base and he watched it fall. With everything happening around it, it felt as though it fell in slow motion. The creaking moan of falling metal echoed across the base. The tower plummeted into the runway, crushing those who fought beneath. The growing cloud of dust spread outward, blinding those in its path, and once it had passed, the fighting continued as though nothing had happened at all. Mike looked closer, past the last remaining layer of dust that lingered amidst the butchery. A sea of people emerged from the other side, storming the front gate. They wore grey battle dress uniforms and were equipped with automatic rifles. There was a glint in his eye, a spec of hope that rekindled the fire inside of him. They were here. The LPA had arrived.

Frank held on, suspended a hundred feet above the north-eastern forest. He felt the grit between his clutching fingers. He looked down, a fatal mistake. The busted jeep was left nestled in the bed of pine trees below. His stomach churned as he saw the ground rushing up to him. He closed his eyes and held his head high. The muscles in his fingers begged for respite and began to edge back over the cliff, burning under the strain of weight to carry. He fought back, pulling himself up to snatch at anything his hand could find, but there was nothing but dirt and sand. His lungs expanded against his body. His desperate fingernails scraped across the cliff's edge. He was free for a split second in time, a moment that would last with him forever, but something stopped him. A firm grasp encircled his forearm. He looked up to see her against the pale sky, a woman in a cloak of black feathers. He felt her sharp fingernails dig into his flesh through the thickness of his jacket. She stared down with piercing eyes and pulled him up to safety.

Frank scrambled up the edge of the rock. He lay on his back, never truly appreciating level ground as much as he did then. They were concealed by the trampled bushes that separated them from the battle. Breathing heavily, he sat up and stared, remembering the woman's familiar face; her long, straight black hair that parted at the centre, her emerald green eyes that glowed against her tanned skin.

"You..." he said. "I saw you in the mountains, and Wolvendale." She looked different now. Her scraggly dry hair and tattered rags were all behind her. He had only pieced it together now. This was her, the woman he released from the shackles of the raiders.

"And I saw you," The Raven replied. Her accent was similar to that of someone who had grown on him over the gruelling expedition. "I saw you in the mountains. I saw you outside Wolvendale. I saw you sewing your crops on the outskirts of Merribank and I saw you when you first set foot on this land."

Frank squinted, surprised by the fluent nature of her tongue and knowledge. He gazed out across the distant ocean to clear his baffled mind. "I don't understand. How did you..."

The Raven struggled to look him in the eye. He could tell there was much she knew, much she had seen that he would never even begin to understand. He saw her contemplating her every word, fearful of revealing too much to him.

"Who are you?" Frank prodded.

"The last of The Beothuk. I guide my people through the eyes of the raven. My brothers and sisters fight to reclaim what is ours." The wild crack of nearby gunfire distracted them in their hidden shelter but Frank ignored it. "Wolves guided by a raven," he uttered to himself. His mind was swarmed, struggling to digest the overload of information.

"Sam..."

She stared back, confused by a name she did not recognise. "We cannot stay here. If my people find you, they will kill you."

"Then why did you help me?"

"Because I know you are not like them. You helped me in my time of need. My people have not seen what I have seen and even when I tell them they do not believe me."

"That's why you left me out there in the mountains, because of your people?"

"Yes. I wish I could have done more, but I had to go, I am sworn to stay with them. Our people have hidden in the mountains for years. We have studied your kind from afar. I met one of you and he taught me to speak your language, but my people did not approve. And then he was taken by them, the monsters within. He and my..." She stopped. She closed her eyes and swallowed hard. "At first my people did nothing but not long after, more of us were taken, and for the first time in many years, we fight back."

The Raven lifted Frank up to his feet and looked him in the eye. Her hand trembled as it touched his forearm. "The boy, you have been keeping him safe."

"I- we have, my wife and I."

"I've seen how he is with you. Even in these darkest of times, you still manage to place a smile upon his face. I have seen it. I come to you for a reason. I need you to do me one thing."

"What is it?" Frank asked.

"You've done more for him than I ever could. I see him with you and her. I see him happy and I could never take that happiness away from him. Please, just grant me this. Let me see him one last time. Let me see my son."

The sudden realisation threw him and all at once everything was clear. *Her son.* He studied her features again, ashamed he had not noticed the resemblance before. The green eyes, strong nose and tanned skin. This was his mother. This was who he was returning the lost child to. "He's your son. He should be with you." She struggled to compose herself against the harrowing prospect. A thousand yard stare, penetrating his eyes and deep into his soul. "He won't even remember me," she said. "He was ripped from my hands days after his birth. My people disapprove, for he is the son of an outsider. If I were to take him back, I fear I will lose him again. I can never allow that to happen."

It was pity that Frank felt for her. When Annie and he had tried for a child all those years ago, they had lost the child before it was even born and they kept trying some time after with no luck. To have been granted the gift of a child and then have that revoked only days after its birth; Frank didn't even want to imagine what that felt like.

"I'll take you to him," Frank said. He held out his hand and she took it willingly. He glanced back into the base and saw the sea of grey flood the gates of the black site. *Oh shit...* Bullets hailed over the runway. The bodies of raiders and the grey wolves dropped in waves. Frank held her hand tight and led her back towards the battlefield.

"We have to get your people to stand down." He tugged forward but she held back. She stood still, terrified.

"They will never yield."

"But they're getting slaughtered!"

"This isn't for you to resolve," she cried back at him. He looked at her, then back at the base, confused. The LPA swarmed like bees defending the hive. He felt lost, defeated. Innocent people were dying and there was nothing he could do. Even if he did run back, there was no way he could put an end to the onslaught of the LPA. He stood there beside her; watching the wolves drive their harpoons and scrapers into the hearts of the raiders, only to be cut down by the thousands of bullets hailing the runway. All they could do was stand on the sidelines and wait for the massacre to end.

# TWENTY-THREE

Annie sat aboard the small wooden rowing boat. It rocked gently over the calm water around them. Sam sat quietly in her lap. She held him close to her, her eyes never leaving the tree line further up the incline. Tracy sat at the other end of the boat, holding onto the rope wrapped around the wooden stump at the end of the boardwalk. She too stared up the sloping prairie of rocks and grass, ready to release them from Autark's shore at a moment's notice. Max sat between them, eyes closed, chin resting over the boat's edge. They had readied two more rowing boats either side of them for the others. The gunfire had ceased for over half an hour. There was no signal, no sign that anybody was coming for them. Annie suffered in silence and patience slowly ate away at her soul.

*Where are you, Frank?*

She ran her tattered sleeve across her running nose and coughed into the damp material of her jacket.

"Where is Frank?" Sam asked curiously.

"He's coming," Tracy told him. "They're all coming." She noticed Annie's silence and together they shared an unsettling look of doubt. Their eyes drifted down to Sam. His spine was stiff and his skin pale. He looked as though he had seen a ghost. His eyes froze, fixated on whatever lay ahead. Max's ears shot up. He barked again and again. The sisters followed Sam's panicked gaze and their hearts struck with terror.

A man stood at the other end of the boardwalk, doused in sweat and blood. His long tattered hair twisted and tangled in front of his devilish eyes. Hands by his sides, stiff fingers curled into claws. His hunched shoulders rose and dropped with every breath. He clawed the hair from his face to reveal his scarred skin, burnt and withered. He moved towards them, eyes on the shell-shocked boy in Annie's lap. The heavy clatter of boots knocked across wooden beams. Tracy shot up, rocking the boat. She grabbed hold of the side to catch her balance and fumbled for the bolt action rifle. The Burnt Man's pace quickened, he locked onto Tracy, already halfway down the platform. Annie squeezed Sam tight. She watched Tracy grab the rifle, her hands shaking wildly as she cocked the bolt into place. The Burnt Man reached the edge of the platform, arms raised and eyes wider than she ever knew possible. Tracy swung the rifle round to face him.

Annie shut her eyes. She heard a thundering weight crash the ocean's surface. Water droplets splashed up against her cheeks and Max's cry echoed through her mind. The deafening gunshot faded away. Her eyes remained shut. She did not open them immediately. She felt immobile, a tingling sensation coursed through her entire body. Max's wet nose prodded her and left a damp residue across her neck and cheek. She wormed her fingers back into motion and her hand reawakened from the prickling vibrations of pins and needles. She ran it across Sam's chest and felt his heart pound from within. Her sister's heavy breaths followed on from the splash of water like an overlaying percussion to the boy's heartbeat. She listened even more closely and noticed the sounds of gentle waves lapping up against the pebbled shore. It had always been there but she had only now just noticed it. Annie slowly opened her eyes.

*Frank...*

He was already halfway down the grassland. He limped down with his body to one side to stabilise himself against the uneven slope. He left behind a single shaded parting that divided the field behind him. Annie shot up inside the boat with Sam in her arms. His skin was returning to its regular shade and the sight of Frank helped thaw him from his frozen state. Sam called out to him through Annie's jagged movements and waved sheepishly out over the prairie. Annie looked up again and saw them emerge from the tree line; Mike, Kara, and lagging in exhaustion behind them, Barry. They lifted their weary heads and the sight of the others filled them with a new lease of energy. Together they ran the rest of the way, hopping over rolling mounds of rocks and boulders to reach them. Annie settled Sam down beside her. She grabbed the boardwalk hurriedly and pulled them in closer over the water. Frank made his way down the boardwalk and Max dived up to greet him halfway. The dog jumped up in excitement, his front paws scratching across Frank's jeans. Annie wrapped her arms around the dock's wooden post and began to pull herself ashore. She felt the large worker's hands of her husband take hold of her arms and tug her forcefully into his own. He squeezed her tightly. An ounce of energy lingered through her body. She laid her palms flat across his back and buried her head into his broad chest. Frank listened to the sobbing rendition of his wife's tears and his heart sank. He promised he wouldn't leave her again. A promise he had broken. This was the last time, he swore it. He held her even tighter and he didn't let go. He wasn't going to leave her again, not ever, and now more than ever he would do anything to make it up to her.

"It's okay. They're gone," he whispered down to her.

"We're going to be okay."

He closed his eyes and buried his nose into the top of her head. Even though they hadn't washed for what felt like an eternity, remnants of freshly scented coconut oil still lingered in the roots of her loosely tied bun. Clattering boots thudded over the wooden beams of the boardwalk. Mike and Kara leaned over the boat. They took Tracy and Sam by the hand and helped them ashore.

Tracy regained her balance and when she raised her head, Barry stood there, only metres away. His shoulders were hunched, his mangled hands presented up in front of his body.

Tracy stared down at his twisted fingers. His eyes were beady without glasses. He squinted, struggled to look her in the eye and before he could muster up the courage, he felt her entire body weight plunge into him. Her arms locked around his own and he stood there, ashamed and embarrassed of what had become of him.

Mike glanced down into the water between the rowing boats. The burnt man laid face down, floating atop the water's surface. His limp body bobbed across the gentle waves. His soaking hair tangled and outspread over his hidden face. The thickness of his blood penetrated the water like a flurry of cigarette smoke through the air. He felt Kara's hand touch his chest. She stood next to him, her eyes distant across the far water beyond. Her hand rose up and wrapped the side of his neck furthest away from her. He felt her tug slightly, as if to turn him away. She didn't want him to look anymore. He followed her direction and together they turned their backs on the drifting corpse of the burnt man.

Sam wriggled between Frank and Annie, joining the everlasting embrace. Frank ran his hands through the young boy's hair and held him close. He peered over his wife's shoulder, up beyond the prairie and into the tree line from which he came and saw the ragged outline of a feathered cloak. The Raven watched from the shadows of the forest. Her cloak of feathers made her shoulder's appear broader in the darkness. It was too dark to see any further detail. She stepped forward and her face caught the light of the pale sky.

"What do we do now?" Annie asked in his arms.

Frank's eye never strayed from The Raven as he spoke. "We go home."

"What about the slaves?" she asked.

"They're free now. The LPA pulled in and Mikes left them working to get people back to their homes."

"And Sam?"

The Raven nodded. Frank returned the gesture; a shared understanding to a previous agreement. He could only imagine the pain she felt. He imagined it to be as it were during Annie's miscarriage all those years ago, but only ten times worse. Frank swallowed hard. He hadn't noticed Annie looking up at him now, waiting for his answer.

"He's coming home with us," said Frank. Sam stared up, bewildered by his response, and Frank made sure to check with the boy. "That is, if you want to?"

The boy's dimples curled through his nodding smile. He threw himself into the couple, an arm around each of their legs as he hugged them tight with undying gratitude. Annie continued to stare. She seemed concerned, unconvinced. It couldn't be true. It was too good to be true.

"What about his parents?" she asked quietly enough for the boy not to hear. Frank glanced back up to the tree line but The Raven was nowhere to be seen. He turned back to Annie, distracted by her concerned eyes so full and wonderful.

He shook his head. "... They weren't there."

"Are you sure?"

"I'm sure."

"But we came all this way to-"

"I know, I know. We asked every one of them. Nothing..."

Annie's attention drew down to the boy. She stroked his hair softly, her expression bland and unfulfilled. It wasn't how he'd expected her to react. In fact, it was just the opposite. She had grown attached to the boy. They had developed a bond that spurred Frank on to see the good in what they were doing. He thought about that night back before Wolvendale, standing out in the darkness with only the cast shadows of the campfire to light them. She had put up a fight that night to protect him, to watch over him and be there for him. He thought that was what she wanted; to have somebody to care for, to know what it is like to nurture a child as though it were her own. Maybe he had made a mistake.

Frank gently hooked his arm around her shoulder.

"At least we tried."

"At least we tried..." she repeated in a dull faded tone. She smiled briefly but couldn't hold it for very long. He knew it wasn't genuine. She wanted to look after Sam but a little part of her was left with disappointment and despair, knowing that the child's true parents were nowhere to be found. It nibbled away at Frank ever so discreetly like a bloodsucking leech. He had lied to her. He'd spent so much time with the boy and he knew how much he made her happy. Allowing The Raven to enter his life now would only confuse the poor child. It wouldn't have been fair. Sam had been through enough. Frank knew it and The Raven knew it also. She had seen them watch over him through the eye of the raven. Frank held Annie close and spoke softly into her ear. "We'll take care of him. He has a gift but it's not for us to say what he should do with it. That's all they wanted him for and he's been through a lot. He's just a boy, we should let him have that; a childhood, a real childhood.

We'll let him decide what he wants to do with his ability for himself when he grows older."

Frank thought about the future. Maybe there was a time - when the boy was old enough - that Frank could tell him the truth. He would not look forward to that day, but until then, he swore to raise the child as if he were his own and that was a vow he would not break.

"So what now?" Kara asked Mike at the edge of the boardwalk. They stood side by side, watching the others re-unite with their loved ones.

"Well, I think the LPA will stick around, help make amends for what's happened."

"What about you, what's next for Mike?"

"You know, despite all that's happened. This land has grown on me. I'm thinking of staying."

"You are?"

"Well since there's no military to keep an eye on this place anymore, I was thinking maybe the LPA could fit the boot. Not to control, but to protect. 'Libertad para Autark.' 'Liberty for Autark.' Javier Paraíso was a good leader, but he was never a fighter. Without someone for the people to look to, they will lose hope in restoring what was once something special. We're already here, I'm here. The LPA can be so much more. They can be the ones to prevent something like this ever happening again. We'll defend. We'll rebuild. We'll grow. What happened back there was wrong. I couldn't stop them from doing what they did to the Beothuk. I couldn't protect the last surviving members of their people and now they're gone forever. I won't let that happen again."

"Not all of them are gone. Despite their way of life, every group of people has those who are cowards at heart. I saw some of them flee back toward the mountains. What happened back there wasn't your fault. There is no way in hell you can pin that on yourself."

"I know, I know... but I still can't help but feel responsible. The least I can do is accomplish what I set out to do when I came here; restore freedom to Autark."

"Sounds very noble. Also sounds like a lot of work. You plan on doing it all by yourself?"

"I'm sure the people will cooperate."

"Elkford is without a leader, Merribank has been burnt to the ground and Wolvendale is a ghost town. You're going to need someone who has lived here long enough to know how things were before this all started; a face the people will recognise as their own to vouch for you when you announce these plans of yours."

"That's true," Mike smirked. She was way ahead of him, but he played ball. "Know anybody?"

"I might."

The wind blew strong and the tide crept in deeper along the stilts of the boardwalk. Frank planted a kiss upon Annie's forehead. He brushed the stray hairs away from her face and tucked them behind her ear. Through all that had happened he had lost sight of the fact that she was in desperate need of care. She needed rest and nourishment to cure her ailments. They all did. They had spent enough time out in the cold for one winter.

"Come on," Frank said. "Let's go home."

Frank and Annie each took hold of Sam's hands. Together they went back up the boardwalk of Autark's harbour, back toward the military base, back home.

# EPILOGUE

Elkford was the first town of Autark to be restored to its former glory. The settlers were forever in debt to the LPA who stayed to guard the land and its people for the sake of a forgotten liberty. The one thing that the people of Autark shared in common was their value of freedom.

Mike and Kara stood in Elkford's courtyard. They were in the middle of conducting a high intensity training course for the men and women of the LPA. They held a course every afternoon for those who wished to attend. Nothing was obligatory in the LPA, nothing except for safety talks and emergency drills. They went through everything that afternoon; cardio, weight training, muscle build and even close quarters combat drills. Mike and Kara ran vigorously up and down the rows of their people with booming voices. They shouted words of encouragement for the people to keep on going just that little bit longer. The toll of the Elkford's steeple signalled them to stop. The people of the LPA quickly formed rows of an orderly fashion. Mike thanked them for their attendance and dismissed them promptly. A banner was situated high above the archway of the stone wall that curved the perimeter of the courtyard's barracks.

*'Libertad Para Autark* - *You are your own being, and so you shall be free.'*

Mike and Kara had worked to instil this motto into the hearts and minds of their people. They weren't soldiers, they were human beings banding together to work towards a different way of life; one where men and women could make use of their trade in exchange for the goods and services of others. The settlers and freedom fighters of Elkford were no different. Each and every individual pulled their weight in the effort to restore Autark. A lonesome raven did watch. It was perched high upon the single cherry blossom of Elkford's courtyard with watchful eyes that observed the many defenders of Autark. As the people of the LPA dispersed through the courtyard to return home to their families, Mike and Kara strolled back up the stone pathway and disappeared through the doors to the keep.

The raven took flight and flew south along the western coast. It rested upon the branch of an apple tree, one of many in an orchard blooming like no other on the island. The sign on the front gate was a little faded, something that had yet to be refurbished. The sign read, *'Frank & Annie's'*. It curved upwards in the middle across a hand-painted picture of assorted fruits and vegetables. The raven caught sight of a young boy with a long nimble stick in his hand. The boy closed the wooden gate and ran up the dusty trail alongside his faithful border collie.

Sam lobbed the stick up towards the glorious two story country house. It had transformed from what once was a simple wooden structure on a platform, into a brick house on a foundation of concrete. A wide trellis filled the space between the top and bottom floor, blooming with confederate-jasmine that twined the wooden diamonds of guidance. Max bolted after the stick. A whirlwind of dust kicked up in his tracks and fluttered back down into the open trail. He heard a monotonous knocking that sounded like it was on the other side of the house but he was soon distracted. He spotted them kneeling in the tomato patches, picking only those that were ready to be picked. The bearded man lifted his head and smiled as he spotted Sam through the garden. Sam caught sight of the black leather eye patch immediately; it was always the centre of focus against the vibrant colours of the garden. He ran through the row of tomato plants held up by support posts and fell into the woman's arms. Frank hugged him tight and Annie turned round to see what was going on through the vines of tomatoes.

"Where have you been?" he asked curiously. Sam smiled and dived in to help Annie pick the tomatoes that he knew were most ripe, a skill he had learned from his time in the garden with Frank.

"To the stables."

"Again? I hope you said thank you to Callum for showing you the horses."

"I did."

"And how is he?" Annie asked.

"Good."

"And the girls?"

"Yeah. They let me sit on the horse, but we didn't go though, just to sit."

"That's nice of them. That place sure has come a long way."

"Henry would've been proud," said Frank.

A rapid knock against the kitchen window turned the heads of the three in the allotment. Sam peered past the light and saw Tracy; her head hunched low beneath the curtains and she waved them all in as she did every evening. That was her signal. Supper was ready. Sam darted back up through the narrow patch of soil and into the clearing. Max returned to him with the stick and placed it by his feet. He turned back to see Frank, his neck craned up to the roof where a ladder was propped up by the downspout.

"Baz, come on, mate," Frank shouted up to the roof.

Sam looked up. Barry's balding head popped out from the concealment of the roof. The sky was bright and cast a shadow across his excited plump face. He wore a set of thick bottle-rimmed glasses, courtesy of a new optician in the outskirts of Merribank. They weren't the most stylish of spectacles, but they allowed the man to see again.

"I-I-I-I'm coming," he yelled back down the ladder. Frank held onto the base of the ladder and Barry descended, one foot at a time. The plump man held a wooden hammer in his stiff hands. His bones had healed but his fingers were now stiff. He had told Sam before about how he struggled to move them. Sam remembered not to stare and he ruffled Max's fur in adoration. The adults gathered inside the house and he heard Annie call his name.

"I'm coming," he yelled back through the front door. As he stroked the dog's chin, he looked out and scanned the land around them; the rolling hills of fields that held pockets of trees dotting the surrounding landscape. He had seen it all before during the dark days, but seeing it in this way, with these people, it was as though he was seeing Autark again for the first time. He smiled to himself and looked down at Max who stared back up, patiently awaiting the command so that he could dive in for the meal. "Come on, Max." Together they hopped up the porch and ran into the house. Sam shut the door behind him and the sun began to descend behind the horizon.

The raven remained silent, watching from afar. There was a glint in its eye, something that held it from leaving right away. It continued to stare at the house, hesitant to leave. It had perched on that same branch every other day for the past six months. Behind its deep, black eyes lay an array of emotion. There was guilt and sacrifice in its falter. It seemed to struggle with it every day, but above all, after seeing those who cared for the boy; those feelings were soon overwhelmed with acceptance. The raven croaked softly, readying its wings for flight. It took off suddenly and returned east to its home in the mountains. Those people would never be forgotten. They were the ones who restored Autark, the ones who gave the people their freedom.

Printed in Great Britain
by Amazon